WAS THIS ANY WAY TO START A MARRIAGE?

Eliza had never been so angry in her life.

"I demand that you put me down this instant, Matthew Decker!"

She had suffered more humiliation at the hands of this man than any woman should have to endure. Now she was hanging upside down over his shoulder as he carried her onto Main Street.

She whacked him once, as hard as she could, in the center of his back. He ignored her and kept walking. Since beating on him with her fists seemed ineffective, maybe there was another way to get his attention. She took her thumb and forefinger and grabbed as much of his hind end as she could through his denim pants.

"Hey!" He jumped. "You shouldn't be doing things like that in public!"

Winter Bride

⚔ TERESA SOUTHWICK ⚔

HarperPaperbacks
A Division of HarperCollinsPublishers

HarperPaperbacks   *A Division of* HarperCollins*Publishers*
10 East 53rd Street, New York, N.Y. 10022

Cover illustration by Jean Monti

First printing: March 1995

Printed in the United States of America

HarperPaperbacks, HarperMonogram, and colophon are
trademarks of HarperCollins*Publishers*

❖ 10 9 8 7 6 5 4 3 2 1

To Susan Macias, an exceptional writer and dear friend. I'm grateful for the Friday phone calls that kept me focused on this book. As always, your input from start to finish was invaluable.

To Jolie Kramer, a wonderful writer and friend who showed me early in this book that conflict provides a journey which forces our characters to grow and change. I hope I've learned my lesson well.

Winter Bride

1

Silver Springs, Wyoming Territory—October 1, 1875

"*How could a hat this ugly* bring good luck to a bride?" Eliza Jones stared at the ivory-colored, wide-brimmed monstrosity resting on her carpetbag and shook her head.

"What's that you say, ma'am?"

Eliza whirled around, startled. "I didn't think anyone was there." The balding man with the thick black mustache stood in the doorway of the Silver Springs stage office. "What do you think of that hat, Mr.—"

"Whitaker, ma'am, Ed Whitaker." His gaze lowered to the object in question. Eliza thought it was the most horrendous blend of satin and lace that she had ever seen. "Well, now, I don't rightly know much about female attire."

"I do. Take it from me, it *is* awful. I can't see a blessed thing through that veil. It's as transparent as a tablecloth. And I've promised to wear it at my wedding today."

"Do tell, ma'am."

"That's right. I've come all the way from Boston to marry Matt Decker. His mother arranged everything, including the headwear," she said, chuckling at the offensive hat. She'd rather die than let Mrs. Decker know how she felt about it. Her laughter faded as she glanced up and down the street, hoping to see her bridegroom. "He was supposed to be here to meet me. I hope nothing's happened."

"Don't worry, ma'am. The stage was early today. I can't remember the last time it was on schedule. Early's as unusual as ice in July."

"Really, Mr. Whitaker?" She wanted very much to believe that.

He nodded. "He'll be here. I know Matt."

"So do I. And I hope you're right." Eliza wasn't convinced, even though his mother had been certain he'd forgiven her.

So she'd come to Wyoming to marry him. As a young girl, she'd followed him everywhere. It seemed she hadn't lost the habit. But this time she would make sure he didn't have cause to regret it.

"What're you goin' to town for? Ain't run out of supplies yet."

"I got my reasons." Matt Decker looked in the small mirror on the kitchen table and wiped away the last traces of shaving soap. His cheeks and chin were pale compared to the tan on the upper half of his face.

"And why in tarnation did you shave off those whiskers with the weather turnin' cold?"

Drops of water clung to the hair on his bare chest and Matt rubbed them away before tossing the towel into the tin basin. He took a deep breath and looked at his ranch foreman. Wiley Powell was his right-hand man. More. He was like a father. Matt knew he'd get an earful from the older man after explaining why he was going to town. Best get it over with and say it straight out.

"I'm getting married."

The older man's gray eyebrows shot up. "Didn't know you was keepin' company with anyone," he said, his tone calm. Too calm, Matt thought.

"I'm not. In case you haven't noticed, there's not a whole lot of available women in Silver Springs to keep company with."

"Then you best fill in the particulars, boy, or I'll be thinkin' you got into the locoweed along with those cows we rounded up today."

"Mail-order bride. Sort of."

Wiley lifted his sweat-stained brown hat and set it on the back of his head. His faded blue eyes narrowed with disapproval. Matt braced himself. He figured sticking his fingers in his ears wouldn't help. Folks clear down in Cheyenne would know what Wiley Powell thought of his marriage plans.

"You're fixin' to get hitched to a female you never even laid eyes on before?"

"That about sums it up."

"How'd all this happen?"

"My mother knows her and arranged everything. It's not like the lady's a complete stranger."

Wiley nodded as if something was finally clear to him. "So that's what all them letters was about. Since I've known you, you've never sent more'n three or four letters a year to your mama." He squinted at Matt. "You know her name?"

"'Course I do. Laura Decker."

"Not your mama's name, you knothead. The woman you're fixin' t'marry."

Matt hadn't felt this cornered since the night his father threw him out and told him he wouldn't ever amount to a pile of horse manure. "Her name is Miss Jones."

"She got a first name?"

"'Course she does." Matt stared him down and hoped he'd leave it right there. Several seconds passed while they eyed each other.

Wiley's grizzled chin jutted forward. "You gonna tell me what it is?"

He should have known. When the old man wanted something, he was like a hungry steer pawing through the snow to get at the sweet grass below. Matt shifted uncomfortably. "When she tells me, I'll pass along the information."

"Jehoshaphat, boy! You don't even know her given name?" He rubbed a hambone-sized hand over his salt-and-pepper whiskers. "Forget her name. What if she's got a face that would stop a stampede? You considered that?"

"She's got green eyes, brown hair, and freckles."

"How d'you know?"

"Ma's letters. I told her I wanted a sensible, sturdy woman. Life's hard. I need a woman who won't turn tail at the first sign of trouble."

"What about the widow Buchanan? She's had a heap o' heartache and still keeps that boardin'house goin'."

"Her life's in town. Mine's the ranch."

"Then what about Bertha Dutton? She's runnin' that spread of hers practically single-handed since Cal passed on."

Matt shook his head. "Too old. Besides, I don't need more land to worry about."

Wiley's brows lifted in surprise. "You *want* someone you don't know. So you don't care too much for her."

"No. You're wrong." Matt grabbed his best white shirt from the high back of the pine chair and held it up. An iron-shaped brown mark scorched the broad back of the material. "This is why I want a wife."

"You're gettin' married because your shirt's burned?"

Letting out a long breath, Matt shook his head. "No. Because I don't want to do it alone anymore." He pointed to the pile of food-crusted pots and pans spilling over the sides of the basin by the window. "There's not a clean dish in the place." Then he gestured toward the hall that led to his bedroom. "There's a pile of dirty clothes in there as high as the Laramie Mountains. It's time there was a woman around here."

Wiley shook his head. "You don't need a woman you never seen before."

"I do if I aim to make this spread the biggest in the territory."

"Still set on provin' somethin' to your pa?"

"No, to myself. I can build this place, but if there's no one to do it for, what's the point?" He ran his fingers through his long hair. "Carrie's been gone two years next month. I'm finished mourning her and the child that took her from me."

"Nobody can fill her place."

"I'm not looking to do that. I want a partner, someone to keep house while I tend the ranch."

"Get yourself a housekeeper."

"No. I want a wife, legal and proper." He poked his arm into the long sleeve of his burned shirt.

"What the hell for?"

"To give me a son."

"What if you don't like her? Ain't no place for a young 'un in a marriage like that."

"Ma says she's sure we'll like each other just fine."

He looked out the window above the pile of dirty dishes. He was proud of the ranch—the barn, blacksmith shack, harness-and-tack building, and the three-bedroom frame house he stood in. He had taken land with nothing but grass that was belly-high to an oxen and the money he'd saved after a year of cowboyin' and from them he'd carved out this place. And he was making it bigger all the time. But he wanted an heir to carry on after the good Lord saw fit to take him. He didn't intend for anyone who wasn't blood to get their hands on the Double C.

Ben Colter had been his closest neighbor. Matt had come to love his daughter, Carrie, then married her. After the old man died, the acres of grazing land Matt had started out with doubled in size. He'd often wondered what would have happened if old man Colter hadn't had a child to leave it to. Matt didn't want to find out.

"Would it make any difference if I said this whole business is a bad idea?"

"Nope."

"Anythin' I can say to talk you out of it?"

Matt shook his head. "Too late for that. She's comin' in on today's stage from Cheyenne. Can't leave the lady to fend for herself when it was my idea for her to come out here in the first place."

Wiley nodded. "You want me to trim up them wavy locks of yours so's she don't think she's hooked up with a grizzly?"

Matt looked in the shaving mirror at his shoulder-length brown hair. He appreciated his old friend's support, especially when he knew the man was dead set against the marriage. "No time. She'll be waiting."

"That Cheyenne stage ain't never on schedule."

"I'm counting on that. Thanks to those strays, I'm already late." He looked at the stack of dirty dishes. "Wish I had time to clean this place up so she's not scared off as soon as she sets foot inside."

"Don't look at me," Wiley said. He walked out the door and added over his shoulder, "You got yourself into this."

"I thought I could count on you. What's she gonna think when she sees that mess?" Matt followed and watched the older man hurry off, chuckling. When he looked at the wide, wooden porch that spanned the whole back of the house, he had an idea. That old coot had helped him out after all.

He grabbed an armful of pots from the kitchen and tossed them out the back door. Then he went inside for the dishes and stacked them more carefully. After he finished, he inspected the now tidy room and nodded with satisfaction. That was one taken care of. He could just shut the rest of the doors. Except for . . .

"Oh, God, the bedroom." He went down the hall and

groaned at the mound of dirty clothes. "Got no choice," he said as he shoved everything under the bed. Then he quickly threw the quilt up over the pillows and smoothed it once before racing out the door. That would buy him some time.

Eliza paced the wooden planks outside the Silver Springs stage office. Three hours had passed since Mr. Whitaker had assured her Matt would be there, and she was beginning to worry that he wasn't coming.

Mrs. Decker had first mentioned a marriage to her son as a solution to Eliza's difference of opinion with her father. After that one unfortunate incident, he thought she needed a husband to keep her in line and he'd picked one out. A banker. Eliza had said she'd only marry Cornelius Fairbrothers over her father's dead body or Cornelius's. That redheaded, pasty-faced prig didn't have an ounce of fun in him, and he ordered everyone around like a general commanding his army. Why, he'd fired that poor young woman from her teller job just because she'd stayed home with her sick child. No, she could never spend the rest of her life with a man like that.

Then Matt's mother had come to her rescue. She said he had recovered from his wife's death and was looking to marry again, except there were few women in Wyoming. Eliza couldn't understand why that was. Since women there had the right to vote, she'd thought more would venture to the territory. She liked the idea of having a say in things.

Eliza had been certain he'd never agree to wed her. The last time she'd seen him, he'd said he never wanted to lay eyes on her again. But Mrs. Decker had said he'd forgotten all about that and had eagerly consented to the union.

Eliza looked up and down the street now. Horses, wagons, and people kicked up the dust, but no one paid any attention to her. And there was no sign of Matt Decker.

She'd left Boston a week before, barely able to control her impatience to see him again. After so many days of traveling, she was rumpled and weary and anxious to plant herself smack-dab in the middle of her new life with him even in uncivilized Wyoming. Although she'd only been twelve when he left home, she hadn't met a single man who could hold a candle to Matt. Would he look the same as she remembered? Would she recognize him? She could still picture his brown hair shot with golden lights. And his eyes—they were as blue as the sky. He was the handsomest man she'd ever seen. And now there she was, right there in Silver Springs, because he'd asked her to come all this way to marry him.

But he hadn't been there to meet her. She was starting to get a little scared.

She hadn't had any qualms about leaving the East— until now. A brisk wind pulled at the pins holding her hair on top of her head. She shivered and clutched her shawl more closely around her. She'd rather be scared in Wyoming than marry the man Papa had picked for her. She shuddered, not from cold, but at the thought of Cornelius Fairbrothers. She'd sooner starve or freeze to death than marry him.

"It's gettin' late, ma'am. You can't stay out here all night."

She turned away from the street and glanced at Mr. Whitaker, who had poked his head out the door. She didn't need him to point that out. The sun was going down, along with the temperature. Besides the man had a sign in his hand that read CLOSED UNTIL MORNING. It didn't take long for her to come to the conclusion that he was anxious to get home for supper, and he didn't feel he could leave with her standing there. She looked in her reticule and counted the remainder of her money. Matt had sent enough for her fare and expenses, but there wasn't much left. What would she do if he didn't come?

"Is there someplace I can get a room for the night? An inexpensive room?" she added.

He nodded and jabbed his finger in the air. "Down on Main Street."

She turned her gaze in the direction he indicated. "There's only one street."

He grinned. "Why do you think we call it Main?"

"I see your point," she said, smiling back.

"The other side of the mercantile. Ethel Buchanan takes in boarders. Ever since her husband Walt got kicked in the head by his horse and died, she's been rentin' out rooms to care for her three young 'uns. Try there."

"I'll do that. Would it be all right if I leave my trunk here until tomorrow?" she asked. He nodded, then started to put his sign in the window. "One more thing," Eliza said. "If Mr. Decker comes looking for me—"

"He'll go to Ethel's. But if it'll make you feel better, I'll leave him a note."

Eliza nodded. "That would relieve my mind. Thank you ever so much."

"Don't mention it, ma'am." He put the sign in the window and a note on the door, then slapped his hat on his head and headed up Main Street.

She looked at her carpetbag with the big, ugly ivory-colored hat sitting on top. Matt's mother had given the hat to her. Eliza had tried tactfully to decline, but the woman had insisted, and issued very explicit instructions besides: Eliza was to have the thing on, with the veil over her face, when she first saw Matt.

The hat was a Decker family tradition. Brides always wore it or faced a future with bad luck. Laura Decker swore she'd had it proudly on her head on her own wedding day. Eliza had thought it best not to point out that their luck had deserted them when Matt and his father had quarreled, sending the son west. He'd never been back, but he kept in touch with his mother. Maybe that was its own brand of luck.

Eliza couldn't imagine a hat so ugly bringing *good* fortune, but who was she to argue? The woman had saved her from a horrible fate by arranging for Eliza to marry her son. If all she had to do was wear that hideous hat, it was a small price to pay.

She glanced up Main Street to her left, then to her right. It was practically deserted. What if something had happened to him? After all, this was uncivilized territory. And unless he'd changed a lot in the last eight years, Matt was a man who never shied away from danger.

That's why he'd come west in the first place, and she hoped he'd forgotten—or at least forgiven—her very small part in all that. When her father had looked at her with his minister's expression that said she was going straight to perdition if she didn't tell everything she knew . . . Well, what was she to do? But Matt had refused to listen to her. His mother had said that everything would be fine just as soon as Matt saw her again.

But she'd also promised to wear the hat when she first saw him and the part that covered her face was so thick he wouldn't be able to see her. She sighed. She was too tired to puzzle it out now.

Eliza picked up her bag and the hat on top, and started toward Ethel Buchanan's boardinghouse. In the morning, she'd find some way to track Matt down. And if he was in trouble, she'd just get him out of it. That's what a wife did.

A knock on the door startled Eliza into wakefulness. It took her a minute to remember that she was in her bed at the boardinghouse. She was amazed that she'd dozed off when she was so terribly worried about Matt. Maybe whoever was outside her door had news of him. Another knock sounded.

"Who is it?" she called.

"Miss Jones?" It was a man's voice, deep and hushed.

"Yes. Who's there? Have you come about Matt?"

"It is Matt, ma'am. Matt Decker," he added.

She jumped out of bed and lighted the oil lamp beside

her. Then she ran across the room before she realized she was wearing nothing but a cotton nightdress. She'd packed her duster in her trunk, and the trunk was still at the stage office.

With her hand on the knob, she whispered through the closed door, "Are you all right? I was so afraid that something had happened when you didn't meet me."

"I'm real sorry, Miss Jones. I planned to be here, but I was late getting away from the ranch, and then the wagon lost a wheel."

"But you're all right?"

"Yes, ma'am."

Eliza was puzzled. Why was he behaving so formally, as if they hadn't practically grown up together? He was treating her like a complete stranger. He'd never called her "Miss Jones" or "ma'am" when she'd known him back East. More often than not he'd called her "pest" or "pain in the . . ." But that was a long time ago. Maybe his courteous ways were a sign of maturity. She would match his good manners and show him she was far from the twelve-year-old girl he'd hardly noticed before he went away.

"I'd invite you in, Mr. Decker, but I'm not exactly dressed to receive a gentleman caller. It wouldn't be proper."

"It would if we were married. I've got the preacher with me. Ethel wouldn't let me in without him."

"Is Mrs. Buchanan out there too?"

"No, she went back to bed. She put the shotgun up when the reverend convinced her I was dead serious about this wedding."

Boots scraped and shuffled on the wooden floor outside her room. "Hello in there, miss. It's Reverend Wilson. Welcome to Silver Springs."

"Thank you." This was crazy, conversing with her intended and the minister through a door in the middle of the night. But then, this entire courtship, if one could call it that, had been crazy.

"Mr. Decker, am I to understand that you want to get married now? At this time of night?"

"Reverend Wilson's leaving town before sunup, Miss Jones. When he gets back in a couple weeks, I might not be able to get into town because of the weather. We're all awake; might as well get on with it. The reverend brought the Good Book with him."

Matt had never been one to let grass grow under his boots. Apparently that hadn't changed. Everything he'd said made perfect sense to her. She'd come a long way to marry him and she couldn't do that if the preacher left town.

"Just let me put my dress on."

"If it's all the same to you, ma'am, I'd just as soon not wait for that. I've had a hard day and the reverend here was rustled out of a warm bed. Could you just throw a blanket around you or something?"

He was obviously in a big hurry. He really was going to let bygones be bygones. Why *not* throw the quilt around her? she thought. Nothing about this wedding was traditional. She spotted the hat on the dresser beside her. Except that. She'd promised to have it on when she first saw him, and she couldn't break her word—especially to Matt's mother.

She sighed as she lifted the hat brim, gathered her braids, and stuffed them under the crown before lowering the veil over her face. She'd been so anxious to see Matt again. Now she'd have to wait until after they were married, because she could hardly see her hand in front of her face through the thick lace.

"Miss Jones? You ready?"

It seemed Matt was anxious, too.

"One minute." She grabbed the quilt from the bed, refusing to think about the picture she made. She'd always thought she'd be married in a long, pretty gown. She just hadn't expected it would be a nightgown.

Matt waited impatiently in the hall with the preacher beside him. The short, wiry man had resisted presiding over such a hasty wedding and he had tried to convince Matt that "groom's nerves" were making him act like a lunatic. Nothing in his life had made Matt less nervous. This was right; it was logical. There was no reason to be jittery.

He didn't understand why the preacher had raised such a fuss about saying the vows so fast. Matt had work to do at the ranch and the reverend wanted to get on the road at dawn. Neither of them wanted the matter of a wedding to slow them down.

The door finally opened and there she stood—wearing a blue-and-white quilt around her shoulders and the most godawful wide-brimmed hat with a thick veil over her face. It was the color of dirty snow and looked like a bird-cage with a brim. The thing was almost as big as she was. He could see her, sort of. But her features were indistinct through the veil. He recalled Wiley's fretting that her face might stop a stampede.

"No offense, ma'am, but could you take the hat off?" he asked, removing his own and holding it in his hand.

She shook her head. "That would be bad luck. Your mother gave it to me. She said she wore it at her wedding and that I mustn't break tradition."

He didn't recall ever seeing that hat. And he was certain he'd remember it if he had. "But, Miss Jones—" he said.

"I promised." She clutched the blanket to her neck with one delicate hand and, through the opening in front, held out the other one. "Hello, Ma—Mr. Decker."

"Ma'am," he said, swallowing her hand in his much larger one. The touch of her made him forget everything else.

Her palm and fingers were fine-boned and soft. On the list of wifely requirements he had given his mother, he had specifically stated well built and sturdy. He was afraid she might have missed that part. This woman—he looked down and saw that she wasn't wearing shoes—stood about as tall as the middle of his chest in her bare feet. The quilt hid the rest of her. So he could still hope she was big-boned and strong.

Her hand was so soft, he did wonder whether she was used to hard work. Then she squeezed his fingers and he couldn't think about anything but taking air into his lungs.

"Let's get on with it," he said gruffly. With her hand in his, he turned to face the preacher.

Reverend Wilson cleared his throat. "May we go inside? I don't think the rest of the boarders would appreciate a wedding at this hour in the hall."

Matt tossed his hat on the chair beside the door and led her farther into the room. He stopped at the foot of the bed and turned his back to it. "This better?"

"Yes," the reverend said, quietly closing the door. He came to stand in front of them. "Dearly beloved, we are gathered—"

"Look, Jim, the three of us hardly constitute a congregation and it's the middle of the night. Can we just get to the 'I do' part?"

Her hand tightened in his. "Mr. Decker, due to circumstances beyond my control, I'm being married in a quilt. The least you can do is let Reverend Wilson say some words."

Matt looked down at her. She sure was a bossy little thing. He was glad, though. She'd need every ounce of that spunk on the ranch. "It seems the lady wants words, Jim."

"I reckon I can do that." The man smiled. "We're gathered in the sight of God to unite these two people in wedlock. Marriage is a holy state and should not be entered into lightly. . . ."

The *lock* part of *wedlock* made Matt just a shade more nervous than he'd been before. He looked down at his bride. "I'm not entering into anything lightly. Are you, Miss Jones?"

She shook her head. "There's nothing light about coming all this way to get married."

"Then I say get on with it. What do you say, ma'am?"

"I'd like that fine."

"All right with you, Jim?"

"Whatever you say, Matt." He opened the Bible. "Do you, Matthew Decker, take this woman for your lawfully wedded wife?"

"I do."

The preacher looked at the woman. "Do you, Miss Jones, take this man for your wedded husband?"

She hesitated, then looked up at him. He held his breath. She smelled as sweet as a field of wildflowers in spring. It was all he could do not to remove that veil himself to see what she looked like. He towered over her, and her hand, so small and cold in his, trembled. He smiled and nodded slightly, encouraging her.

"I do," she whispered.

"By the powers vested in me by the territorial legislature, I now pronounce you man and wife. You may kiss your bride."

"Jim . . ." Matt looked back at her. "Do you need to witness that part for the vows to be legal?"

The man grinned like an idiot. "Don't guess I do need to be here for that." He held out his hand. "Congratulations and best of luck to the both of you."

Matt shook his hand, then quickly ushered him to the door. "'Bye, Jim. And thanks."

"Glad to, Matt."

He closed the door. Taking a deep breath, Matt turned to his new wife. She stood with her back to the bed and the lamp behind her sent her flickering shadow across the floor to his feet. He realized it wasn't her; it was the outline of the hat.

He stared at the ridiculous contraption and said, "I think I'd like to see you without that thing."

She laughed. The sound was sweet as sugar and cheerful, like the water bubbling over the rocks in the brook on the Double C. Something about the tone was vaguely familiar. That disturbed him.

"I believe I'd like to be seen without it," she said. "In fact, if it wasn't a family tradition, I'd like to let the wind blow it so far away I'd never set eyes on it again." She paused for a breath, then continued, "I'm so excited to be here. I've never seen more spectacular land in my life. It's no wonder you fell in love with it and stayed."

She was right about that and his mother was right about her. Something told him this woman would do him proud and they'd have a good, full life together.

He held his breath while she lifted the veil, but was disappointed when he still couldn't see her. Her face was in shadow, and he couldn't wait one second longer to see if her features matched her soft, feminine hand and sweet voice.

"Miss Jones—I mean Mrs. Decker, would you mind turning toward the light?"

Her laugh washed over him again and set every nerve on edge.

"Of course," she said, moving beside the lamp.

Matt stared at her. She was beautiful, even with the hat still on her head. This was not a face that would stop a stampede, but more likely start one. Her eyes were definitely green, the color of the grasslands that stretched across his valley. A trail of freckles crisscrossed her little turned-up nose.

There was something familiar about that nose and those freckles. The memory made him even more uneasy. As he studied her, the bad feeling grew.

She removed the hat, and two brown braids tumbled over her shoulders, halfway to her waist. Suddenly he went back in time. A vision flashed into his mind of a freckle-faced twelve-year-old girl begging him to stop and listen to her, racing after him with tears streaming from her green eyes, brown braids flying behind her. He had yelled over his shoulder that he never wanted to see her again.

Standing before him was the little pain in the ass who had once made his life hell. And he had just married her.

"Eliza Jones," he said through gritted teeth. "What the hell are you doing here?"

2

"*Matt . . . I don't understand.* I'm here to be your wife."

He shook his head and his eyes darkened dangerously. "I agreed to marry Miss Jones. If I'd known that was *you . . .*"

Eliza felt as if she'd been pushed off the top of the hard, jagged mountains she'd admired from the stage-coach on her way from Cheyenne. Matt hadn't known he was marrying *her.* Why had his mother done this to them?

Her knees felt wobbly, but she refused to give in to the weakness. Besides, there were only two places to sit—the bed and the chair beside the door. She couldn't think about the bed until things were settled between them. Matt stood in the center of the room. She'd have to pass him to get to the chair. The way he was clenching his hands told her it would be best to stay where she was.

"Please listen to me," she said.

"What can you say, Eliza? You tricked me."

"No." She took a step toward him, just a few feet away at the end of the bed. If she had any sense, she would be afraid, but the Matt she knew would never hurt her. He couldn't have changed that much.

The oil lamp behind her cast her shadow across the floor, all the way to his feet. She couldn't see his features. In spite of everything, she was anxious to compare the man he was now with the boy she'd known years ago. She moved slightly to the side, so that she could study him in better light.

The intensity in his expression did frighten her some, especially the anger in the blue eyes she remembered. He seemed bigger, somehow, broader through the chest, and dark hairs peeked out from the vee of his white shirt. His hair was longer, giving him a wild, uncivilized look. It suited him. He was still the only man she'd ever met who could make her heart race like an out-of-control train. He was even more handsome than the day she'd last seen him. In fact, the emotions racing across his face were exactly the same as they were then—he wanted to throttle her now, just as he had eight years ago. She had to make him see that what happened this time wasn't her fault.

"You tricked me all right. I've seen wedding tintypes of my folks and I've never laid eyes on that damn hat before."

"It's the most hideous thing *I've* ever seen. Your mother made me promise to wear it the first time you saw me. I thought that was a little strange, but she said it was good luck. I see now what she was up to."

"Yeah. The question is how in the hell did you get my mother to help you?"

"It was her idea, you ninny."

"Why would my own mother betray me like that?"

Eliza glared at him. "For some reason she must think we belong together."

"And you think *I'm* a ninny."

"The fruit doesn't fall far from the tree."

"Careful. You're talkin' about my mother."

"I'd never say anything unkind about her. She's the dearest woman I've ever known, next to my own mother. You, on the other hand—"

He turned away for a second and raked his hand through his hair. There was a brown mark on the material between his shoulder blades, just about the size and shape of an iron.

Eliza couldn't help smiling as she pointed to his burned shirt. "That's why she did it."

"What? Why?" He twisted his head, straining to see the spot she indicated over his shoulder.

"You need a wife."

"That's what my mother said. But I don't need a trouble-maker like you." He thought for a minute. "Now I understand why my intended never answered my letters. Ma said 'Miss Jones' was too busy caring for an invalid father."

"That's not true. There's nothing wrong with his constitution. I never knew about any letters. Don't you see what she did? She convinced me that you'd agreed to marry me and told you that I was a complete stranger. Then she made me promise to wear the hat."

Matt hated the fact that she might be telling him the truth. Why in hell would his own mother play him false this way? He'd told her he needed a woman who could help him on the ranch. He'd had it all figured out. This time, marrying would be like buying a horse. A man grew to count on and respect his horse, and even had an attachment for it. But if anything happened to that horse, he could get over it quick.

Eliza was completely unsuited for ranching. He knew his mother had always had a soft spot for the pain-in-the-neck tomboy who had turned his life upside down. But enough to betray her own flesh and blood?

"I can't believe she'd do this. She never once let on in her letters—"

"Oh, my gosh." Eliza slapped her cheek, then dropped the quilt from around her shoulders and moved to her carpetbag. She picked it up and threw it on the bed. "I completely forgot."

"What now?"

Matt watched Eliza as she stood in front of the oil lamp, rummaging through her bag. With the light shining behind her, her woman's body was clearly outlined through the thin nightgown. His eyes opened wider and he swallowed. That was not the body of the tomboy he'd known. She'd filled out into a woman. Even worse, he couldn't control his response to her. It made him madder than a wounded bear that Eliza Jones, of all people, could make him feel that hardness in his loins.

"Here it is." She pulled an envelope from her carpetbag. "Your mother gave me a letter for you to read after we were married."

"You look at it already?" he asked suspiciously. "Or maybe you forged it."

"I wouldn't do that."

"Why should I believe you?"

"Because I never lie. My father's a minister, for goodness' sake. If that's not enough, think about it for a minute. If I was a good liar, would you be in Wyoming now?" She put her hands on her hips. The movement pulled the thin material of her nightgown tight across her bosom. "I did not open this letter. Here." She held it out to him.

When Matt took the sealed envelope, she dropped her hand as if she was afraid he might touch her. He wanted to. God help him. In spite of this whole mixed-up marriage mess, he wanted to touch her . . . all over.

He opened the letter and immediately recognized his mother's familiar, curlicued scrawl. He quickly read the one page and it confirmed everything Eliza had said. They had both been tricked. His mother's only excuse was that she knew best. In a pig's eye, he thought angrily.

He handed the letter back to her. "Go ahead and read it."

She did, then looked up at him, smiling. She wasn't the least bit upset that they'd been bamboozled. "I think you owe me an apology."

He hated it that she was right. Even more, he hated the way her smile turned his gut to mush. But she *was* right.

His mother had said clearly that Eliza thought he'd known who he was marrying. They'd both been tricked and he'd misjudged her.

"Sorry," he mumbled.

She cupped her ear with her hand. "What did you say? I didn't hear that."

"Sorry," he said, only slightly louder.

"You know, the elevation here has sort of addled my hearing. Could you repeat that once more?"

"I'm sorry," he said, both words loud and distinct. If he spoke any louder, everyone in the boardinghouse would hear him. He clenched his teeth, then ground out, "And I'm not gonna say it again."

"That's quite all right," she said sweetly. "I accept your apology." She studied him intently as she folded her arms beneath her breasts. "You look wonderful, Matt. Your hair's longer, but otherwise you're still the most . . ." She stopped and looked down for a second.

"I'm still what?"

"Never mind." She picked up the braid resting on her breast and tossed it over her shoulder.

He couldn't take his eyes off her bosom; he could almost see the soft curves there. His palms tingled from the need to touch her. He reminded himself that she was a pest, and she always would be. He and his father hadn't spoken since the night Matt had stalked out of the house. It was all her fault.

"Even though this mail-order marriage isn't your doing, once a pain in the ass, always a pain in . . ." It was damn near impossible to think straight with her standing there dressed like that. He picked up the quilt in front of her and dragged it around her shoulders. Then he moved far enough away that he couldn't touch her.

A sad look settled in her green eyes as she clutched the thick material at her neck. "You haven't forgiven me for telling my father about you and Emily O'Leary."

"Why did you?" He waited for the anger to rush through

him and was surprised when he felt nothing, that he wasn't mad about it anymore. He just wanted to know why she had tattled to the reverend. He hadn't been willing to listen years before. "Couldn't you have said you never saw me that night?"

"That would have been a dead giveaway. He knew I followed you everywhere."

Before Matt could stop it, a corner of his mouth lifted. "You did, didn't you?"

She nodded. "You wouldn't let me explain that I tried to lie to my father. But he's a minister. Matt, he gave me that stare—do you remember it?" She shuddered, then continued. "One look and I knew he could see clear into my black soul and I was going straight to hell. I told him everything."

"You could have said nothing."

"I was just a child, Matt. I couldn't defy him. Not then." She looked spitting mad for a second, then her gaze rested on him. A sorrowful expression replaced the anger. "I feel terrible about what happened between you and your father."

"We never did get along. I don't think it bothered him so much that I spent the night with a girl who wasn't my wife. It was because she was the town tramp. Whatever happened to Emily?"

"She took up with a soldier and followed him to the Arizona Territory."

He crossed his arms over his chest. "I hope she's found what she wants."

"What about you? Have you found what makes you happy? Your mother says your letters go on and on about Wyoming, the ranch, the potential for raising cattle on this land."

He had big dreams, no question about that. He was close to seeing them come true. But only lately he'd realized that that didn't mean a whole lot if he was by himself, and without anyone to pass it on to.

"I found something worth working for. I suppose I

have you to thank for my being here at all. Like you said, if you were a good liar, my father would still be trying to make a businessman out of me."

"But you already are—a businessman, that is. Ranching is business."

"Not according to my father." He turned away.

"I can't wait to see the ranch. The land I saw on the way from Cheyenne was so beautiful, I can't even put it into words. And from the looks of that shirt, you need me to keep house for you."

He whirled around. "But we're not married."

"Not more than a half hour ago, we both said 'I do' and that man with the Good Book pronounced us man and wife. No one held a gun to your head."

"But I didn't know I was marrying *you*. That changes everything."

"It doesn't change the fact that in the eyes of man and God, we said vows."

"We'll just have to unsay them, get unmarried. Then you can go back where you came from."

She flipped her other long braid over her shoulder and shook her head. "I can't go back."

"Why the hell not? We'll get the thing annulled. We can do that as long as we don't—" He looked at the bed, then at her with the quilt still wrapped around her. A lot of good that blanket did. The image of her body outlined by the light was burned into his mind as surely as the Double C brand that marked his cattle. It would take a whole lot of willpower not to do with her what married people were supposed to do.

She was all grown up and she'd turned into a pretty little thing. But why his mother had thought Eliza Jones would make him a good wife he couldn't imagine. His list of qualifications had included sturdy and sensible.

He already knew he couldn't use the word *sensible* to describe Eliza. And sturdy? He didn't have to touch her to know she was small and delicate. Carrie had been strong, born and raised in Wyoming, and she hadn't survived. Eliza was used to a comfortable life back East. She was completely unsuited for the harshness of this land. No way was he going to hold her to her vows.

He stoked his animosity, built it up bright and hot even though he knew most of it had nothing to do with the past. If he let go of his anger, he'd have a bigger problem. He'd have to deal with the fact that she *wasn't* a stranger.

"I don't want the marriage annulled," Eliza said firmly.

"I do."

"I thought here in Wyoming, where women can vote, I'd get more say-so about my life."

"I guess you thought wrong."

She lifted her chin in the stubborn way he remembered. "Well, I can't stop you from getting an annulment. But that doesn't mean I have to go back where I came from."

"'Course you do."

She shook her head.

"Why the hell not?" he asked. "You can't stay." He knew she was too dangerous.

She looked sheepish. "It's a long story."

"It looks like we have all night." He sat on the bed and rested his elbows on his thighs, then dangled his hands between his knees. "Spit it out."

She sighed. "If I go back, I'll have to marry Cornelius Fairbrothers."

Matt willed himself to patience. It wasn't easy. Something told him she was starting in the middle or even at the end of her tale. "Why?"

"Father thinks I need a husband."

He took a deep breath. "Why?"

"Because things happen to me, and I—"

"What things?"

"Well, it wasn't a lot of things, just one particular thing."

"Tell me what it was. Sometime tonight."

"All right." She cleared her throat. "It was May, and unseasonably hot for that time of—"

"Dammit, Eliza. Get to the point. Sooner or later I've got to get some sleep before starting back to the ranch. Why was your father so all-fired anxious to marry you to this Fairweathers?"

"Brothers."

"What?"

"Fairbrothers. His name is Cornelius Fair*brothers*—"

"Eliza," he said, gritting his teeth. Two more seconds and he'd put her over his knee. Never in his life had he been tempted to lift his hand in anger toward a woman. Except for Eliza. He'd lost count of the times he'd wanted to throttle her. She always could provoke him like no one else could.

"You're not going to like it."

He snorted. "There's a surprise. Just tell me."

"All right. I was in jail."

"Holy shit." Of all the things he'd expected, that wasn't it. She could drive someone else to commit murder, but she was basically sweet, honest, and straightforward. She was just a girl, for God's sake. What could she possibly have done? "Why were you in jail?"

"I went to a rally."

Here we go again. "What kind of rally?"

"A women's suffrage rally.

"*Women's* suffrage?" He lifted a brow. "You're still wet behind the ears. Why would your father let you go?"

She frowned at him, then ignored his comment and went on with her story. "A friend asked me to go with her."

"What happened?"

"What makes you think something happened?"

"You don't go to jail for dusting the parlor, little girl."

"I'm not a little girl." Her mouth tightened and she speared him with a look, then went on. "Anyway, at the rally we heard the suffragettes speak about why women should have the vote. Wyoming men are forward-looking and reasonable, if you don't mind my saying so."

"I do mind. I just want to know why you went to jail,

how long you were there, and what that has to do with why you can't go back home to marry Fairweathers." His voice rose a notch.

She put her finger to her lips. "Shh. You'll wake the whole boardinghouse with your shouting. You certainly haven't learned patience, have you?"

"Eliza—"

"I was arrested along with everyone they could catch after the riot started. I spent the night in jail. My father got me out and said I had to marry Mr. Fairbrothers. I refused. That's when your mother stepped in and said you'd gotten over your wife's passing." She paused. "I was sorry to hear about your loss, Matt."

"Thanks." He looked down, then back at her. She was staring at him with those big green eyes of hers. "Get on with your story," he said gruffly.

"That's all there is. Except that whatever you decide to do, I'm staying in Silver Springs. I can't go back and face my father," she said with a shiver. "He'll make me spend my life tied to that pompous, condescending, hard-hearted, grim-faced banker. And those are Mr. Fairbrothers's good points."

Matt knew a lot about Eliza. One thing stood out above all the rest. She was stubborn as a mule. He could have the marriage annulled, but if she said she was staying, she meant it. What would become of her? How would she survive in Wyoming?

"There must be another man who wants a wife," she said as if she could read his mind.

"I get the feeling you're picky about men if Corny What's-his-name couldn't sweet-talk you into matrimony."

"I'm not picky." She adjusted the quilt around her shoulders and gripped it more tightly. "I'll do what I have to."

He didn't like the sound of that. "What are you talking about?"

"I'll get a job until I can find a man I like who will have me."

Matt could think of at least twenty men who'd have her, maybe more, and the thought of any one of them putting their hands on her was more than he could stand. She wasn't old enough or tough enough to handle a rough-around-the-edges territory man. Besides, he felt responsible for her. His mother had gotten her there under false pretenses.

"Have you seen the size of this town?" he asked. When she nodded, he went on. "It's not exactly the big city. You can't just go out and find a way to support yourself."

"I'll ask Mrs. Buchanan. She has her hands full with three children and the boardinghouse. Maybe she'd take me on, in exchange for working here."

"Ethel is barely getting by now. She can't take on another mouth to feed."

"Maybe Mr. Whitaker down at the stage office can find some work for me."

"Ed Whitaker?" For all his timid look, the man was the biggest womanizer Matt knew. Letting Eliza within ten feet of him would be like leading a baby lamb to the slaughter. He cursed the wagon wheel that had kept him on the trail and allowed her near Whitaker in the first place. "You're not to go to him for a job. You hear?"

"Then what is it you want from me, Matt?" She glared at him. "You don't want me for a wife, and you don't want me to be anyone else's wife."

"You're not old enough to be married. What in hell was your father thinking of to let you come out here? What possessed my own mother to send a little girl like you out here to marry me?"

She pulled herself up to her full height and squared her shoulders beneath the blanket. "I'm a full-grown woman, Matt Decker. Women younger than me are married with several children. No one forced me. I came out here because I wanted to."

"I want you to go home, Eliza," he said. Suddenly he

was tired, clear down to his bones. It was the middle of the night and he'd been up nearly twenty-four hours.

"No." She shook her head emphatically. "You don't have to worry about me. You go back to the ranch. I came out here on my own, I'll take care of myself the same way. If this is any indication of what to expect from married life, I don't think I want any part of it."

He studied her for a long time. He knew he wouldn't be able to get the annulment until the circuit judge came through. And he couldn't stay away from the ranch waiting until that happened.

If it killed him, and it probably would, he intended to send her back East in the same condition as when she'd arrived in Wyoming. He promised himself he wouldn't touch her, except to protect her.

"You're coming with me."

Eliza wasn't sure she'd heard him right. "What did you say?"

"I want you to come to the ranch."

"Why?" Her eyes narrowed. If this was about him thinking she was still a little girl, she'd tell him a thing or two.

"Because I want you to," he said.

He stood up and the bed creaked after being relieved of his weight. He was a big man, bigger and broader than her father. That was saying a lot, because she'd always thought the minister must be as tall as God. Matt stretched as if his muscles had been cramped and tensed for hours. His shirt pulled tight across his broad chest and the gesture was so very male that she held her breath. She wasn't the little girl he left behind. She was a grown woman with feelings and desires.

She wanted to stay with him. She wanted to see the ranch he'd built. She wanted to make a home for him—with him—and be his wife, in every way. He said he wanted her to go with him. After everything that had happened, she was afraid to hope that he'd changed his mind about her sharing his life.

"Why should I go with you?"

"I can't leave you here by yourself."

"What if I said I'd rather stay in town than go with you?"

To her amazement, he grinned. He'd been nothing but intense and grim-faced since she'd first opened the door to him. The amusement transformed him and brought back the twenty-one-year-old man she'd followed around as a lovesick twelve-year-old. Lord, but he was handsome.

"I'd know you were lying," he said.

"How?" She couldn't possibly be that obvious. Surely he couldn't see her heart fluttering.

"You came out here to get married. Why would I believe you wanted to work in town?"

"But—"

"It's settled." He held up his hand to stop further argument. "I'm tired, Eliza. And you must be, too. I need some rest. We're leaving for the ranch early."

"What about the annulment?"

"I'll check into it before we go."

He walked to the chair by the door and picked up his hat, then put his hand on the doorknob.

"Where are you going at this time of night?" she asked.

"Ethel must have another room in this boardinghouse."

"I think I got the last one. Besides, you can't wake her again. Isn't it bad enough you got her up once and forced her to get out her shotgun?"

"I can't stay in here—with you. It's not proper."

"We're married, for goodness' sake."

"In name only." His gaze darted to the bed. "And I aim to keep it that way."

"That's fine with me," she said. For once in her life she hoped she was a good liar. She turned away from him so he wouldn't see the tears gathering in her eyes. "Don't wake Mrs. Buchanan. You take the bed. I'll sleep on the floor."

Eliza let the quilt fall away from her shoulders so she could straighten the sheets on the mattress. She heard his boots on the wooden floor behind her. She felt his hands on her shoulders as he turned her to face him.

"I can't let a lady spend the night on the floor," he said.

"It doesn't matter. I'm so tired I could sleep on a rock."

"Eliza," he said with surprising gentleness, "I'm too tired to argue. I'll be the one sleeping on the floor and I don't want to hear another word on the subject."

She nodded. She was worn out. Bending over, she picked up the quilt at her feet and handed it to him. "This will make it a little softer."

"But you'll need it. It's cold in here."

"I'll be fine. This is a thick nightgown."

"No, it's not. Why, when you were in front of the lamp, I could see clear—" He stopped and swallowed hard.

"I don't need the quilt, Matt. I just want to sleep." She'd had about as much as she could stand for one day.

Eliza put one knee up and crawled into the soft feather bed. It was cold. She lay on her back and pulled the sheet up to her neck. Then the room went black as Matt blew out the lamp.

Chills shook her, and even when she rolled to her side and pulled her knees up, wrapping her arms around them, she couldn't get warm. She couldn't stop her teeth from chattering. But the darkness and the damp air were nothing compared to the emptiness inside her.

The odors of trail dust, axle grease, and bay rum mingled together and told her that he was near the foot of the bed. She heard his deep, even breathing. Darn it. He'd turned out the light only a few minutes before. How could he forget everything that happened and go to sleep so fast? She certainly couldn't.

This was not how she'd pictured her wedding night at all. A wave of sadness washed over her and pressed against her heart. She'd had such wonderful, silly, foolish dreams of a new life with Matt. Her fingers curled around the sheet at her neck. She would have a new life, all right. It just wouldn't include him. Her teeth chattered again and she clamped her jaw tight to keep from making any noise.

Then she heard him grunt and swear under his breath. This was followed by a scraping noise. The next thing she knew, she felt the heavy, snug warmth of the quilt as Matt settled it over her.

She sat up. "I don't want this."

He let out a long, slow breath. "I can't sleep for all the racket you're making. Take the damn thing."

She shook her head, then realized he couldn't see her. "I won't be able to sleep knowing you're on the floor without even a blanket."

"Don't worry about me."

"I can't help it."

In the darkness, she could almost hear his mind working. The next instant, the mattress dipped as he rested his weight on it.

"What are you doing?" she asked.

"I'm coming in with you."

"You are?" Had he reconsidered his decision about a real marriage with her?

The mattress bounced and swayed as he settled in. "Don't go getting any notion that things between us have changed. We can share the blanket and the bed to get some rest. But that's all. Wyoming gets damn cold. You might as well know that for the short time you'll be at the ranch."

"Boston was cold, too," she said, her teeth still chattering.

"Oh, hell," he said. "Turn over on your side, away from me."

"I already am."

He moved right up against her. He hesitated and his arm hovered near her for a few seconds. Then he fitted his hand to her abdomen and pulled her to his chest. "There. That better?"

"Yes," she lied. In a heartbeat his arm was removed and their bodies only touched where his chest met her back. She was warmer, all right. But it was cruel of him to taunt her like this when he had no intention of letting her be his wife.

"Good. Now go to sleep."

"'Night, Matt," she said softly.

"'Night."

Almost immediately, she heard his breathing grow soft and even in sleep. As his body relaxed, his arm slipped down and came to rest lightly over her stomach.

Through his shirt and her nightgown she could feel the muscles in his broad chest. His sleeve was rolled up and she let her fingers explore his bare arm, discovering that his wrist was wide and strong. Her buttocks nestled against his muscular thighs and even through the pants he still wore, she knew his power and strength. In sleep, he pulled her more tightly against him and his forearm brushed her breasts. The intimate touch made her heart race.

She'd never slept with a man before. Now she realized she'd have been better off if she never experienced it, for knowing that the joy of his big body wrapped so tightly around hers would be for just this short time was more than she could bear. From now on, she would compare every night to this one. If she had never seen Matt again, she wouldn't have missed feeling safe and secure. She would never have known how good contentment and the warmth of a man felt if she hadn't spent this short time in his arms.

He'd made it clear these were things she shouldn't get used to.

The sooner she settled into a life of counting only on herself, the better off she'd be. Earlier, she'd stopped arguing with Matt even though she had a lot left to say. There was no point in wasting her breath when his mind was made up. It was time he learned she could be just as stubborn as he was. In the morning he'd find out that she meant every word she'd said to him. No matter what, she was in Wyoming to stay. No matter what, she wasn't going to the ranch with him.

3

Matt rolled over and groaned, groggy from a deep sleep, the best rest he'd had in a long time. It took him a minute to remember where he was. This wasn't his bed, but it was soft and the feminine fragrance of wildflowers drifted to him. He stretched his hand out across the mattress. When he came up empty, he opened one eye.

The space beside him was vacant. He sat up, rubbing a palm across his stubbled chin as he looked around the room. Eliza's carpetbag was gone. On the dresser sat the hat that had hidden her when they had said their vows.

So it hadn't been a nightmare. The hat was a nightmare, but it wasn't a dream that he had married Eliza Jones. He also remembered telling her he was sleeping on the floor. What was he doing in the bed? He lifted the covers and looked down. At least he still had his pants on.

Then it came to him. He had awakened and heard Eliza's teeth chattering. The only solution had been to share the blanket and their body heat.

Somehow, he'd managed to keep his self-control while

holding her in his arms. And somehow, she'd managed to slip out of his embrace without his knowing.

Where the hell was she?

"Let me get this straight," he muttered to himself. "I got married less than six hours ago. I'm in a bed, with my pants on, all alone." He shook his head. "Somethin's wrong. Real wrong."

There was a knock on the door and he quickly got up to answer it. No doubt it was Eliza. He turned the knob and pulled the door inward.

"I'll be with you in—" It wasn't his wife, but the woman who owned the boardinghouse. "What are you doing here, Ethel?"

"For one thing, this is my house."

Ethel was a big woman, sturdy and sensible, the sort he should have married. Her black hair was pulled straight back from her ruddy face in a tight bun at her nape. Her dark eyes studied him speculatively as she stood there with her hands on her ample hips, very ample hips. Eliza was nothing like her. Somehow that was a comforting thought, although he liked and respected Ethel Buchanan.

"I mean, why are you here in my room?" he asked.

"Three reasons. First, breakfast is ready. Has been for hours and if you don't get your lazy behind out of that bed, you won't get none. Second, thought you might like to know your new wife has been up and out since dawn, askin' for work, all up and down Main Street."

"She's what?"

"She's lookin' to find a job here in town. 'Pears to me your mail-order bride took an instant dislike to that face of yours."

"What's the third reason you're here?" he asked, trying to keep his anger toward Eliza at bay.

"Saw Reverend Jim early this mornin', just before he left. Just wanted to give you my congrats on your weddin'."

"Thanks," he said through gritted teeth.

*   *   *

Eliza plopped her carpetbag down on the wooden planks outside the saloon. She'd been everywhere else and nobody could give her any work. If she couldn't find a job in the Silver Slipper, and it had to be a decent job, either she would have to go to Matt and eat crow, or go back home and do the same thing. She wasn't about to do either.

She placed a hand on the door.

"Excuse me, ma'am."

Eliza turned around. A little girl of about ten sat on the planks with her back leaning against the hitching post, facing the unsavory establishment. She had straight blond, almost white, hair and brown eyes. Her calico dress was patched and worn. The crocheted sweater she had on was far too small and not nearly warm enough to protect her from the cold wind blowing down the street. A tattered book lay open in her lap.

"Yes?" Eliza said. "Can I help you?" She walked over to the child and crouched down in front of her.

"No, ma'am. I'm fine. But looks like you need some help."

"Why do you say that?"

"'Cause my pa told me a lady doesn't ever go in a place like that. And you were just about to."

"Where's your pa now?"

She pointed to the door Eliza had almost entered. "In there."

"Is that why you're out here? Because a lady doesn't belong in a saloon?"

The girl nodded.

"What's your name?"

"Jenny. Jenny Evans."

"Well, Jenny Evans, your pa's right. A lady doesn't have any business in a place like that unless she can't find a job anywhere else in town."

Jenny tipped her head to the side and brushed a straight strand of hair from her cheek. "Why do you need a job, ma'am? Hear tell you married Mr. Decker."

"How did you know who I am?"

"I been sittin' here for a long time and everybody's talking about Mr. Decker's pretty little bride lookin' all over town for work. You're awful pretty, ma'am. You are the one that married him, aren't you?"

"In a manner of speaking."

"So why do you need a job? He's got a fine ranch. Lots of cattle and horses. Folks say he's gonna have the biggest place in the territory someday."

Eliza puzzled over that question for a minute. How did one explain that she'd made a huge mistake by getting married? How could she tell this child that Matt couldn't stand the sight of her and she couldn't go home?

There was no reasonable explanation so she sidestepped the question. "Where do you live, Jenny?"

"Here and there. We go all over and my pa looks for work. He's a cowboy."

"Does he have a job now?"

"No, ma'am. We was at the Double C a couple days ago. Mr. Decker told my pa that with winter comin' on he wouldn't have anything until spring roundup."

"Where's your mother?"

"She died of fever when I was three."

Eliza's heart went out to the little girl. "I am sorry, sweetheart."

"It's all right." She shrugged. "I don't remember her much. Can't miss what you never knew."

So young to have known such loss. Eliza wanted to wrap her arms around Jenny, but she sensed a core of pride in the girl that wouldn't permit it. The door in front of them opened, and a man staggered out without closing the door behind him.

"Is your father in the saloon looking for a job?" Eliza asked.

She had to admit that if there was work to be had, Jenny's father needed it more than she did. He had two mouths to feed.

Jenny looked at the opened door with eyes wise beyond her tender years. "No, ma'am. I'm real sure that's not what he's doin' inside."

The wind blew and Eliza pulled her heavy woolen shawl more snugly around her shoulders. Jenny hunched her slight body in an effort to stay warm.

"Do you have something warmer to put on, child?"

The girl shook her head. "I'm fine, ma'am. Truly."

The door in front of them banged closed and they both jumped. Eliza looked past Jenny to the mercantile on Main Street and made up her mind.

"Jenny, will you watch my carpetbag for a little while? I'll give you a nickel."

"I'll watch it, ma'am. But it wouldn't be neighborly to take money."

"Thank you. I'll be back very soon."

Matt pulled the wagon to a stop in front of the stage office. He'd been all over town looking for Eliza and had just missed her wherever he went. He'd picked up supplies while he was at it and this was his last chore. He wanted to have her trunk with him when he found her. The sooner he left Silver Springs with her, the better. Everywhere he stopped, people snickered behind their hands when they saw him. What the hell was she up to?

He jumped down and went inside. Ed Whitaker sat behind a cluttered desk, a tin cup filled with coffee at his elbow. The wooden walls were littered with paper, schedules, notices, and the like. Clustered in the corner, he saw a strongbox and mail sacks waiting to go out on the next stage to Cheyenne.

Ed looked up when Matt slammed the door shut. "Howdy, Matt. What can I do for you?"

"Came to fetch Eliza's trunk."

"Hear congratulations are in order." The other man smiled. "Your bride was in here a little bit ago. Asked for a job. Things so bad on the Double C, Matt? You gotta take a mail-order bride so you can send her out to work?"

Matt lifted his hat, then pulled it low over his eyes. One more word, Ed, he thought, and I'll ram that waxed mustache down your throat. "My wife has a mind of her own."

"Can't hold that against her. She's a right pretty little thing. I'd take a wife through the mail, too, if I knew I'd get me one who looks like her."

"That her trunk over in the corner?" Matt managed to keep his voice steady—barely. But anger burned through him bright and hot. He'd warned Eliza about this man, yet she'd come to him for a job. It was time to get her out of town. He would check with the sheriff and see if the circuit judge was due anytime soon. If not, he would take her back to the ranch where he could keep her out of trouble, for her own sake.

"That's hers. Need a hand, Matt?" Whitaker started to get up.

Matt stooped and lifted one end of the trunk, then shoved his shoulder beneath it and stood up. "No. I can manage this. See you, Ed."

"Congratulations again. And good luck. Somethin' tells me you're gonna need it."

He turned at the door. "You didn't happen to see which way Eliza went, did you?"

"Didn't see, but she said the only place she hadn't asked about work was the Silver Slipper."

"Thanks, Ed." With an effort, Matt kept his face expressionless. He left the stage office and dumped her trunk in the back of the wagon beside that hat. He secured the tailgate, then slammed his fist into it. Anger and apprehension twisted and turned inside him.

Surely she knew better than to go into a saloon and ask for a job. He had one more stop to make before he caught up with her.

*   *   *

Eliza handed Jenny the package she'd just bought at the mercantile, then went into the Silver Slipper. She waited by the door until her eyes adjusted to the dim interior. A haze of gray smoke hung in the air and burned her eyes and throat. The place was practically empty except for the proprietor and the man seated in the corner, face down on the table. His hat had tumbled off and she could see that his hair was sandy colored. Was he Jenny's father?

The man started coughing and couldn't seem to stop. Finally the spasm passed and he was still again. He was drunk as a skunk while that poor child waited patiently in the cold outside. Whether she found work here or not, Eliza was glad she'd used the last of her money to buy Jenny a warm coat. It would give her even more satisfaction to give the girl's reprobate father a tongue-lashing he would never forget. Unfortunately, that would have to wait until he was sober.

"What are you doin' in here?" asked the man wiping off the long bar that took up one whole wall of the establishment.

Behind him were shelves of liquor. In the center, between the bottles, was a painting. Eliza's eyebrows rose. It was a likeness of a naked woman. All of a sudden her face felt hot.

"Like my painting?" he asked, grinning at her.

"It's very big. I'm sure it's clearly visible from every single corner of this room."

"That it is," he said with pride. Then he stopped wiping and put both hands on the bar. "What do you want?"

Eliza swallowed hard and moved forward on shaky legs. "I'm in need of a job and I was wondering if you had work for me. Serving drinks, perhaps? Or food?"

The man looked her up and down. "Come closer so I can see you better. Over here under the lamp."

She stopped in front of the wooden bar. It was high

and she had to lift her elbows to lean them on the scratched and burned surface. The place smelled of liquor and sweat and smoke. She wrinkled her nose and her stomach turned over, but she decided she'd better get used to it. Her choices were severely limited.

The man studied her. "You ever worked in a saloon before?"

Eliza looked him straight in the eyes and hoped he couldn't see the lie in her own as she nodded. "Back East."

"You know how to keep the customers happy?"

"Of course." She didn't have the vaguest idea what he was talking about.

"You ever drink before?"

"Lots of times."

He turned away and pulled a bottle filled with amber liquid from the shelf behind him. He poured some into a tumbler and shoved it across the bar. "Prove it."

She stared at the glass as if it were a snake. "It's awfully early. Perhaps coffee would be—"

"This is a saloon, lady." He pushed the drink a little closer. "Do you want the job or not?"

Oh, Lordy, now what? Did she have a choice?

Matt stopped the wagon in front of the Silver Slipper. Two disturbing pieces of information had put him in a foul temper. He hadn't been this angry since that drifter he'd hired had gotten drunk and set fire to the barn.

After leaving the stage office, he'd stopped at the sheriff's and learned that the circuit judge wouldn't be back for six weeks. If he wanted an annulment, he had to go all the way to Cheyenne. Since he couldn't afford to be away from the ranch that long, he had to wait. And if the bad weather came early this year, as it showed every indication of doing, he'd probably have to wait till spring to end this marriage. That was the first thing that had set him off.

But what had really pushed his temper to the boiling point

was learning that Eliza was in the saloon looking for a job. He wrapped the reins around the brake handle and jumped down from the wagon. After adjusting his hat low over his eyes, he stepped up on the planks outside the saloon.

"Mr. Decker?"

He looked down at the little girl who had some opened brown wrapping with a new coat right in the center of it resting in her lap.

Matt hunched down beside her. "How did you know who I am?"

"I peeked out of the wagon when Pa and I stopped at your place a couple days ago. He was looking for a job."

He nodded. "I remember him." The man had had a fit of coughing and Matt knew he wasn't strong enough for cowboyin' even if he'd had the work to give him. Matt had sent him into town where he would be better off. "Did he find anything?"

She shook her head. "He will, though. Somehow we always make out."

"I guess so," he said, nodding at the new coat.

"Pa didn't get me this. It was the lady."

"Which lady?" His eyes narrowed.

"The one who went in the saloon."

"Do you know her name?" He was sure he already knew when he noticed Eliza's carpetbag sitting next to the girl.

"She didn't tell me. Said she married you 'in a manner of speakin'.' What does that mean?"

"It means she was real happy."

"The lady didn't seem too happy. She wouldn't own up that she married you at first." She studied him somberly for a minute and Matt wondered what else Eliza had said about him.

"Was the lady mad?" he asked.

The girl thought for a minute, then shook her head. "No, worried, more like. I told her a lady shouldn't go in the saloon, but she said she had to if she couldn't find a job anywheres else."

"That's Eliza."

"I told her not to go in."

"You're a sensible girl, unlike another female I know." He glanced over his shoulder at the saloon door. He looked back and took the coat from her lap, then held it for her to slip her arm in. "You put this on. There's a cold wind blowing."

When she was snugly buttoned up, Matt stood and grabbed Eliza's carpetbag, which he tossed into the back of the wagon with her trunk.

"Mr. Decker, I promised the lady I'd take care of her bag," the girl said. She was standing now beside the hitching post, and there was a fierceness in her blue eyes. She looked ready to do battle. Eliza had won her over in a hurry.

"You did a good job. I'll handle it now."

Matt patted her shoulder, then walked past her into the saloon. It took a few seconds for his eyes to become accustomed to the darkness inside. When he could see clearly, he got mad all over again. Eliza stood in front of the bar staring at a glass of whiskey. Brad Slicker, the barkeep, was grinning at her. Before Matt could stop her, she picked up the glass and gulped the contents.

Instantly, she started choking. Matt ran across the room, his boots ringing on the wooden floor. He patted her back and grabbed the glass from her hand as he glared at the other man.

"What in the hell are you doing, Brad? You know better than to give liquor to a lady."

"She was askin' for a job. Anyone who works here has to be able to drink with the customers."

"She won't be drinking with your customers."

"You can't . . . run my life," Eliza said between spasms of coughing. She wiped her eyes and looked at the barkeep. "I drank the whiskey. Do I get the job?"

Matt slapped his hand on the bar and stared down at her. "It'll be a cold day in hell before any wife of mine works in a saloon."

She brushed a hand across her mouth and glared straight up at him, her eyes big and angry. "It'll be a cold day in hell before I'll be a wife to the likes of you."

"Don't be swearing at me."

"Then don't you swear at me."

"I think we need to discuss this in private," Matt said, turning away from the man behind the bar, who was still grinning like an idiot. Brad Slicker was enjoying his predicament far too much and was bound to spread this story all over town. In Silver Springs, that would take all of half an hour. Matt moved between her and the barkeep.

"You gave up any right to tell me what to do, Matt Decker. Now get out of my way," she said, hiccuping loudly as she tried to get around him. "I need to see this gentleman about a job."

The bartender chuckled. "She's got spunk, Matt."

"She does that. I'd settle for a little less spunk and a lot more sense. She's coming with me."

"I'd say the lady doesn't want to go with you. I could use someone like her in my place. Give it a little class."

"Thank you, sir," she said, moving around Matt. She held out her hand. "Then we have a deal? When can I start work?"

The slow burn that had been kindling inside Matt since finding her gone from the bed now ignited into flames. There was no way he would permit her to work in a place like this for a two-bit womanizer like Brad Slicker. Everyone in town knew Matt had married her. She was his responsibility now. Since she didn't seem inclined to be reasonable, he had to take drastic measures.

Matt took the hand she held out to the bartender and turned her. He pulled her toward him, then stooped down, wrapped his arms around her waist, and lifted her off the ground. He heard her gasp as the air left her lungs.

"You put me down!" She started to squirm in an effort to break his hold.

"Not on a bet." He slapped a hand against her backside

and left it there to hold her in place. He felt her stiffen in outrage.

"The lady is declining your offer," Matt said. "She's going to the ranch with me."

"Matt Decker, you put me down this instant. I'm not going anywhere with you."

"Offhand, I'd say you don't have a choice." He nodded to the barkeep. "Good day, Brad."

The man laughed. "I have every chance of a good day. Sorry I can't say the same for you, Decker."

Matt felt her small fist land on his lower back. Brad was right. It was not going to be a good day.

4

Eliza had never been so angry in her life.

"I demand that you put me down this instant, Matthew James Decker!"

She'd suffered more humiliation at the hands of this man than any woman should have to endure. Now she was hanging upside down over his shoulder as he carried her onto Main Street. Blood rushed to her head, making her ears buzz and her cheeks tingle.

She whacked him once, as hard as she could, in the center of his broad back. He ignored her and kept walking.

"Did you hear me? You let me go or I'll . . ."

"You'll what?" Matt stopped, but she continued struggling.

"Mrs. Decker?" It was a child's voice.

Eliza went still. Mrs. Decker? That was her.

"Mrs. Decker?"

"Jenny?" She tried to lift up and see around Matt, but she couldn't. "Is that you?"

"Yes, ma'am." Footsteps shuffled on the planks as the

little girl walked around to stare at Eliza. "Are you all right?"

Eliza could hear the worry and uncertainty in Jenny's tone. And no wonder. What kind of man would carry a woman from a saloon in such a manner? She needed to reassure the little girl even though her undignified position hardly confirmed her words.

"I'm just fine," Eliza said. Then she hiccuped. After that, she started to giggle. What was wrong with her? There was nothing at all humorous about her situation.

She looked at the child, but all she could see was the middle button of the new blue coat she was wearing. "Jenny, please don't call me Mrs. Decker. My name is Eliza Jones. But you can call me Eliza."

She wanted to glare at Matt as hard as she could, but her only view of him, besides the iron-shaped burn in his shirt, was his backside. She stared at it for a moment as an idea struck her. Since beating on him with her fists seemed ineffective, maybe there was another way to get his attention. Her eyes narrowed. She took her thumb and forefinger and grabbed as much of his hind end as she could through his denim pants.

"Hey!" He jumped. "What the hell are you doing, woman?" He tried to look at her over his shoulder, but her derriere was in his way. "You shouldn't be doing things like that in public."

Aha! she thought. She pinched him again as hard as she could.

"Eliza!"

He tried to bat her hand away, but with her on his shoulder he couldn't. Then she felt his body tense. People walking by stopped. Since she could see only their legs, she assumed they were curious about what was happening between her and Matt outside the saloon. She couldn't fight him with sheer brute strength, but he would pay for humiliating her like this. She pinched him again and he jumped again.

"Show's over, folks." His tone was low and she suspected he'd gritted his teeth, although she couldn't see for sure. He probably glared at them, too, because the people moved on.

"Eliza, I'm warning you," he growled.

"Then put me down, you big bully. Or I'll keep it up until you do."

He loosened his grip, and she slid down his hard chest, feeling his muscled thighs through her thick green wool skirts. She staggered, whether from the whiskey she'd drunk in the Silver Slipper or too much blood to her head, she wasn't sure. Matt reached out and held her upper arms until she was steady. His hands felt warm and strong and sure.

Eliza looked up at him. "I'm glad you finally saw the error of your ways."

"*My* ways? You're the one drinking whiskey for breakfast."

"And I had that job, too. But thanks to you, I'm not sure I'll get hired now."

"Damn right you won't work there."

She tied the ends of her shawl in a knot over her breasts and jammed her hands on her hips. The wind blew, but she was so mad, she hardly felt its bite.

"Eliza?"

She glanced down and saw that Jenny was beside her.

"What is it, sweetheart?" she asked, crouching down to the little girl's level.

"I'm glad you're not going to work in the saloon. I wish my pa wouldn't go in there either."

Eliza swallowed against the lump in her throat. This poor little girl was waiting alone out in the cold for a man who was dead drunk and collapsed on a table inside.

Matt looked down at the child. "Jenny, your father will probably be in there for a while. Can you do something for me?"

"Depends." With eyes big and blue and old for a child her age, she solemnly stared up at him.

He reached into his pocket and pulled out some money. "I want you to go over to the boardinghouse and get a room. Tell Mrs. Buchanan I sent you. There's enough money here for a couple days. That should give your pa time to rest up and get well."

"How will he know where I am?"

"I'll tell the barkeep to see that he gets to Ethel's when he's sober—when he's ready to leave." He smiled at her. "You just go on over there. Mrs. Buchanan will take good care of you."

"I don't know if Pa would want me to do this, mister."

"Consider it payment for watching the lady's bag." He glanced at Eliza. "And for telling me what the lady was up to."

Eliza managed to keep her anger in check, only because Matt was doing a kind and generous thing for this needy child. "Jenny, thank you for taking care of me. You earned every cent of that. Now run along and get warm. And have a hot meal."

"Yes'm, if *you* say so. Thanks, Mr. Decker." She smiled, then shyly took the money from Matt before turning toward the boardinghouse. After a slight hesitation, she whirled around and threw herself into Eliza's arms. "Thank you."

Eliza hugged her close for a minute, then let her go run down the street.

Matt pointed a finger at Eliza. "You stay put while I tell Brad Slicker to get her pa to Ethel's when he sobers up." He disappeared inside the saloon.

In a pig's eye she'd stay put. Eliza wasn't about to obey any order Matt gave her. She started up the street but didn't get more than a few feet before she heard his heavy boots on the boardwalk behind her. She quickened her pace, but then she felt her arm gripped, pulling her up short.

"I told you not to move." Matt's voice was tight with anger. "Where do you think you're going?"

She looked up at him. "I don't have the slightest idea. But anywhere you *aren't* will be fine with me."

"We have some things to talk about."

"I thought we'd settled everything."

"Not by a long shot. Get in the wagon."

Eliza looked at the big wooden ranch wagon up the street a ways beside the saloon. There were supplies in the back of it, along with her trunk, carpetbag, and the hideous hat that had gotten her into this mess in the first place.

"Why should I?"

"I'm taking you to the ranch with me."

"I'm not going."

"You're my wife. You'll do what I tell you." He glanced up and down the street.

For the second time that day, people slowed down and eyed the two of them. His discomfort gave her great satisfaction.

"No man is going to tell me what to do." She stuck her chin out and met his gaze. "This is Wyoming. Women have the right to vote."

"This is not an election. You're my responsibility."

"Not anymore." She started to walk away, but he hadn't released her arm. "Let me go."

"No."

"Why? You made it clear you don't want any part of me."

"I can't leave you to fend for yourself when it was my mother's idea for you to come out in the first place." With that, he bent at the knees and lifted her the way he had inside the saloon.

"Oh, no, you don't. Not again." She tried to twist out of his grip, but he was too fast and far too strong. "Let me go!" She cried.

"This is your own fault, Eliza. You left me no choice."

He marched up the street, climbed into the wagon, and dropped her on the seat.

She tried to scramble out the other side, but he grabbed her with his left hand. With his right, he pointed to a coil of rope at his feet.

"One more move, Eliza. Just one, and I'll tie you up." His eyes were like blue fire. She didn't think she'd ever seen him so angry, not even the night he'd fought with his father.

"You wouldn't dare truss me like a Thanksgiving turkey."

"I was thinking more of hog-tying you. Have you ever seen a hog tied, Eliza? They're slippery little critters, so they bind the front legs, then the rope goes—"

"You win, Matt. I'll go with you."

He stared hard at her for half a minute, then nodded and released her arm. After sitting beside her, he unwound the reins and slapped them against the two horses impatiently tossing their heads. They started forward.

Eliza refused to say one more word to him as they rode out of town. The air between them fairly crackled with hostility.

Finally, she spoke. "This is kidnapping. There must be laws against that, especially in Wyoming."

"It's not illegal for a man to take his wife home."

"What if she doesn't want to go?"

"It's for your own good."

"If you cared about what was best for me, you would have stayed out of it and I'd have a job now."

"In a saloon? Little girl, you don't have the slightest idea what you were letting yourself in for. You're a minister's daughter."

"I'm smart. I learn fast. And I'm not a little girl. How many times do I have to tell you I'm a grown woman?"

"The things you'd learn in that place no decent woman should know."

This was getting them nowhere. Eliza glanced over her

shoulder. The little town of Silver Springs was growing smaller as they moved relentlessly forward. She needed to get back there. If they traveled too far, she knew she'd never find it again. She wasn't stupid enough to think she could survive on her own in the wilderness, but she was hurt enough to be very sure that she didn't want to go anywhere with Matt. She forced herself to relax and consider her options.

She leaned over and looked at the ground slowly passing by. They weren't going very fast. It wasn't so very high up. Why, she wasn't even as high as the tree she used to climb and hide in to spy on Matt when she was a child. She could make it.

"Matt, it seems you've left me no choice." She smiled sweetly at him.

"I'm glad you finally see things my way. The ranch is the best place for us to work this out." His eyes narrowed.

He was uneasy whenever she was reasonable, but this was the best solution. With luck, in six weeks the circuit judge would come through Silver Springs. By then, everyone would have forgotten today's little scene. He could get a quiet annulment, then put her on a stage back to Cheyenne, and from there she could catch the train to Boston.

"You'll see. Things will work out." He settled the reins in both hands. As soon as he had rested his elbows on his knees and looked at the road ahead, she stood up and placed one foot up on the side of the wagon. In that instant, he knew exactly what she had in mind.

"Eliza, don't!" he hollered.

He reached out for her, but managed to grab only her woolen shawl as she jumped. He stared at it in his hand for a second, then reined in the horses and set the brake. Damn her! He should have tied her up in the first place. He was too godawful tired of chasing her all over kingdom come. But he had no choice, since the only place she could go was back to town.

He grabbed the rope and leaped down. This time he'd make sure she stayed put.

He found her sitting in the tall grass beside the road, rubbing her ankle.

"Eliza, this is the last straw."

She looked up at him, then her gaze lowered to the coil in his hand and her eyes grew wide. She got unsteadily to her feet, but when she put her weight on her right leg, she staggered and nearly fell.

"Shit." Matt took a step forward.

She glanced over her shoulder, then lifted her skirt and half skipped, half ran from him. She was beaten. Why couldn't she just go quietly? Eliza Jones was still nothing but trouble. He stomped after her.

That was the last time he would ever confide in his mother. All he'd wanted was a sturdy, sensible woman to be a partner with him in the ranch. He'd thought the *sturdy* requirement the most important. Now the *sensible* part had taken on a whole new meaning.

"Eliza! Stop. Don't be a fool."

She kept right on going as if she hadn't heard him. She could hardly walk, let alone outrun him, but that's what she was trying to do. Idiot woman! She was headstrong and impetuous. Still, deep inside him, a spark of admiration for her spunk flared to life.

As he went after her, he wondered what he was going to do with her. She'd nearly killed herself trying to get away from him. No matter what she said, he had to look out for her, at least until the annulment. He had to convince her to go with him to the ranch. He shook the rope in his hand. A sturdy length of hemp could be pretty persuasive.

With little effort, he caught up with her and fell into step beside her. So far, manhandling her hadn't gotten him anything but pinched on the behind in public after following her all over town. Now he was chasing her down the road. Things had sure changed since they were kids. *He* was the one trailing after *her* this time.

She turned her head to look at him and lifted her small chin high. That stubborn expression was way too familiar.

"You wouldn't dare tie me up." She hobbled forward and he could tell by the way she clenched her teeth that she was hurting bad. He got mad all over again.

"What the hell did you jump for? You could have broken your neck."

"If I had, then all your problems would be over." She continued walking, until she stepped in a rut in the road. She cried out as she crumpled to the ground.

He went down on one knee beside her and held out a hand. When she ignored it, he curled his fingers into a fist and rested his forearm on his thigh. Did she have reason to be so upset? He was the one who'd been tricked. So had she, a damn rational little voice argued back. If he had known getting a mail-order bride would be this much trouble, he'd have bought a horse instead.

"Dammit! You're the most stubborn, pigheaded woman I ever saw. Are you prepared to crawl all the way back to town? Or are you ready to let me take a look?"

"Don't swear at me." She glared at him. "If I let you look, you'll likely tie that rope around me."

She took a deep, shuddering breath and turned her head away. Had there been a quiver in her voice? When she brushed the back of her hand near the corner of her eye, he wondered if she was crying. He realized he'd seen her cry only once before. The day he'd left home.

He'd only told her what to do because it was best. That didn't seem so important now. He could fight her contrary determination, but he had no weapon against her when she was like this.

"All right, Eliza. You win. I'll take you back to town."

She sniffled but said nothing.

He waited, but she just sat there biting the corner of her lip. He guessed this was how she kept herself in control. This was more than the discomfort from her ankle. He'd slammed the door on her finger once, trying to keep her from following him, and she hadn't shed a single tear. Physical pain wouldn't reduce her to this.

He was sure it had more to do with the fact that she'd come halfway across the country expecting to marry a man who wanted her. It had a lot to do with not wanting to go back to the life she'd left. Though he hated to admit it, she was probably upset because he hadn't given a single thought to her feelings since she'd lifted the veil on that hat and he'd recognized her.

"I'm sorry I bullied you. I'll drive you back to Ethel's. Give me your hand." He stood and held his palm out to help her to her feet.

"I c-can't go there."

"Why not?"

She bit her full top lip again and blinked hard.

"Doggone it. What do you want? I'm ready to take you anywhere. Just stop crying."

"I'm not crying."

"Doesn't much matter whether you are or not. I'll take you wherever you say except Ed Whitaker's or the Silver Slipper. I didn't know how strongly you felt about things. I won't force you to go to the ranch. So say the word and—"

"I have no m-money. I used the l-last of what you sent to buy Jenny's coat."

"Then why in the hell did you nearly kill yourself to go back?"

"I figured I could get Mr. Slicker to give me the job. But now . . ." She massaged her ankle and shook her head. "You made me so darn mad. Telling me what to do. Carrying me around as if I was nothing more than a s-sack of flour."

What a mess he'd made of things. He'd only tried to take care of her because he was responsible for her. He was responsible, all right—for pushing her to the point of desperation so that she felt her only choice was to jump and hurt herself. He felt lower than the slime on the underside of a rock.

"I'm sorry, Eliza." He went down on his knee again and gently turned her chin toward him with his index finger. Her eyes looked greener than ever, as well as red and puffy from crying. "It's just that, with you going up and down Main Street looking for a job when everyone knew we just got married . . . Hell, I was pretty mad, too. Guess I wasn't thinking straight."

She stopped rubbing her leg. "I didn't know what else to do. I need to earn my keep."

"You ready to let me look at that yet?" he asked, pointing to her injured leg.

She sighed. "I suppose."

"Let's get you out of the middle of the road." He stood and offered her a hand. This time she let him pull her up.

She took one step and sucked in her breath.

Matt put his arm around her waist and pulled her arm up across his back, so she could grip his shoulder. "Hold on and I'll help you over to that rock."

They took a few halting steps, then he stopped so she could rest.

"Matt, this might be easier if you just played the bully again and threw me over your shoulder."

"Might be at that." He grinned. Some of her spirit had returned. He was glad.

He lifted her in his arms, gently this time, and carried her to the side of the road before carefully setting her down. He hunkered beside her and took her heel, setting it on his knee. Now what? It wasn't right for him to look at a woman's leg. He glanced up and saw the freckles across the bridge of her nose. Hell, this was Eliza. One time they'd gone swimming in the river back home and he'd seen her legs all the way up to her knees. A little further, in fact. Wasn't anything special. How improper could this be?

Pushing her skirts up, he cautiously touched the thick wool stocking encasing her leg. He tried to study it objectively, the way he would a horse or steer. He swallowed hard. No horse he knew of had limbs that looked as good as Eliza's. Even through the thick material, he could tell that she was shapely and slender. Except from the middle of her calf down. There her leg looked like a stuffed sausage. There was an awful lot of swelling. He didn't think he could pull her boot off without causing her pain. He told himself she deserved what she got, but then he couldn't put her through it.

He slipped his knife from his boot.

"What are you going to do?" she asked.

"I'm sorry, Eliza. There's no other way. I need to cut it off."

"My leg?" she cried.

"Of course not. Your shoe."

"Oh. In that case, go ahead. My foot hurts like the very devil."

He lowered his head and grinned. It was only the second time he'd ever heard her swear.

Very carefully he sliced through the leather and pulled the shoe away. He couldn't tell much through her heavy stocking and he started to cut that, too.

She touched his hand. "No, Matt. I don't have enough stockings for you to ruin these." She pushed her skirt higher and fiddled with the fastenings.

It was far too much like being married. He stood and looked away.

After a minute or so she said, "You can turn around now. I'm ready."

He did turn, but he wasn't prepared, at least not for the sight of her leg bared nearly up to her . . . Whoa, that's as far as he cared to go with that kind of thinking. After all, this was Eliza. Still, the sight of her feminine curves filled him with longing, a feeling he hadn't had for some time. The sight of her graceful thigh and knee made his hands sweat and his chest ache. The delicate limb sorely tested his control.

Standing a foot away, he studied the injury. He didn't

dare touch her bare flesh. Especially since she was hurt. He was almost grateful for the swelling and the purple already spreading around her ankle.

"Doesn't look too serious. Can't be broken since you were able to walk on it and all. Probably just a sprain."

A chill wind rustled the grass beside them and whistled through the trees nearby. He smelled the weather turning colder and was anxious to get back to the ranch. The repair on the wagon wheel was as flimsy as the patch on a schoolboy's britches. He wasn't sure it would hold, and he was less than eager to spend the night on the trail with Eliza.

She shivered and he remembered that her heavy woolen shawl was in the wagon.

"Put your clothes on. We need to get going." He turned away again.

"Where, Matt? We haven't settled anything. What about the annulment?"

"I still plan to get it. You can't stay, Eliza. Life's too hard here. You're not cut out for it." He pushed his hat back and waited until he knew she had to be completely covered. Then he turned, squatted beside her, and looked at her uncertain expression. "Just before I found you in the saloon, I stopped at the sheriff's. The judge won't be back for at least six weeks, if the good weather holds."

"What are we going to do?"

He put his hand on her knee, a friendly gesture of comfort, nothing more. "I've been thinking. You need a way to earn your keep and I need help on the ranch. That's what got me into this predicament in the first place."

That and his yearning for a son. Without thinking, he'd moved his fingers toward her thigh. Then suddenly he removed his hand from her leg as if it burned him like a hot coal.

"This really is a mess, isn't it?" The look in her green eyes was so lost that for a second she reminded him of Jenny. He wouldn't abandon Eliza the way the child's father had done her. No matter what, he'd see that Eliza was all right.

"It's not that bad. Things will work out. You'll see." He ran his fingers through his hair, then pulled his hat low on his forehead. "We'll go to the ranch. Give your leg a chance to heal, wait until we can see the judge and end this marriage."

She bit her lip again and he held his breath. Then she nodded. "I guess there's no other choice."

"None that I can see."

She shivered again. "Then I guess we'd better get going."

"I'll help you," he said, holding out his palm.

"All right." She looked at his hand and tried to smile. "I never meant for things to go so wrong, Matt."

"It's not entirely your fault."

He picked up the rope he'd set aside and watched her slowly limp toward the wagon. It had taken half the day, but finally he'd convinced her that his way was best. He'd take her to the Double C where he could keep her out of trouble. Six weeks would pass like lightning. Things couldn't get any worse.

5

"Whoa!" Matt said.

He pulled the horses to a stop in front of the ranch house. He was cold and hungry and angry because he would have been asleep by now except for Eliza's foolishness. It didn't sweeten his temper any that *she* was sound asleep with her cheek resting on his thigh. Her snuggling had been driving him crazy for the last three hours.

"Wake up," he said, shaking her shoulder none too gently.

She moaned and burrowed further into the jacket he'd thrown over her. The moonlight outlined her smooth skin, the long lashes that shadowed her cheek, and her small, pointed, stubborn chin. That chin had been defiantly lifted in the air a lot today. At least until she'd begun to sway in her seat. She'd finally toppled sideways into his lap and he'd let her stay there. He had been just too damn tired to move her.

Lucky for her the full moon had given them enough light to travel by. He'd made the decision to keep going after sundown because he didn't want to be stuck on the trail with her. He was glad to be finally home. Only now that they were here, he was nervous. It seemed very important that Eliza approve of his ranch. She was the first person from home to come to Wyoming. When she went back, he wanted her to be able to tell everyone that he'd amounted to more than a pile of horse manure.

He realized it was more than proving himself to the people back home, though. He wanted to impress *her*. He just wasn't sure why it mattered that he did.

"Eliza?" He touched her shoulder.

She groaned again, but didn't open her eyes. She must be completely worn out between the long trip from Boston, a restless night at Ethel's, and her job hunt all over town. Or maybe it was the whiskey that had put her under. Eliza had almost certainly never touched a drop of liquor in her life and she'd tried to convince a leather-tough old barkeep that she could hold her own with his customers. Hard as he tried, Matt couldn't stifle a grin at the memory. He'd forgotten how she could liven things up. A pain in the ass she might be, but she was never boring. The smile faded quickly. She wouldn't be here long enough to liven things up.

"Eliza? Come on now." He shook her.

She stretched and pulled one hand from beneath his sheepskin lined jacket. As soon as the cold hit her, she shivered and groaned and quickly put her arm back under the warm coat.

"I don't want to wake up," she said, her voice hoarse from sleep as she burrowed against his thigh.

Something tightened in his chest like wet rawhide drying in the sun. He wanted to pull her onto his lap and wrap his arms around her. He fought that feeling with everything he had. Caring about a woman wasn't something he'd ever do again.

Eliza had tagged after him when she was a child and he hadn't the heart to send her packing then. Because of that, he already had too many shared memories with her. With her big green eyes and cheerful smile, she was more dangerous to him now than when she'd blabbed his secrets to her father.

Hell, what was he fretting about? He kept forgetting—*this was Eliza.* She was still that little girl. But when she sleepily rested her hand beside her cheek and her fingers trailed down the inside of his leg, his instant physical response proved he didn't think of her as a child. No matter what, he wouldn't let himself think of her as a woman. Everything would have been so much easier if she were a stranger.

"C'mon, sleepyhead. Get up."

Eliza yawned and lifted her head. Beneath her hand she felt the rock-hard muscle in Matt's thigh. She felt so safe and snug, she was unwilling to move and lose the feeling.

The last thing she remembered was Matt helping her into the wagon. She was surprised to find herself sleeping in his lap. The way he'd treated her, she would have expected him to throw her in the back of the wagon with the sacks of flour, sugar, and coffee.

She sat up and the jacket fell away from her. It had to be Matt's, and he had to be freezing without it.

She handed it back to him. "Thank you for this."

He looked at her beside him. "Put it on until I can get a fire going in the house."

She shook her head and pulled her woolen shawl tighter around her shoulders. "I'm fine."

He stared at her for a second before taking it and slipping first one, then the other, arm into it and turning the collar up around his neck. "How's the ankle?"

She rotated her stockinged foot and winced. "Throbs like the devil when I move it."

"Let's get inside." He stood and crossed in front of her, then jumped. He raised his arms to help her down.

Eliza hesitated. She hadn't wanted to come to the ranch with Matt mostly because he'd hurt her and rejected her. Now that the house loomed before her, she knew there was more to her reluctance than bruised feelings.

She had to go inside and see the rooms he'd shared with his first wife, the bed he'd slept in with the woman he'd loved and lost.

Eliza had come to Wyoming with high hopes for a lifetime with Matt. Six weeks was all she would get.

She remembered his arms around her in bed last night and realized then that it would have been better to never have known such pleasure. She had a feeling that seeing his home, and what they could have shared together, would make her feel even more regret. She sighed. Sooner or later she had to face it.

She stood up, carefully keeping her weight off the injured ankle. Matt put his hands at her waist and she braced herself with her fingers on his shoulders. He lifted her down, then instantly released her to move to the back of the wagon. She heard the creak of the tailgate as it was lowered.

Unsteadily, she turned and looked at the one-story frame house. A wide porch and overhang fronted the structure. The windows on either side of the front door were dark. She shivered. Best get it over with and go in. She started to hobble and a sharp pain shot from her ankle all the way up her leg.

She sucked in her breath. "Lord Almighty."

"Eliza?" Matt called.

"I'm all right."

"What's wrong?" he asked, coming up beside her.

She looked at him uncertainly. "I might need some help. I'm sorry."

His hat hid the expression in his eyes, but she saw his lips thin to a straight line. He put one hand behind her knees and the other across her back and lifted. "Put your arm around my neck."

She nodded. "I heal fast, Matt. Honestly. Why, tomorrow I'll race you the way we used to. . . ."

"Doesn't matter. I'll rig up a cane or something to help you get around. Telling you to stay off it would be like asking a jackrabbit not to move a muscle."

Eliza heard the curtness in his voice. Was he having second thoughts about bringing her here? He was taking her into the house where he'd lived with the woman he'd expected to be with forever.

"That's not true. I can follow orders as well as the next person as long as the orders are sensible." Her breast brushed against his chest where his jacket gaped open.

"Didn't the minister teach you that you go to hell for telling lies?" he asked. He shifted her in his arms so the contact was less intimate.

He carried her to the porch and up the three stairs. After crossing the wooden planks, he awkwardly opened the front door and pushed it wide with his shoulder. He started to bring her inside, the way a bridegroom traditionally carries his wife over the threshold of her new home.

"Put me down, Matt." She tried to disentangle her legs from his grasp.

"What's wrong with you?"

"Nothing. I just want you to let me go."

"Quit wiggling. I'll set you down when we get inside."

Eliza knew there was no point in resisting. He was far too strong.

Tears welled in her eyes. She didn't feel like a bride. How she wished things could have been different. She'd dreamed of being a bride in a home of her own since she was a girl. She'd imagined magic and excitement, and love. This moment was nothing like she'd fancied it would be.

Matt's ranch would never be her home. If she wasn't practically crippled, he would have let her march in under her own power. She squirmed in his arms, wanting to be anywhere but there.

"Hold on," he said. "I'm going into the kitchen. I'll light a lantern and the fire in the grate so we can get warm."

The moonlight shining through the windows and into the hall was his only guide. Without hesitation, he carried her through the house.

He stopped in a big room and seated her on a wooden chair. She heard the screech of the lantern chimney as he lifted it, then the scratch of a match before she saw the flare of fire he used to light the lamp. He brought it to the table and set it down beside her.

"Welcome to the Double C," he said. "Sit tight while I get a fire going."

She nodded, shivering. The cold inside the house penetrated her body the way the wind hadn't been able to do. Before long he had a blaze roaring in the hearth that sent warmth and light creeping out into the room. It was surprisingly bare. She'd expected to see evidence of a woman's touch, but there weren't curtains at the windows or even a cloth on the table. For some reason, that made her feel better.

"I'm going to bring in your things," he said.

She started to say she'd help, then felt a throb of pain in her ankle. He'd had to carry her inside; there was no way she could handle even her carpetbag. Guilt flashed through her as she watched his broad back disappear in the shadows down the hall.

She heard him moving through the house. She could tell he made several trips to the wagon before he appeared in the kitchen again.

She glanced around. "This is a nice room, Matt."

"Yeah." He took his hat off and hung it on a peg by the back door. Seconds later, his jacket was beside it.

"With all the outside chores you must have, how do you find time to keep the house so tidy?"

His shoulders moved slightly as if she'd startled him with the question. "It's not really all that neat."

"It is. Why, there's not even a dirty glass anywhere to be seen."

He shrugged and jammed his hands in his pockets. "You hungry? When we stopped to water and rest the horses, you didn't have any jerky."

"I didn't want any. Now I'm just exhausted."

She thought he looked relieved. The less time he spent with her the better, she guessed.

"I'll show you where you'll sleep," he said.

Eliza felt a small catch in her chest. She'd known they wouldn't be sharing a bed, but a part of her thought that maybe if he had a small one-room house, there wouldn't be any choice. Matt's home was big and looked to have several extra bedrooms. It would be no hardship at all for him to put her in one of them.

"Follow me," he said. Then he looked at her. "Let me carry you."

She took one look at his face and knew the prospect was as welcome as a dust storm on wash day. She shook her head. "I'm sure I can make it."

"Suit yourself." He turned and went into the hall.

She stood and tested her ankle. Pain shot up to her knee and she winced. Then, careful to put very little weight on her foot, she hopped more than walked after him, using the wall for support. He never once glanced back to see if she was all right.

"This is it," he said, turning into a doorway on his right. It was the room closest to the kitchen. A lighted lantern rested on the pine dresser against the wall on the far side of the bed. She saw her trunk and carpetbag sitting at the foot of the four-poster that matched the other furniture.

"It's very nice."

"That's what you said about the kitchen."

"Was there something more you wanted me to say?"

"I guess not."

"I'm sure I'll be very comfortable here."

He leaned against the doorframe. "If you need anything, I'll be right across the hall."

She looked past him and nodded. "Thank you. I think I have everything."

He shifted as if ready to leave, then hesitated, and hooked his thumbs in the waistband of his denim pants. "You might hear some noises."

"What kind of noises?"

"Howling. Up in the hills. I just wanted to warn you so you wouldn't be afraid. It's just coyotes. Nothing to worry about."

She blinked and went very still. "Coyotes?"

"Yeah. But they hardly ever come around here."

"That's good."

He nodded. "When they do, the dogs scare them off."

"I'm glad to hear it."

"Coyotes are darn smart, though."

"They are?"

"Yeah. They work in pairs. Sometimes one will howl like a whole pack and attract the watchdogs while the other sneaks in for the kill." He crossed his arms over his chest. "Clever."

"Are they smart enough to open the door and come in the house?"

A slow half smile turned up the corners of his mouth. "Don't reckon they are."

"Good." She nodded emphatically. "Then there's nothing to be afraid of."

He started to turn away again, then stopped. "One more thing."

"What's that?"

"If you hear the windows rattle, it's only the wind."

She smiled. "We have wind in Boston. I think I'd recognize it."

He looked sheepish. "Yeah, I guess."

"In fact, I even survived a hurricane once. With you."

"Oh. Yeah. I forgot."

She stared at him for several moments. "Anything else?"

"Nope. Guess not."

"Good night, then."

"'Night." He went out and closed the door after him.

Eliza grabbed her carpetbag and set it on the bed, then pulled her cotton nightgown from it. There was a knock at the door.

"Matt?" she called.

"Yeah. I brought you some water for the morning."

"Come in."

He entered the room with a white pitcher and placed it beside the basin on the dresser. He looked uncomfortable and ill at ease. "Thought you might need this."

"Thank you. That was very thoughtful." She felt stiff and uneasy around him. What had happened to the young man she'd always been able to tell anything to? She wanted him back. This handsome, tight-lipped stranger made her more than uncomfortable. He made her sad.

She limped to the end of the bed and sucked in her breath when she forgot not to put her weight on the injured foot.

"Ankle's really bothering you, isn't it?"

"Only when I'm not careful. In the morning I'm sure it'll be good as new."

He nodded. "I'm sure it will. Good night."

He left her then. Relieved to be alone, she picked up her nightgown. The chill in the room forced her to undress quickly so she could get under the thick, inviting patchwork quilt on the bed. Before she blew out the lantern, there was another knock on the door.

"Yes?"

"It's me again."

Now what? He'd covered water, wind, and wild animals. Why didn't he just leave her be?

Hope flared inside her. For a man who couldn't stand the sight of her, he was paying her an awful lot of attention. Had he changed his mind about the sleeping arrangements? "Yes?" she said.

"I brought something to wrap your ankle. I think that will give you some relief so you can sleep better. There's a lot to do tomorrow."

So he was only interested in giving her a good night's sleep so she could give him a fair day's work. She should have expected that.

She had a good mind to tell him to leave her alone. But it *was* throbbing painfully. She sighed. "Come in."

There was a loud creak as he came in once again. He had changed his shirt, and in his hand he held several lengths of material. There were some brown marks on the white strips that she recognized as the burn mark she had seen on his back.

"Did you rip up your shirt?"

He met her gaze. "It was ruined anyway. Get on the bed and I'll fix you up." His words took a second to sink in, then he went still. "I mean I'll take care of you."

"I know what you mean." Eliza smiled. She'd swear his neck was red and the color was spreading up into his cheeks.

"I'm not sure you do." He cleared his throat. "What I mean is, this will make you feel better."

"What are you talking about?"

"Just sit down and stick your goshdarn leg out so I can—"

"Why, Matt. You're such a sweet-talker. You make me swoon."

"Dammit, Eliza. You know what I mean."

"I'm sorry." She laughed and limped to the bed, then sat. "I couldn't resist. I forgot how much I liked to tease you." The Matt she used to know would have teased her back.

"I haven't forgotten." He went down on one knee in front of her.

As fierce as he looked in the lantern light, his touch was surprisingly gentle when he cupped the heel of her injured foot in his big palm and lifted it, resting it on his thigh. The feel of his fingers sent shivers straight up her leg. Her breath caught.

"Did I hurt you?" In his upturned eyes, she could see concern.

She shook her head. "You tickled me, is all."

"I'll be more careful." There was a huskiness to his voice.

He gripped her calf, and she could have sworn his hands shook. Then he wound the strip around her ankle and beneath her arch, over and over. Finally, he ripped the material and firmly tied it.

"Is that too tight?"

She shook her head. "It feels fine."

He nodded and stood up. "That will give you some support." He lifted his chin toward the bed. "Put that extra pillow underneath it tonight. By tomorrow I think most of the swelling will go down. Might be painful for a couple days but you'll be fine in no time."

"I'm sure I will. Thank you, Matt." She stared up at him, waiting for him to go.

His gaze lowered to her mouth, then lower still to the bodice of her nightgown. Her heart pounded against her ribs and she was sure he must be able to see it, or at least hear it.

"Was there something else you wanted?" she asked.

He took a step back. "No. Nothing. Sleep well, Eliza."

He turned away and was out the door in seconds.

Eliza shivered and crawled beneath the covers. She waited, wondering if he would come back again. But when she heard the door across the hall close firmly, she let out a long breath and shut her eyes. She was sure she would fall asleep instantly. Instead, she kept seeing the expression on Matt's face when he'd taken care of her ankle. He'd looked intense, fierce, and almost hungry. If she didn't know how much he hated having her here, she would have sworn he was reluctant to leave her bedroom.

That couldn't be. He'd made it clear that he didn't want her anywhere near him. Then what *did* he want from her?

She yawned. It was late and she was exhausted. She would look for answers in the morning.

The sun streaming through her window woke Eliza the next morning. She got up, washed quickly with the water Matt had brought the night before, then put on an old calico dress and an apron over it. Her wrapped ankle was still sore, but she could get around slowly, enough to do all the chores Matt wanted her to.

Since she only had one good shoe, she limped into the kitchen in her stocking feet. The room was empty and as neat as it had been the night before. She wondered if Matt was up yet. It didn't look as if he'd made breakfast. Then she noticed the hooks beside the door were empty of the sheepskin coat and dusty black hat he'd left there the night before. He must have gone out to do whatever it was that he did on the ranch.

"Time to start earning my keep," she said to herself, looking around the kitchen. Cooking would probably be one of the things that Matt wanted her to do. The way to a man's heart . . . Only she didn't figure there was enough food in the territory of Wyoming to soften his attitude toward her, let alone show her the way.

At the thought of food, Eliza's stomach growled. Between looking for a job the day before and traveling at a pace fit to kill the hardiest body, she'd eaten very little. She found a pantry off the kitchen where supplies were stored and gathered all the things she'd need for a batch of flapjacks. Then she looked through the cupboards for a bowl to mix it in. She couldn't find anything. There were saucers and an odd plate, but no pots, pans, or other utensils.

Just then, Matt opened the door. He whacked his hat a couple of times against his thigh to remove the dust, came inside, and hung it on the peg next to his jacket. Before closing the door, he reached back outside and grabbed a funny-looking stick from the porch.

"'Morning," he said.

"Good morning." She pointed to the thing he'd brought inside. It looked like a *T,* with some cloth wrapped around the smaller horizontal piece on the top. "What's that?"

"I made it for you." His voice was gruff.

"To beat me with?" she asked, grinning.

His glance quickly shifted from the contraption to her.

When he saw her amusement, he almost smiled. "Not a bad idea. But no. This is a crutch. Sort of. How's the ankle this morning?"

"Sore. But better." She leaned back against the kitchen table and folded her arms. "Are you hungry?"

"Starved. Breakfast ready?" He glanced around the kitchen.

Dressed in denims and a long-sleeved plaid flannel shirt, he looked rugged and capable. Though he hadn't shaved and stubble darkened his jaw, he was handsome enough to steal the breath from her body. Where she came from, the men drew a straight-edged razor across their whiskers every morning before they went to their place of business. The sight of him fairly took the strength from her knees and she recalled the sensations he'd evoked with his hands on her leg last night.

"Eliza?"

"What?" She shook her head to clear it of the unwanted images.

"Breakfast?"

"Breakfast? You want breakfast? Of course you do. It could be ready in two shakes, but I can't find any dishes. Do you keep them in the barn or something?"

Matt glanced at the door. "Damn!"

"Really, Matt." She stood up on both feet and put her hands on her hips. "About your swearing. As you've pointed out on several occasions, I'm a minister's daughter. I'm not accustomed to men's profanities. I'd appreciate it if you'd refrain from certain words, unless you have a very, very good reason. I don't think asking where you keep the dishes is good cause. Do you?"

"It could be."

Matt wasn't so sure she would think it was a good reason, but he did. Between a pile of chores left over from yesterday and trying to forget the picture Eliza made in her nightgown, he'd forgotten that every dish, bowl, and cooking pot on the place was dirty and piled high on the back porch.

She waited. When he glanced over his shoulder at the door again, she finally asked, "What is it?"

"Nothing," he said more sharply than he intended.

A spark of interest leaped into her eyes at his tone. "Guess I'll go look for myself."

"No." He stepped between her and the door that hid the mess from her.

She grabbed the crutch. "You'd better get out of my way."

It was a losing battle and he knew it. Not because she was prepared to bash him over the head with her stick, but there was no way to hide what he'd done. He stepped aside and let her pass him without saying anything. He reckoned one look was worth a thousand words and Eliza would have more than a few thousand to say when she saw what was out there.

On the porch she limped over and picked up the blue speckled coffeepot. He watched her back closely, waiting for a sign, ready to duck if she decided to throw it at him. For a long time she didn't say anything. Just when he was beginning to breathe a little easier, she turned in his direction.

Her green eyes snapped angrily. "This explains everything. You brought me here forcibly because you wanted slave labor."

"That's not true. I truly think . . ."

"Hogwash! You don't *think* at all." She hobbled past the pile and studied it. Her knuckles turned white as she gripped the coffeepot. "What was all that rubbish about feeling responsible for me? And that nonsense about not leaving me to fend for myself? It seems to me you prattled endlessly about what's best for me." She stopped and turned, pointing at him with the pot still in her hand. "I can tell you what's *not* best for me. A stack of dishes that's almost as tall as I am."

"What did you expect, Eliza?" he asked defensively. "This is Wyoming Territory, not your parlor in Boston."

He lifted a hand toward the stack. "I have more important things to do than wash pots and pans."

"So do I. Like going back to town." She hobbled forward with her finger still pointed at him.

He backed up against the wooden siding of the house. "Don't you dare pinch me, woman."

"I have no intention of pinching you." She pushed the pot into his hands, then stooped down and rummaged through the stacks of things.

"What are you going to do?"

"Put you to work." She handed him a frying pan without looking at him.

"Doing women's chores?"

"If you want to eat any time soon, you can just help."

"You sound like my mother."

She looked up at him and her eyes turned thoughtful. "Remember the time we caught all those fish and she made us clean them before she'd cook?"

A corner of Matt's mouth turned up. He'd forgotten about that. "What do you mean 'we' cleaned them? You couldn't take one off your hook, let alone cut the heads off."

"Because they're slimy little critters." She shuddered at the thought, then picked up several plates. She put a bowl on top with spoons, forks, and knives sticking out of it. "Let's wash these up. I'll do the rest later."

As she limped back into the kitchen, he noticed that she had no shoes on. When she moved, her skirts swirled around her legs and he caught a flash of her ankle. Beneath her black stockings, he could see the outline of the wrap he'd put on the night before. He remembered the feel of her leg in his hand and how much control it had taken to keep from sliding his palm up under her thin gown.

"Did you have a good night's rest? After I wrapped your ankle, I mean."

"Yes," she said. "Thanks for asking."

She took the blue speckled pot from him and washed it

out, then measured coffee into it and left it on the stove to boil.

At least one of them had slept well. He couldn't get his mind off Eliza's shapely leg and imagining the parts of her he hadn't seen. He remembered the outline of her body when she'd stood in her nightgown before the lamp that night at the boardinghouse. He pushed the thought away.

"What can I do?" he asked. He felt guilty after forcing her into this godawful mess.

She stopped pumping water and looked over her shoulder. When she smiled at him, the sweetness of it nearly turned him inside out. Damn. It felt good to have a woman in this house again. But he couldn't get used to her. She was the wrong woman. He'd known Eliza for a lot of years. She was definitely the wrong woman.

She stepped aside and made room for him at the pump handle. "Fill this pot with water and heat it on the stove. I'll wash a bowl and mix up some batter. Quick as a wink, we'll have hot food and clean plates to eat it on."

He did as she told him, then stood back and watched her. She adjusted her apron around her small waist while she waited to turn the flapjacks. It was a fine, homey sight, Eliza cooking for him. A man could get used to having a woman around, even the wrong woman. Give him too much time, and he might even like it. With a vengeance, he began scrubbing dishes and spoons, forks and knives.

Together, they made short work of the job and were soon sitting down at the table to eat.

Matt sliced off a big piece of light, tender flapjack with a fork so shiny he could see his face in it. "I'm hungry enough to eat a bear." He put the food in his mouth, chewed, and swallowed. He raised his brows. "This is good."

"You sound surprised."

"I can't help remembering those cookies you made."

"You mean the ones that sat in your stomach like bullets?"

"Yup."

"I've been practicing since then." She put her plate on the table, then sat across from him.

He looked at her. "I'm sorry about the mess, Eliza."

"It can't be easy running this ranch alone," she said as she poured maple syrup over the steaming pancakes. "Your mother told me why you wanted to marry again. Now I've seen the truth of it for myself."

Had his mother also told her that he wanted a son? Good Lord, he hoped not. Eliza was honest as well as relentless. She'd do her best to fulfill any agreement she thought she'd made and would keep at him until it was accomplished. Matt wasn't sure how long he could hold her off. He just knew they couldn't do *that* or he would never get the annulment. Eliza was not staying in Wyoming Territory. That's all there was to it.

"I have to get back to work," he said, pushing his empty plate away.

"Don't you want more to eat?"

He shook his head.

She finished her food. "I have a lot to do, too. Think I'll start with that pile of dirty clothes under your bed."

His eyes widened. "How did you know?"

"That's where you always put them," she said, grinning.

He smiled back. He couldn't help it. No one had a sweeter, livelier grin than Eliza. Then his amusement faded. "You know me too well."

"It's a good thing you made me that crutch. If I'm going to get all this work done, I'll need it to get around."

"You're in no condition to do all these chores. They've waited this long, they can wait until your ankle's better."

"I won't do more than I can handle." She carried their plates over to a bucket by the pump.

When she reached for the dishpan hanging on the wall,

her skirt lifted and he saw her ankles and slender calves and her stocking feet. He was reminded that she had no shoes. She'd need another pair.

"I've got things to do in the barn," he said gruffly.

She quickly looked up and a troubled expression stole into her eyes. "I'll have a meal ready for you at midday."

He nodded, then grabbed his coat and left. Breakfast with Eliza had been more pleasant than he wanted to admit. That made him uneasy.

As he walked away from the house, Matt turned up the collar of his jacket against the chill. He headed for the barn where he'd put Carrie's things. When he entered the dim interior the odor of dust and hay and animals surrounded him. After climbing the ladder into the loft, he pulled the canvas covering away from the two trunks, a big one and a smaller one containing baby clothes.

He remembered the hopeless agony he'd felt when clearing Carrie's belongings from their bedroom. He lifted the brown lid and saw her shoes, right on top. Right where he'd left them. He hated seeing her things again, and he despised the pain and emptiness she'd left him in. But he'd learned to live with it.

A vision of Eliza's freckled face, green eyes, and long braid flashed into his mind. It brought a feeling of pleasure so sweet and strong it nearly took the air from his lungs. He pushed the thought away.

The harsh land had taken his wife and baby from him. He'd promised himself he wouldn't let any woman matter to him again. His meddling mother had dropped Eliza in his lap and he'd do his best to make sure she was safe. But there would be no more intimate meals and shared childhood memories. He would get the annulment and send her back home before anything happened to her.

6

"Here." Matt held out a pair of sturdy brown boots.

Eliza looked from the shoes to his face, then set the broom against the wall by the door. "Thank you. How did you know I needed these?"

He glanced at her feet. "You always walk around barefoot?"

"No."

"Besides, I was the one who cut your shoe off." He handed her the shoes and tucked his fingers in the back pockets of his denims. A look of raw pain crossed his face. "Those were Carrie's." He looked again at Eliza's feet. "You'll probably have to stuff the toes. She was a tall woman, a lot bigger than you."

He said it as if her being smaller than Carrie was the worst thing in the world. Eliza told herself not to mind. Obviously he hadn't gotten over his wife's passing. The look in his eyes told her more than words.

"Matt, I don't want to wear these. I can see that it upsets you."

He shook his head. "Carrie's gone. They can't do her any good, and you need shoes. They'll do until we go to Silver Springs for the annulment."

Annulment. The death blow to all her hopes and dreams. During breakfast, she and Matt had teased and talked, and she'd forgotten for a little while that she was only playing at being his wife. The man who'd just come through the door was not the same one who had acted like a husband when he'd joked with her about her cooking. This man wanted to end their marriage as soon as possible. The pain and disappointment sat like rocks in her chest.

She turned away and set the shoes on the floor beside the pine trestle table. If he saw her eyes, he would know what his words did to her. She couldn't let that happen.

The sound of stomping boots on the back porch seemed to vibrate through the kitchen floor before the door opened. An older man in a brown hat that looked like it had seen a lot of days, not necessarily better ones, came inside.

"'Mornin'," he said. He glanced at Matt, who was still standing by the pegs near the back door. Then he walked straight over to Eliza, stopped in front of her, and didn't bother to hide the fact that he studied her from the top of her head to the tips of her toes. His gaze came to rest on her eyes and he pointed, practically touching her face with his finger. "That there won't be stoppin' any stampedes."

Her brows pulled together as she shot Matt a puzzled look, then stared at the newcomer. "Good Lord, I hope not."

He chuckled as he continued to size her up. "Brown hair, freckles, and the prettiest pair of green eyes I ever did see. Matthew, your mama didn't lie."

"Oh, yes, she did," Eliza and Matt said together.

"Maybe she fibbed a mite. This little lady ain't the sturdiest miss I ever saw, but she don't look like she'd turn tail at the first sign of trouble."

"Look again," Matt said. "Eliza, show him your ankle."

Her cheeks felt warm as she recalled how she'd injured herself the day before. The old man would probably agree with Matt that she was willful and childish. Still, she stared him straight in the eye and asked, "Just who would I be showing my ankle to?"

"Wiley Powell, ma'am. Foreman of the Double C." He lifted his hat in salute, then dropped it back down on his head. "Matthew, she may not be sturdy, but she's got spunk."

Matt winced. "Yeah. That's what Brad Slicker said."

"How the hell did the barkeep get a look at her?"

Eliza sighed. "It's a long story."

"That's the best kind." Wiley brushed a large, leathery hand across his chin and she heard the rasp of his whiskers. His pale blue eyes lit up when he spotted the pot of coffee on the stove. "Sure could use a cup o' that. It's colder than a witch's tit—"

"Wiley," Matt interrupted. "There's a lady present."

"Sorry, ma'am. Forgot my manners for a second."

"You're not the only one. Matt's language could use a lick and a polish. And my manners, too. Heavens, I should have thought of offering you coffee, Mr. Powell." Eliza hobbled over to the stove and used a cloth to grab the hot metal handle. She poured some of the steaming black liquid into a tin cup and handed it to him.

"Call me Wiley, ma'am."

"Only if you'll call me Eliza."

"So that's your first name. Wasn't sure you had one."

"She's got one, all right," Matt said. "If my interfering mother had thought fit to mention it, Eliza wouldn't be here now."

"How's that?" Wiley pulled out a ladder-backed chair, turned it around, and straddled the seat with his arms resting on the back.

"Eliza is the pest who trailed after me back home. This marriage is a mistake, and when the circuit judge comes back through, we're getting the whole thing annulled."

Wiley shook his head. "Whoa, boy. I can't keep up with you. First you can't wait to git t'town and tie the knot with someone you ain't never laid eyes on. Now you're gonna *un*tie the knot 'cause you know the lady. You been in the locoweed?"

"It all makes perfect sense to us. Doesn't it, Eliza?" She started to say something, but Matt kept talking. "Until we can end the marriage, we thought it best that she stay here at the ranch."

"That was *your* idea," she said.

"So what happened to your leg? And does it have anything to do with the saloon?"

"Yes," Eliza said.

"No," Matt said at the same time.

The old man looked from one to the other. "Which is it?"

"I wanted to stay in town and get a job. The only place I found work was in the saloon. Matt didn't take kindly to the idea—"

"That's putting it mildly," he grumbled.

"I didn't like being told what to do. I hurt my ankle trying to get away." She and Wiley both turned their gazes on Matt. The way he squirmed under his foreman's direct questions and curious looks gave her immense satisfaction. "So, I'm here to wash dishes and do laundry for the next six weeks until the judge says we're not married anymore."

Wiley stared at Eliza. Then he speared Matt with a narrow-eyed look. "What about the young 'un you want t'have?"

"Old man, you've got a big mouth. Now there's going to be hell to pay."

"Young 'un? You mean a baby?" Eliza asked, her eyes widening as she stared at Matt.

"Shit." He sat down on the chair across from Wiley.

"Matthew, your manners could use more than a lick and a polish," Wiley said, then took a slurping sip from his cup. "Sure can tell it's high time there was a woman on the place."

"That's the second time today, Matthew Decker. I trust you have another very good reason?"

"I believe so, Eliza."

"You'd best explain."

"No. I don't think that would be best. It would be best for me to go clean out the barn." He got up quickly and walked out the back door.

Eliza crossed her arms and looked at Wiley. "Would you care to explain about the baby, Mr. Powell?"

"No, ma'am. That's somethin' you'd best discuss with Matthew." He shifted uncomfortably. "Thought we just settled this first name business. I'd take it kindly, Eliza, if you'd call me Wiley. A widow woman down in Texas was the last one t'call me Mr. Powell." He grinned suddenly. "I'll never forget that night and the way she sure curled my—"

Eliza held up her hands. "Spare me the details."

"Sorry, ma'am." He self-consciously scratched his whiskered chin. "Guess my manners need some more airin' out, too."

"That's all right." She sat down in the chair across from him that Matt had vacated. It was still warm from his body.

While she was here on the ranch, she wanted to get to know as much about Matt as she could. It was probably not the smartest thing she could do and would only hurt her in the long run. But she couldn't help being curious about the successful rancher he'd become. He'd told her it was a hard land, yet from what people said, the part of it he owned was flourishing. She wanted to know what kind of man he'd become since leaving home. One minute he was gentle and thoughtful; the next he was gruff and autocratic. Was there anything left of the fun-loving, devil-may-care, handsome-as-sin boy she'd once followed everywhere? Or had he become as hard as the land and tough as the life he'd carved out of it?

Wiley took a sip from his tin cup, then caught her eye. "You got an awful funny look on your face, Eliza."

"Would you show me the ranch? I want to see how much Matt's accomplished." And what had changed him.

"I don't know." He brushed a hand over his face. "What with your bad ankle 'n' all."

"He loves this place so, and I need to see it and understand why." She touched his arm. "Please, Wiley?"

"It's too dang big to see all in one day. And it's too godawful cold to spend the night out there unless ya got no other choice."

"Just a short tour. Please? It would mean so much to me."

"Gee whiz, Eliza. You make it awful hard on a man."

"I'm sorry. I didn't mean to make you uncomfortable. It's all right. You don't have to take me." She stood up and turned away. "I'll go by myself."

"Jehoshaphat!" He slapped his hand against the table. "You ain't goin' nowhere by yourself. I'll take you."

Eliza whirled around and grinned. "Thank you, Wiley."

"Don't thank me," he mumbled. "I just hope Matthew will be as pleased."

"I'm sure he won't mind. Why, we'll be back before he even knows we're gone."

It was late in the afternoon when Matt finally emerged from the barn. Since that morning he'd tried to keep himself too busy to think about Eliza, and how Wiley had told her about the baby Matt wanted.

There wasn't enough backbreaking work on the whole Double C to keep those things out of his mind.

He hated that he couldn't quit remembering the feel of Eliza snuggling against his thigh in the wagon. Or the way he wanted to move his hand higher when he'd held her leg and tended her sprained ankle. Or the cordial meal they'd shared that morning.

He wondered if, after he'd left them, Wiley had spilled his guts and explained to Eliza that Matt had wanted a mail-order wife to give him a son. Knowing that loose-tongued old man, she knew all about it by now.

She'd always liked children. Even in her tomboy days, she'd had little ones trailing after her for stories or the sugar hards she carried in her pockets for them. The way she'd taken to Jenny Evans told him she hadn't lost her knack. Eliza had grown up, filled out, and left behind her girlish ways, but her soft spot for kids was still squishy as mud. If she knew he'd gotten married because he wanted a child, she'd try relentlessly to give him one.

He was still doing it, thinking about Eliza. Since he couldn't get her out of his mind, he decided he'd just go in the house and see what she was up to. It was getting mighty cold out here. Maybe she'd put a fresh pot of coffee on the stove. He hoped she hadn't felt she had to do all those dishes or wash every stitch of the dirty clothing he'd shoved under the bed. How was her ankle? She should have rested and put it up most of the day. Knowing her, she hadn't.

He also hoped that maybe along with that pot of coffee she might be fixing supper. That caught him up short and yanked his temper. She'd been on the Double C less than twenty-four hours and he was actually looking forward to seeing her in the kitchen. How the hell was he going to get through the next six weeks?

He told himself the only reason he was eager to get up to the house was because he was sick and tired of his own cooking. It had nothing to do with Eliza.

"Hello?" he called, opening the back door. The kitchen was dark; there was no fire in the stove, no glowing embers in the hearth. No food was being prepared. No woman was there with a bright, sweet smile.

She must be resting in her room.

Matt stomped up the hall, making enough noise to wake the dead. "Eliza?" he hollered as he went. "Are you awake?"

He frowned. If she wasn't, she would be soon. He scowled when he stood in her open doorway and saw the room was empty and her bed neatly made. Evidently, she hadn't rested on it all day.

"Are you here, Eliza?" His voice was louder this time and there was an edge to it he didn't want to name. From any place in this house she should have heard him. Why hadn't she answered? He went to the parlor and front room. Both were dark and empty. Where the hell was she?

Matt opened the front door and walked out on the porch. Looking around the quiet, empty yard, he had a bad feeling. Something was wrong, but he couldn't put his finger on what it was.

He walked down the three steps and stood looking at the road. The sun was sitting almost on top of the peak in the distance. He noticed grooves from the wagon's wheels headed south. Had Eliza taken the wagon to go back to Silver Springs, away from him? If she had, she was going the wrong way.

He shook his head. He'd thought she'd given in and more or less accepted their situation. She even seemed to take to Wiley. Then something else occurred to him. He hadn't seen his foreman all day, except when he'd come into the barn shortly after Matt had started cleaning out the stalls with the pitchfork. With so much on his mind at the time Matt hadn't paid much attention. Now he could kick himself in the backside. Or he'd give a lot if Eliza were there to pinch it. He remembered the old man saying something about going to the south pasture of the ranch. Had he taken her out there?

Wiley wouldn't have wanted to put Eiza on a horse since her ankle was hurt. Come to think of it, Eliza didn't know how to ride; she was afraid of horses. The south part of the ranch was the easiest to get to by wagon. He'd forgotten to tell Wiley about the repairs to the wheel. That patch wouldn't hold up to much bumping and bouncing and the road south was better than most, but still rough.

They could be stuck out there all night if that wheel fell apart. A knot of worry pulled tighter in his gut.

"Damn!" He wished Eliza were there to tell him to watch his language. It was getting late. He had to go after her.

He went into the pantry off the kitchen and grabbed a burlap bag of supplies. They probably wouldn't be needed, but a man couldn't be too careful. Then he raced out of the house toward the barn.

He threw a saddle on his horse, tied on the bag of provisions and a couple blankets, then swung up onto the animal's back.

"She'll be all right," he said firmly.

That old man had been taking care of himself for a lot of years now and done a fine job of it. Surely he could manage to watch over Eliza. They shouldn't be hard to track with that nick in the bad wheel, and the thing wouldn't hold up long. He probably wouldn't have to go far to find them.

He dug his heels into the horse's flanks and the animal leaped forward as he guided it south.

"Wiley, open your eyes. Please speak to me," Eliza said. Desperation clawed at her the way the wildcat had ripped at his leg.

She cradled the man's head in her lap. The bobcat had attacked without warning after the wagon wheel had broken, stranding them. Wiley had managed to shoot and kill the beast.

She shivered again, partly from the memory of the snarling cat and partly from cold. In spite of the fire she'd managed to start, she was freezing. She'd put her shawl over the injured man to keep him warm, but it wasn't nearly enough. She could feel the temperature drop along with the sun.

More than anything she wanted him to wake up and

ask for a cup of coffee, but he was as still as death. He had lost so much blood. She'd ripped strips from her petticoat to tie around his thigh and stop the bleeding. It had helped some, but he hadn't opened his eyes, and she was near the edge of panic. She'd taken care of him the best she could; she didn't know what else to do. She needed help. She needed Matt.

He didn't know where they'd gone. She had to go find him. On foot she would never make it.

The wagon was broken down, but the horse was still in the harness. She could ride for help. A shudder racked her. Who was she fooling? Ever since she'd almost been trampled to death by a horse, she couldn't even bring herself to get near one. Matt had saved her then. Would he find her now? If he didn't come, she wasn't sure what would happen. She could no more get on that horse than she could flap her arms and fly back to the ranch. Because of her weakness a man might die. She hated herself for it.

"Please wake up, Mr. Powell." Maybe if she could remind him of that widow woman from Texas, the one who had seemed so special to him, just maybe she could get through to him.

She'd never felt so alone in her life. Would Matt miss them and come looking? He might miss Wiley, but he'd be glad if she didn't come back. She'd been nothing but trouble to him her whole life. Now she'd brought trouble to Wiley, too. He hadn't wanted to bring her out here. She'd known exactly what to say to convince him. If she'd listened to him, he wouldn't be lying here now. If he died, she would never forgive herself. She could never forgive herself anyway—and certainly Matt never would.

The sun finally disappeared behind the mountains that threw a purple blanket over the valley. Eliza shivered again. In the intense quiet, she thought she heard a horse's hooves, but she was certain it must be her fancy because she wanted so badly to believe someone was coming.

In the next moment, she felt the ground vibrating. She hadn't imagined it. Someone *was* coming. Thank God.

Gently, she eased Wiley's head from her lap and stood by the side of the road. She started waving her hands. "Over here," she called.

When the rider came closer, she realized it was Matt. His hat was pulled low on his forehead and his shoulder-length hair fanned out behind him as he drew nearer. The jacket he wore was the same one he'd put over her on their trip from Silver Springs. She could almost see his forbidding expression and knew it would be the most wonderful sight she'd ever laid eyes on in her life.

Matt yanked on the reins, bringing his horse to a rearing stop, then leaped from the saddle. He'd seen the fire a ways off and had pushed his horse to the breaking point.

He gripped Eliza's shoulders and looked into her eyes. "Are you all right?"

"I'm fine." She bit her lip. "But Wiley . . . He's hurt. It's all my fault."

When he saw the man on his back by the fire, he hurried over to him and dropped to one knee beside him. After finding a pulse, he let out a long breath. "What happened?"

"A bobcat. He killed it and I dragged it over there." She pointed to a place on the far side of the fire.

"You dragged it?" he asked, surprised that she would touch the dead animal.

"I couldn't stand looking at it." She shuddered. "Wiley's gun was by the wagon when the thing attacked him. Matt, there's so much blood. Help him."

"If it had him, how did he shoot the thing?"

"I created a distraction."

"The cat went after you?" The thought stopped him cold.

"Only for a second. Wiley was able to get his rifle and he killed the thing."

It didn't make him feel any better that it was only a

short time that she was close to the wildcat, but he didn't have time to contemplate the facts. He had to see to his friend.

There was a pale cast to the old man's face that had nothing to do with his gray whiskers. In the flickering light of the fire, he saw Eliza's shawl covering Wiley's chest and the strip of material high on his thigh that she'd used to stop the bleeding. Beneath it he saw the torn pants and jagged wound where the animal's claws had ripped the flesh.

He pulled his knife from his boot and cut away the denims to see the damage. The bleeding had stopped. Until they could get him back to the Double C, he could do nothing more than wrap it.

"Eliza, give me your petticoat."

"Of course." She turned away and lifted her skirt, then wriggled out of the garment. "Here."

Matt tore it into wide strips and wound it around the man's injured leg. "We need to find something to prop his leg up with in case it starts bleeding again."

Matt walked over to his horse, unfastened the saddle and set it on the ground. When he'd settled Wiley's leg on it, he pulled the supplies and blankets he'd brought into the circle of the fire. He squatted beside the injured man and covered him with one of the blankets. Then he opened the canteen of water, lifted his foreman's head a little, and tried to give him a drink. It was no use.

Eliza stood beside him. "Is there anything more we can do?"

He was puzzled. Wiley had lost a lot of blood, but it didn't explain why he was still unconscious. "I wonder why he hasn't come to yet?"

"I think he hit his head. He fell and there's a big lump on the left side."

He leaned forward and checked; he found the bump. It *was* big.

Matt shook his head and offered her the water. After

drinking she returned the canteen, and he screwed on the cap. He leaned back on his heels. "All we can do now is sit tight."

"We have to get him back to the ranch." She twisted her hands together.

"I can't fix that wheel until first light. We'll take him home then."

"How did you know the wheel was broken?"

A stab of guilt cut him. "I figured that was the only thing that would keep Wiley out after nightfall." He stood and stared down at her. "Never mind the wheel. What are the two of you doing out here in the first place? You said it was your fault."

She stood just out of the fire's glowing circle, so he couldn't tell for sure, but he had a strong suspicion there were tears in her eyes.

"Spit it out, Eliza. What did you do?"

"I wanted to see the ranch. Wiley didn't want to bring me, so I told him I'd go by myself."

"Why was it so all-fired important?"

She stared at him. "In town, everyone told me what a fine spread you'd built here. I remember the things your father said before you left home. I wanted to see for myself how wrong he was." Her voice cracked. "I never meant for Wiley to get hurt. He won't open his eyes. Is he going to be all right?"

"Can't say for sure. He's strong as an ox. That's in his favor. We'll just have to wait."

The injured man groaned and she went to him and knelt beside him. She felt his forehead and brushed the hair back. Then she pulled the blanket up around his neck. "Matt's here, Wiley. He says you're going to be fine. Just concentrate on getting better so you can go back to Texas and that widow woman someday."

"What are you talking about?" Matt asked, coming up behind her.

"Something he told me earlier." She shivered as

the wind blew, picking up more cold as it raced over the valley.

Matt grabbed a blanket and brought it to her. She stood and he started to drag it around her shoulders. His gaze dropped to the skirt of her dress and what he saw there nearly stopped his heart.

"Goddammit it to hell! That's blood. Why didn't you tell me you were hurt?"

"I'm not." She frowned as she looked down at the dark stains.

His hands started to shake. This land had taken too much from him already. Now Wiley lay wounded and Eliza . . . He had to do something.

"This is blood. Where's it coming from?" He grabbed her upper arms and frantically scanned her from shoulder to shoe. He couldn't see anything wrong. He shook her. "Where did it get you?"

"I'm not hurt, I swear. It must be blood from the bobcat." She put her hands on his chest. "It didn't hurt me. Wiley's the only one injured."

Matt let out a long breath. "He's fighting for his life."

Her fingers curled into his shirt and grabbed the material over his heart. "If I could switch places with him, I would. Believe me, Matt, I wish Wiley wasn't lying there. I wish it was me."

He shook his head. He couldn't think about her lying there like that. He felt helpless to keep her from harm in this God-forsaken territory. There was only one thing he could do to protect her.

"Nothing will happen to you, Eliza."

"Of course not. I won't ever be so stupid again. I promise to be more careful in the future."

"There's not going to be a next time. I'm not waiting for the annulment. I'm sending you home as soon as we get back to the ranch."

7

Eliza's eyes burned with fatigue as she carefully watched Wiley for any slight sign of improvement. He was lying completely still in the guest-room bed—too quiet, and too pale. His normally ruddy cheeks were gray as the silver stubble on his face. That worried her more than the two and a half days of fever he'd endured.

"Please say something, Wiley." She moved her rocking chair closer to his side. Desperation grew inside her, even bigger than it had been before Matt had found them.

She had helped Matt stitch up the deepest gashes in the old man's leg as best they could. Matt had told her that since he couldn't leave Wiley long enough to take her back to town, she'd have to stay at the ranch for a while, but as soon as his foreman's condition stabilized, one way or the other, she was going back to Silver Springs. When they got there, he intended to put her on the stage to Cheyenne with enough money for a one-way ticket back to Boston.

The thought of leaving Matt hurt her terribly. Even though she'd known her stay was limited, she hadn't let herself think about what would happen at the end of it. But as much as she hated the idea of going back to Boston, she would gladly give up any of her time left with him if Wiley would just open his eyes.

"Wake up, Mr. Powell. You just have to get better."

He moaned and moved restlessly as if he'd heard her. Or as if he was in pain.

Knowing she was responsible for his suffering weighed heavily on her. If only she hadn't forced him to take her out there. If only the wheel hadn't come apart. If only . . . If only Matt could look at her without despising her.

A sob caught in her throat and she swallowed hard to keep it silent. This was no time for tears.

She stood up and placed her hand on Wiley's forehead. The skin was cool; the fever had burned itself out. Now that it had, his deathly quiet frightened her more.

She looked at his face, the wrinkles smoothed out in peaceful sleep. She'd tried everything else, maybe she should talk sternly. She put her hands on her hips. "Enough of this lying abed, Mr. Powell. Do you think Matt can run this ranch by himself? He needs you. You wake up right this minute." His restless movement was her only response.

Feeling helpless, she dropped to her knees beside the bed and clasped her hands together on the blue-and-white patchwork quilt. She closed her eyes.

"Lord, I've been talking to you all along, but I don't think you've heard me. You just have to help Wiley. You're the only one who can. If you can see your way clear to do that, I promise from now on, I'll do whatever Matt says without one word of argument." She nodded her head, satisfied that it was a good bargain. She looked up at the ceiling. "Amen."

Suddenly she was utterly exhausted. Her head felt so heavy, she could hardly hold it up. Eliza buried her face in her arm on the bed. She was bone-tired, discouraged, and feeling more hopeless with every silent second that passed. The bed moved, but she didn't look up. He was still restless. Was that a good sign? How she wished she knew more about healing. The sheets rustled as he moved again.

"Miss Eliza." He coughed. "S'cuse me, ma'am?"

She wasn't certain that she hadn't imagined his voice. She'd wished and begged and prayed for so many hours to hear him say something, she was terrified that her mind was playing tricks on her.

"You sleepin', Miss Eliza?"

There it was again. She raised her head. He was staring at her.

"Ma'am, could a wounded old codger get a cup of coffee? If it ain't too much trouble?"

She looked at the old man in the bed, smiled, and promptly burst into tears.

"Now, there's no call for that."

She laughed once, a sound that came out more like a choke.

"Miss Eliza." He patted her arm. "Please don't—"

She sniffled and brushed her knuckles beneath her eyes. "I'm sorry. I didn't mean to go to pieces like that." She laughed again. "It's just that—"

"What in tarnation's wrong with you, ma'am? I know you ain't given to hysterics. Not after what you did to that bobcat."

"So you do remember."

"Yes'm." He frowned. "Don't recall anythin' else, though, until wakin' up just now. This ain't my bed."

"No. Matt and I brought you here so I could take care of you. You've been delirious for several days."

His gray brows raised. "Do tell?"

"I've been frantic about you, Wiley. So has Matt." She put a hand to her cheek. "I forgot. I have to tell him the good news." She stood up.

"No need," Matt said behind her.

She glanced over her shoulder to see him standing in

the doorway. She returned her gaze to the bed and sat down. Behind her she heard his boots as he approached the bed. She knew when he was close. The smell of horses, hay, leather, and sunshine settled in the air around her.

"Isn't it wonderful? He wants coffee."

"I'm a mite hungry, too," Wiley said.

"That's a good sign. You need food to regain your strength," Eliza said. She stood up and her shoulder brushed against Matt's chest as she turned toward him. A step back let her breathe again.

She was ever so grateful that Wiley was awake. But that meant she would have to leave the ranch. A great, deep sadness settled in her heart, but she couldn't go back on her bargain. She sniffled away the last traces of her tears and looked Matt in the eye. "When he's strong enough, I'll be ready to go."

"Good."

Matt studied her. Strands of shiny brown hair straggled around her face, and dark circles stained the hollows beneath her eyes. The sparkle had gone out of the green depths and he wondered if it was from fatigue or if he had smothered it. He started to reach for her, then folded his arms over his chest. No matter how guilty he felt, she couldn't stay. It was too dangerous for her.

"Where you goin'?" Wiley pushed himself to a sitting position.

Matt moved to the foot of the bed. "Boston. I should have put her on the first stage back to Cheyenne. It was a mistake to bring her here."

"Mistake for who?" the old man asked.

"You, for one. If it hadn't been for Eliza, you wouldn't be laid up now."

"She's not to blame. If it wasn't for that broken wheel we wouldn'ta been stuck."

"If she hadn't talked you into taking her out there—"

"Matthew, how come you never told me the wagon wheel was busted?" Wiley's eyes narrowed on him.

Matt ran his hand through his hair. "I forgot." That was Eliza's fault, too. He shot her a glare. He'd been so preoccupied with her learning he wanted a baby and what she might do now that she knew, repairs to the wagon had completely slipped his mind.

"If she had kept to the house the way she should have, none of this would have happened."

"Might-have-beens are a waste of time."

"She doesn't belong here, Wiley. She was raised back East where things are more civilized. Letting her stay would be like turning a puppy loose against a grizzly." Matt shook his head. "I don't have time to run the ranch and nursemaid a tenderfoot."

"This here tenderfoot she-pup has some mighty sharp claws."

"What are you blabbing about?"

"She saved my life out there."

Matt's gaze instantly jerked to the other man's face. "What?"

"You heard me, boy. If hadn't been for that little lady there"—he pointed to Eliza who still stood quietly beside the bed—"I'd a been a goner."

"I don't believe it."

"It's true. That wildcat was snarlin' and slashin' at my leg and like t'ripped it to pieces. She started screamin' and yellin', throwin' rocks. If I recollect rightly, she picked up that crutch you made her and whacked that ole bobcat smack on the back with it."

"Good Lord. It's a wonder the cat didn't turn on her." Matt went cold as death at the thought of what could have happened to her.

"It did." Wiley paused and speared him with a look, letting the information sink in.

When the full meaning got through, anger and guilt raged through him. She could have been killed. And it was his fault. He had brought her here. He had insisted she stay at the ranch until they could get the annulment. He had stopped her from going back to town when she jumped out of the wagon. If any harm came to her, he would never forgive himself.

"What happened then?" he asked. He might as well know everything.

"She hollered and beat on that cat until it let me go. While she distracted it, I got my rifle and shot that varmint." The old man rubbed a hand over his grizzled face. "If she hadn't been there, I'd be deader'n a doornail."

"Because of her, you were out there in the first place. I'm not changing my mind about sending her home." Matt was more convinced than ever that it was the right thing to do. For her own good. For his good, too.

"Just tellin' you what happened, Matthew. What you do now is your business."

Matt glanced at Eliza. She hadn't said a single word during this whole thing. That wasn't like her, especially when they were discussing her. More than once she'd said she thought women in Wyoming had a say in things. Her silence made him uneasy.

"Is that the way it happened, Eliza?"

She nodded.

"Why didn't you tell me all this?"

"It wasn't anything. I did what anyone would have."

Matt shook his head. He'd seen men run from less danger. He couldn't imagine a woman doing what she'd done. Didn't matter, though. Things could just as easily have gone from bad to worse. She'd been lucky this time. He couldn't count on her luck holding.

"In a day or two, when Wiley's on his feet, we're going to Silver Springs."

She stared at him for several seconds. He could almost see the wheels turning and braced himself for the arguments stacking up inside her head, just waiting to be spit out to make him change his mind. She finally nodded without a word.

He frowned. "What's wrong with you? Cat got your tongue?"

"Very funny, Matt." She lifted that stubborn little chin.

"Well, don't you have anything else to say?"

She opened her mouth, then shut it again and shook her head.

He should have been glad she was so agreeable. But he couldn't let it drop. After all, this was Eliza. "You always have the last word. There must be something."

"No."

"Why?"

"I promised. I swore that if Wiley got better, I'd do whatever you said without a word. I always keep my promises."

"Good. It's settled, then. When Wiley's back on his feet, you're going back to Boston."

He should have been relieved, but he wasn't. There was a part of him that wanted her to fight him the way she had the bobcat and convince him to let her stay.

She didn't, though. She just nodded again. But that defiant chin was raised higher than he'd ever seen it before.

"Miss Eliza, could I trouble you for another cup of coffee?" The voice came with a surprising amount of strength from the guest room down the hall.

In the kitchen with the sun streaming through the window, Eliza looked up from mending Matt's torn shirt. She sighed. "One minute, Wiley."

It had been several days since he'd opened his eyes and begun his recovery. Eliza had expected to see him moving around by now. He had been eating like a horse, but he hadn't budged from that bed, not even on his good leg. He told her that every time he tried, he was wobbly as a newborn calf, and if he fell, it would be that much longer before he could get back to work.

In the meantime, Eliza had hardly seen Matt. He'd been doing the chores of two men, then he'd come in late at night, eat the supper she kept warm for him, and go to bed. He'd be up and out before the sun. She had offered to fix him breakfast, but he had told her not to bother.

So her only company was the invalid in the other room. Eliza put aside her mending and stood up. She took a mug from the cupboard and poured coffee into it. Then she grabbed some cookies from the jar on the sideboard. Invariably she'd get down the hall and he'd want something besides his strong, black coffee. Fortunately her ankle had healed and didn't trouble her anymore.

She carried the tray into the guest room and placed it on his lap. "That's the last of the sugar cookies I baked. They keep disappearing. I think Matt's been eating them for breakfast."

"Knew that boy had more smarts than he lets on." Wiley's deep chuckle filled the room and made her smile.

"Is there anything else you need?"

"Please, Miss Eliza. Could you stay awhile?" Pale eyes pleaded with her. "I'm gettin' mighty tired of my own company."

She thought of the mending she'd put aside. The morning light was best to see by and she hated to waste it. "Just let me get my sewing."

"Sure thing, ma'am."

When she returned with her basket of thread, needles, and scissors and Matt's white cotton shirt, she pulled the rocking chair closer to the bed and settled in. "How are you feeling today? Any better?"

"Some." He rubbed the quilt resting over the thigh of his injured leg. "Guess I'm gettin' old. Takes longer to heal when a man gets on in years."

She glanced up from the stitch she was taking in the ragged rip in the shirt. "You're far from old, Mr. Powell."

His eyes twinkled when she called him that. She grinned back. "Why, I'd say you're in the prime of your life."

"Then why in tarnation is this leg takin' so all-fired long to get back to the way it was?"

"That was a nasty wound. And you were feverish for several days. It just takes time."

"That there Matthew's shirt?" he asked, sipping his coffee.

"Yes. When I washed the pile from under his bed, I found quite a few in this condition. If I'd known, I'd have brought some material from town and made him some new ones." She studied the uneven tear. "Since I didn't, this is the best I can do."

"Don't know how that knothead got so lucky to marry you."

"Wasn't luck at all. It was his mother's interference. And my eagerness to come here for a fresh start." After the way she'd parted from her father, that old life was closed to her. "Mrs. Decker must have thought he'd take to the idea once it was done. She was mistaken."

"Don't be too sure."

"How can you say that? Everything's a big mess."

He took a bite of cookie and chewed thoughtfully. "You got any feelin's for Matthew?"

"What do you mean?"

"You came a long way to get hitched. Must have had some powerful feelin's for him. Or those problems you mentioned were powerful bad."

She thought for a moment. "It was both. When I was a girl, I adored Matt. I followed him everywhere. That's what got me into trouble with him. He still blames me for his having to leave home."

"How do you feel about him since seein' him again?"

"What are you getting at?"

"I want t'know if you're gonna turn tail and run away from him without a fight."

"He doesn't want me."

"I wouldn't be too sure of that. I've seen the way he looks at you. He wants you all right. He ain't happy about it, but he wants you real bad."

She shook her head. "He only wants me out of his life."

"No, ma'am. That ain't precisely the whole truth. He aims to get you out of here before he learns to care more than he already does."

"Horsefeathers."

He grinned. "Why, Miss Eliza. I do believe that was mighty darn close to swearin'."

"As close as you'll hear me come," she said, trying to look prim. She couldn't, and burst out laughing.

"If you'll pardon an old man's interference, I reckon you're just about the best thing that's ever happened to Matthew."

"I don't think he'd agree. And I'd be careful if I were you. I'm not sure he'll ever forgive his mother for her role in this."

"She wasn't buttin' in. She was just doin' what any mama would to protect her young 'un."

"That reminds me. What with you getting hurt and everything, I forgot. Explain to me what you meant when you said that Matt wants a baby." She pointed at him with the needle in her hand. "And don't tell me again to ask him. You started meddling and I want to know what you meant. He got upset enough to swear."

"He wanted a wife for two reasons. The first was to help around the ranch." Wiley moved restlessly in the bed.

"What was the second?"

"To have a son."

"Why is that so important to him?"

"Because of the land. When Carrie was alive—"

"Carrie was his wife?"

He nodded. "She was in the family way and Matthew carried on about what he'd teach his son so's he could take over the Double C some day."

"I never knew about the baby. What happened to them, Wiley?"

"Birthin' the baby killed her."

Eliza's eyes widened. "Oh, Lord."

He looked at her over the rim of his cup. "You didn't know?"

She shook her head. "Matt's mother never said how it happened."

"Carrie was a tall woman, but narrow of hip. She had trouble when her time came. Matt lost them both."

"How awful."

He nodded. "Took him a mighty long time to get over it."

"I don't think he has. Maybe he never will."

"He needs you to help him."

"I think that fever addled your mind."

"No, ma'am. Like I said, I've seen the way he looks at you." He pointed a finger at her. "Don't tell me you ain't seen it too."

"You mean that funny dark expression he gets on his face?"

He nodded emphatically as a twinkle gleamed in his eyes. "The very one. That's the same way I looked at that widow woman in Texas just before we—"

"That's quite enough." She held up her hands as the heat climbed into her cheeks. "Anyway, I think you're wrong about Matt's feelings. He doesn't think of me that way. He thinks of me as a little girl. The same little girl who followed him around and made his life miserable. He can't wait to be rid of me."

"Horsesh—" He coughed and cleared his throat. "Horsefeathers."

"It's true. You heard him yourself."

"Change his mind." He smacked his fist into his other palm.

"I can't."

"Can't? Or won't?" Wiley's pale gaze wouldn't leave

her alone and she started stitching on Matt's shirt as if her life depended on it. "Didn't figure you for a quitter."

"I'm not. But I *am* practical. Why put effort into a lost cause?"

"You think Matthew's lost?"

She nodded and sighed. "He is to me."

"That's where you're wrong. I think his mama knew just what she was doin' when she sent you here. You're just the woman to find him."

"I don't know how."

"Did you know how to face down that bobcat?"

She frowned. "No."

"Just did what you had to?"

"Yes."

"So do what you have to with Matthew."

"That would be following him wherever he goes."

The old man grinned. "Sounds like a good place to start."

She stuck her needle through the material of Matt's shirt, then hesitated and looked up. "You think I can get through to him?"

"Did you learn anything about the land when we were out there in the south meadow? Did you find out anythin' about Matthew?"

She settled the mending in her lap and thought for a minute. "I discovered that he's a strong man. He had to be to conquer the land the way he has, to stay here and build the ranch into what it is now."

"He needs a strong woman to be his partner."

"You think I'm strong enough?"

He nodded once, with absolute confidence. "Yes'm. Without a doubt. You're just what that stubborn son of a b—" He let out a long breath. "You're what the doctor ordered. Somethin' tells me you always get what you want."

Her mind raced. His mother must have had something in mind to trick them the way she had, and Wiley's theory about her motives was as good as any. Eliza had agreed to the plan for her own reasons. The most important was that she wanted to start a new life. With Matt. Why should she give up without a fight just because he said so?

There was the small matter of her promise. But her exact vow had been to do whatever Matt said without any *word* of argument. She could still keep the promise she'd made. She didn't plan to speak a word to him about staying on the ranch. Her actions, on the other hand, should say a mouthful.

She looked at the man in the bed. "You're right, Wiley."

"I am?"

"I'm going to show him I belong here, in Wyoming with him."

He made a fist and waved it in the air. "That's the spirit."

"I've never been a quitter and I'm not going to start now. I'm going to show him I'm strong enough to be his wife."

In every sense of the word.

8

Matt brushed his forearm across his brow, then leaned on the pitchfork. Inside the barn, the smell of hay and horses and leather surrounded him, good, solid, earthy odors. His stomach growled, reminding him the midday meal had come and gone hours ago. The sugar cookies Eliza baked had only carried him so far, but he fought against going up to the house for something to eat. Seeing her when he was forced to go in at night was hard enough. He'd made it a practice to avoid her as much as possible during the day.

He stared through the barn door into the dreary afternoon light. Clouds blocked the sun and the smell of rain was in the air. From where he stood, he could see the back porch, where Eliza was sweeping. She looked up frequently and stared in his direction. He knew she couldn't see him and wondered why she kept looking at the barn. From this distance, he couldn't read her expression but her movements were erratic, distracted, fitful—as if she had something important on her mind.

Longing settled over him. He'd gotten used to being by

himself for long periods of time and had learned to be satisfied with his own company. If Eliza wasn't here, he wouldn't have to fight the temptation to wander down and visit with her, see her easy smile, and smell her womanly fragrance. He couldn't let himself do that. Otherwise, when she left, he would have to learn how to be alone all over again. It had been hard enough the first time. He didn't think he could do it a second.

He turned his back on her and, with a vengeance, jammed the pitchfork into the hay, then finished spreading it. After putting the tool away, he went into the corral to put out oats for the horses. His stomach growled again. Sooner or later he would have to go down to the house to eat. He couldn't avoid her forever.

When he walked back into the barn, she was standing in front of one of the stalls, staring at the horse inside it. Eliza's brown braid, shot with strands of red and gold, was wound into a coil at her nape. With her white apron covering her calico dress, she looked like a rancher's wife. He noticed Carrie's shoes peeking out from below the hem of her skirt. Regret and longing twisted and pulled inside him until they came together and pressed on his chest. Eliza didn't belong here. He didn't want her to stay. But the thought of letting her go tore at his soul.

What the hell was she doing in the barn anyway? She was afraid of horses. Intense concentration puckered her smooth forehead, furrowing her brow and pulling her full lips into a straight line. She hadn't heard him come in and he watched her, curious about what she was doing. She let out a big breath and moved forward, not quite close enough for the animal to touch her. She lifted her arm and leaned as far forward as she could without letting her body come into contact with the stall. He noticed the hand she held out toward the horse shook. There was something in her palm.

He walked up behind her and stopped. "Eliza?"

She gasped and jumped back, right against his chest.

Tremors racked her body. Whatever was in her hand scattered in the hay on the floor. Why was she putting herself through this?

He gripped her upper arms to steady her. "It's all right, Eliza."

Her breathing was fast and shallow. "I didn't see you there."

"I thought you heard me. I'm sorry I startled you. What are you doing?"

"Getting acquainted with the horse."

What had forced her to do this? As far as he knew she hadn't gotten within a foot of a horse since one nearly ran her down years ago. Matt had seen it happening and had tackled Eliza, knocking her out of the way. After that he had felt responsible for her, a habit that stayed with him until he left home. Funny how easily he'd picked it up again, even after all the years that had passed.

"Why are you getting acquainted?" When he spoke, the wisps of hair near her temple stirred and her scent drifted to him. It was sweet, a mixture of fresh-baked cookies and wildflowers.

She pulled out of his hold, but didn't turn or look at him. She was still trembling and he watched her shoulders tense.

"Eliza?" he said softly.

"When the wagon broke down and Wiley was hurt, I wanted to go for help. There was a perfectly good horse there, but I was too afraid to go near it." She took in a shuddering breath. "If you hadn't come looking for us, he would have died because of me. I don't ever want to feel that weak or helpless again."

"When you go back home, you won't have to worry about it. So go on back to the house where it's warm and—"

"Don't treat me like a child. I would've died *back home*, if it hadn't been for you. There isn't any place that's completely safe." She looked him in the eye. "And if you hadn't come to find us, Wiley would have died."

"It's not your fault the wheel broke. You didn't make the bobcat attack."

"That's not the point. I want to be able to do whatever needs to be done. I hate that there's something I can't do."

He couldn't help admiring her gumption. "You're determined about this?" he asked, nodding toward the horse.

Eliza glanced over her shoulder at the animal in its stall, contentedly chewing on hay. She swallowed once, hard. Then she gave Matt the fiercest look he'd ever seen from her. "I'm going to be that horse's best friend."

How could he ignore such courage? "Then I'll help you. You don't have to do it alone."

"Thank you, Matt." She tried to smile, but her mouth trembled. She caught her top lip between her teeth and turned away. "Something tells me I'd better do it quick before I lose my nerve."

A whinny and stomping hooves from one of the other horses in the barn made her jump.

He put his arm around her waist and gave her a reassuring squeeze. "That's just one of the other horses. Concentrate on Snowflake right now."

"This horse?" she asked, pointing to the one she'd been trying to feed.

"Yeah."

"Did you name her?"

"Carrie did." She tensed at his words. "Relax. Snowflake won't hurt you."

"Why is she named that? Any special reason?"

"Two. This filly was born during the worst blizzard I've ever seen in my life. And see that white mark on her forehead?" Eliza nodded. "Carrie thought it looked like a snowflake. To me it always looked more like bird droppings."

"Then I'm very glad you didn't name this horse, Matt."

He started to laugh. It felt good, real good. He realized he hadn't had much to laugh about in a long time. He waited for the ache of bad memories to take his breath away the way it had earlier. It surprised him when nothing happened. He felt only a slight twinge, and the pleasant glow of a recollection that made him smile.

A thud followed by a scraping sound drew their attention to Snowflake pawing the ground, almost as if she wanted to be included in the conversation. "Want to say hello?" Matt asked Eliza.

Her hands stilled; she dropped her apron over her dress and looked up at him, her eyes wide and scared. "I wish I could say it from here."

Eliza had grown up, but she hadn't left behind her girlhood fear of horses. He wanted to show her there was nothing to be afraid of. He wanted to see the spunk that had impressed Brad Slicker and everyone else who had met her in town.

"Snowflake is in her stall. She can't get out. You don't have to go in until you're ready. This is nothing like the last time."

Eliza stood up straight and squared her shoulders. "I'd like very much to say hello to Snowflake."

Matt led her closer to the gate enclosing the animal. "You were holding out your hand before. Why?"

"I was going to feed her. I figured the way to her heart was through her stomach." Matt thought he heard her mutter under her breath something that sounded like, "Might work better with horses than men." He wasn't certain that was what she had said and decided to let it pass.

"Feeding her was a good idea. Follow your instincts. What was in your hand when I startled you before?"

She bent down to pick through the hay, then straightened and held out her palm. He saw what looked like chicken meat.

"You can't feed that to a horse."

"I thought you said to follow my instincts."

"Horses don't eat chicken."

"They don't?"

"That's not exactly true. Horses aren't the brightest animals ever put on this earth. They'll eat anything you give them. But chicken would give her colic."

"I'm sorry, Matt. I had no idea. I'd never do anything to deliberately hurt her." She pointed to a cloth covered plate on the bench just inside the barn door. "I brought you some, too. I hope chicken doesn't give you colic."

He shook his head. "I love fried chicken."

He couldn't remember the last time, if ever, he'd had a hot lunch while he was working. Carrie never had brought food out to him, always losing herself in whatever she was doing. He never minded; he always thought going to the house to eat a pleasant break in the day and an excuse to see her.

Now Eliza had brought him fried chicken, his favorite. Had she remembered? He tried to hold back the rush of pure pleasure at her sweet nature and couldn't.

"I've got something else that Snowflake will like a lot better," he said.

"What?"

He went to a bucket in the corner and grabbed a handful of oats. He cupped Eliza's hand in his and let the grains fall into her open palm. "This."

Eliza looked from him to the dried grain in her hand. "You're sure?" Worry mixed with fear in her eyes. "My instincts tell me she'll like me a lot better if I don't give her something that tastes awful."

"I'm sure."

Matt stood behind her and encircled her waist with his arm again. He gently pushed her forward, encouraging her to move the oats closer to the horse's mouth. She started to close her hand.

"Don't," he said. "She could nip your fingers if you curl them up like that."

He brushed his palm over hers to flatten her fingers. A

ripple of sensation jolted him from his wrist to his shoulder. He swallowed hard. This was no time to give in to his attraction to Eliza. She needed his help.

Pressed against him from shoulder blades to backside, she trembled from head to toe. Still, he could feel her determination, could almost taste her courage. When Snowflake leaned her broad face toward the food, Eliza tensed but held her ground. Matt steadied her hand. The horse whinnied softly, then nibbled the food.

Eliza flinched, but otherwise made no move to flee. Her sheer guts and heart made him proud of her.

"That's just fine," he said softly. "There's nothing to be afraid of. This little girl is as gentle as can be. She won't hurt you."

When the oats were gone, the horse's nose and lips moved over her fingers looking for more food. Eliza giggled. "Her nose is like velvet. But it tickles."

They stood there for a long time as Eliza grew more confident. Matt stayed right behind her. She felt so good. He tried not to enjoy the feel of her in his arms but he couldn't help it. Tentatively, she touched the horse's face with the tips of her fingers. Matt inhaled the fresh sweet scent of Eliza's hair and savored for the first time in a long time the closeness of a woman.

He liked how she felt snuggled against him and hated himself for it.

He wanted to pull back, but then he might rob Eliza of this chance to free herself from her fear. He couldn't do that to her.

Slowly, he felt the tension ease out of her as the animal sniffed her wrist, nickered softly, and blinked her big brown eyes.

"Scratch her nose," Matt said, bending close to Eliza's ear. He resisted the almost overwhelming urge to press his mouth to the slender column of her neck and see what she tasted like, know the texture of her skin, find the boundaries of her passion. "Snowflake loves that."

He took Eliza's wrist and placed her palm on the horse's snout, leaving his hand on hers. Something stirred in his chest and came to life, a feeling he hadn't known for a long time, the satisfaction of thinking of someone besides himself.

He moved her palm gently up and down, and when Snowflake lowered her head, he said, "She wants you to scratch her between the ears. She likes you."

"Really?" Eliza glanced up at him and smiled.

He laughed at her innocent delight. The brightness of her face made him feel the same as if the first ray of spring sunshine warmed him after a long, cold winter.

"Really," he said.

"I like her, too. What a pretty girl," she crooned, doing as he'd instructed. "What next?"

He grinned. "One step at a time. Take it slow and easy."

"I can't. I might lose my nerve."

He thought for a minute. "Maybe you should brush her."

"Can I?"

He nodded. "I'll show you how."

Regret washed over him after he let Eliza go. It was as if a cloud had suddenly drifted across the sun, throwing a shadow over him. Shaking off the feeling, he grabbed the brush from the shelf on the wall and handed it to her.

She rubbed her thumb over the stiff bristles. "This means I have to go in there with her, doesn't it?" Eliza's green eyes were wide when she looked up at him. She was so close he could count every last freckle on her nose. Her lips were full and pink and soft looking.

He wondered if she tasted as smooth and sweet as she looked. It suddenly seemed important to find out. Slowly, he lowered his head. Her mouth opened slightly—waiting, welcoming. The horse snorted and pawed at the ground. Matt blinked twice and pulled back.

"You can't brush her from this side of the fence," he said gruffly. He turned away from her.

"Matt?"

"What?"

"You won't go away?" she asked uncertainly. "You'll be here while I do this?"

He wanted to run for the hills and stay there until Wiley was well enough to take her to the stage in Silver Springs. In his whole life, he'd only ever run away from his father's disapproval. He'd come to Wyoming and discovered an inner strength he didn't know he had. He didn't think he was strong enough to resist Eliza, though. His instinct for survival screamed at him to get the hell away from her before it was too late. He started to walk out of the barn.

"Matt?"

He stopped when he heard the doubt in her voice. He couldn't leave her to face down her fear alone.

"I was just going to get more oats," he said, moving to the bucket to scoop a handful of the grain.

He opened the stall and motioned her forward, then closed the gate with the two of them inside. Eliza stood with her back against the slats. He could understand her reluctance. The sheer size of the horse was intimidating to her. Eliza's determined little chin was about even with Snowflake's back. Matt took her hand and tugged her closer to the animal's side, away from her mouth or back legs. He handed Eliza the brush and stood behind her again, ready if she needed him. But this time he didn't hold her or touch her. After wondering what her lips would taste like, looking into her big eyes would be his undoing.

He'd been a fool to think bringing her to the ranch would solve the problem of their marriage, and a worse one to think things couldn't get more complicated than they had been in town.

"Soft and steady, Eliza," he said gruffly. Sort of like gentling a woman before bedding her. He pushed the thought away as quickly as it came. The last thing in the world he should be thinking about was bedding Eliza.

He'd come damn close to kissing her. If he followed his instincts, he'd have her beneath him in the hay until they were both weak and breathless. And if he did that, he'd break his promise to send her back to Boston untouched.

Eliza looked at Snowflake. To keep from trembling she made herself rigid. She wished Matt would put his arm around her again as he had when she'd fed the horse. He stood tall and strong beside her, near enough to reassure her, but not close enough to touch her.

Whether he touched her or not, she had to keep going. If she wanted to be part of Matt's life, she had to be able to do the same things he did. He rode a horse almost every day. That meant, even if her heart beat so hard and fast it wore out, she had to conquer her fear.

"Go ahead, Eliza."

She took a deep breath and tentatively brought the brush down the horse's side. The animal stood completely still, and Eliza did the same thing again. She kept up the movement until her self-confidence grew, squeezing out the fear.

"Is this all right, Matt?" She glanced at him and saw a look of such intensity on his face, she wondered what in the world he was thinking about.

"You're doing fine." His voice sounded strained. "You could talk to her."

She nodded and turned back to the shiny brown coat of the horse in front of her. She was surprised the hide was so coarse; she'd always thought a horse's hair looked soft.

"What a good girl you are, Snowflake." She stroked two or three times, then hesitantly patted the animal's neck. "Does that feel good? Do you like being petted, pretty girl?"

To her right, Matt shuffled his boots and turned away.

"You know, Matt, I think I'd like to try riding her. Do you think I could?"

He rounded on her. "Five minutes ago you didn't want to come inside the stall. Now you think you're ready to ride?" He glared at her. "You don't do anything halfway, do you?"

"I've made up my mind to do this. Why stop here?"

Behind her, Eliza heard Snowflake pawing restlessly and the pungent smell of hay drifted to her. The next thing she knew, warm breath tickled her neck just before a soft nicker sounded close to her ear. She didn't have time to be afraid when she felt Snowflake's velvety nose right between her shoulder blades. With one shove, Eliza pitched forward, right into Matt.

She screeched and he gripped her upper arms to steady her. Her heart hammered so hard it hurt; her knees were wobbly as a rickety old table. He turned her so that he stood between her and Snowflake, then he stared down at her.

"Still think you're ready to ride?" he asked, a note of angry challenge in his tone.

His voice settled over her and raised gooseflesh on her arms. She sensed a dare in his words that had nothing to do with horses.

She lifted her chin and met his gaze. "I'm ready to ride anytime you're ready to take me."

His blue eyes darkened like a midnight sky. His mouth thinned to a straight line and the muscle in his jaw contracted as he hesitated and waged some inner battle. Finally his head lowered toward her.

"Damnation," he muttered, his lips an inch from hers.

"Do you think this is a good reason to swear—"

She felt his unwillingness as his hands tightened on her arms. She knew his surrender when his mouth silenced her.

Her heart pounded against her ribs as his lips moved over hers, slow and sure. Eliza had only been kissed once before, and Cornelius Fairbrothers couldn't hold a candle to Matt. Cornelius's touch had left her cold whereas Matt's warmed her like a prairie fire. He kissed her cheek, her nose, her forehead, then moved back to her mouth. As his breathing quickened, he grew more insistent. He traced the outline of her mouth with his tongue, coaxing her to open to him. She did gladly.

Then he stroked the inside of her mouth and bolts of pleasure zigzagged through her. Heat kindled in her belly and the glow spread outward to her arms and legs. When he settled his lips over hers, the pressure was hard, almost bruising, but she didn't care. A sweet ache throbbed between her thighs and she tried to move closer to him, to rest her palms on his chest. Then his hands tightened on her upper arms and he pushed her away from him, breaking the contact of their lips.

Eliza didn't know whether to laugh or cry. Countless times, she'd imagined him doing this, even though he'd made it clear he would rather chew cowhide into leather strips. But finally he'd kissed her and she didn't want him to stop. "Why are you pushing me away?"

"Because it's wrong. We're wrong."

She tried again to put her arms around his neck and snuggle closer. "Matt?"

"Don't, Eliza. I shouldn't have done that. Just let it go."

"I can't. I liked it. I want you to kiss me again." She pleaded with her eyes. "I want you to show me how to kiss you back."

"Oh, God. Don't do this to me."

"What? I don't understand."

His eyes flared like twin blue flames. "You never know when to quit, do you, Eliza? You really want to know what this is all about? I'll show you. Just remember you asked for it."

He tugged her to him and held her against him with his hands on her buttocks, but he didn't kiss her again. He watched her as he let her get accustomed to the hard ridge of his manhood. This intimate contact with the lower half of his body shocked her, but she'd rather die than let him see it. The Matt she'd always known was gentle. This man had a thread of violence she'd never seen before. She sensed that he was trying to use her innocence against her, to frighten her away, and she wouldn't let him do it.

She pulled out of his arms, her chest rising and falling.

She stared at him. The same mouth she had so liked kissing just moments before thinned to a straight line. Anger and desire swirled together in the depths of his eyes. She knew if he could take back the kiss he would do it in an instant. "Why did you do that?"

"Because it's what you wanted."

"No. You're trying to scare me and I want to know why." He'd been gentle and caring, the man who had once saved her life, when he helped free her of her panic around horses, but now he'd awakened a different kind of fear.

She remembered Wiley's words, *He wants you. He ain't happy about it, but he does.*

"You wanted me to show you how to kiss back." His eyes narrowed. "Change your mind, little girl?"

Her chin lifted slightly. "I'm not a little girl. I've been kissed lots of times." That was closer to the truth than when she'd said the same thing to Mr. Slicker about whiskey.

"You've never been a good liar, Eliza." Matt pulled her to him again. "Prove it," he said, and lowered his mouth to hers.

The touch of Matt's mouth heated her, more intoxicating than the glass of whiskey she'd drunk in the saloon. By God, she would prove to him that she wasn't quite the inexperienced little girl he thought. And she'd show him she wasn't afraid of him, even if she was—just a little bit.

She stood on tiptoe and looped her wrists around his neck. When she traced his mouth with her tongue the way he'd done to her, he sucked in his breath as a shudder moved through him. Then she pressed herself as close to his lean, muscular body as she could. He was still aroused, but she didn't find it shocking this time.

Instead, the contact sent a thrill through her that settled in her breasts and went straight to her core. Over the smells of hay and horses and heat, she inhaled the scent that belonged to Matt alone. The scent of man. The elemental, female part of her responded until she could hardly pull enough air into her lungs, and her chest rose and fell unevenly until breathing was an effort.

Eliza slanted her mouth to make the contact between them more firm. She rubbed her bosom against the unyielding wall of his chest. He groaned and tightened his arms around her.

He lifted his mouth from hers. His harsh, rapid breathing stirred the hair on her face. The look in his eyes made her want to back away.

"Who the hell taught you to kiss that way? And don't tell me not to swear. This is a damn good reason."

Eliza inhaled deeply. He was angrier than he'd been the day she looked for a job in town. Intensity built within him and burned in his eyes.

"Who, Eliza? Fairweathers?"

"Brothers."

"You did this with Fairbrothers?"

"No."

"Wasn't he the one your father wanted you to marry?"

"Yes."

"And he wasn't the one you—"

"No. I hated it when he kissed me."

"Just how many men have you kissed?" He threaded his fingers into the hair on either side of her face and cupped her cheeks in his palms. His expression was ruthless. "Don't lie to me. I'll know if you are."

"Only two. You're the second. You're the one who taught me this."

"I haven't taught you a thing. I could show you a whole lot about being with a man, but you're not ready for that. You have some notion of life that's not real. Grow up, Eliza."

"I'm a woman fully grown, whether you like it or not. I'm not the little girl you saved from that horse. But you've been my hero ever since that day. I kissed you like that because it felt right."

"No." He dropped his hands and stepped away from her. "This is wrong. I'm nobody's hero and I don't want to be. When fate kicks you in the ass, there's no such thing as a hero."

"This is about Carrie, isn't it?"

He shook his head, then ran splayed fingers through his hair and brushed it out of his eyes. "This is between you and me. The sooner we end this marriage, the better for both of us."

"You didn't kiss me like you wanted to end our marriage."

"What do you know about it? I'm the second man you've ever kissed. You're practically a baby. I know what's best. And you promised to do what I say without a word of argument."

How could she keep her promise? If she went away, who would get through to him and show him that he couldn't give up on life? When he'd lost his wife and baby something inside him died, too, and she was beginning to doubt that he wanted it back. Why had he asked his mother to find him a wife? He didn't want to care about anyone. Wiley was wrong. Laura Decker was wrong. Eliza was not the woman for him, because he didn't want a woman or a wife. In fact, she didn't know what he wanted.

"Speaking of going home . . ." He ran his fingers through his hair again. She remembered how he'd always done that when his exasperation with her had grown to the breaking point. "How is Wiley today anyhow?"

So, he wanted to talk about anything but her. She wrapped her arms around her waist. "I'm not sure. He eats like a horse, but when I suggested he get up and walk around, he said he's still too weak."

His brows drew together. "If it was anyone else, I'd say he was trying to get out of work. But I've known that old man for eight years. He's the only one I know who works harder than I do."

She felt the need to reassure him. "He lost a lot of

blood, Matt. And that bump on the head was pretty bad. I'm sure it won't be much longer until he's up and around."

He stared at her. "Can't be too soon for me."

Eliza blinked hard to keep the tears gathered in her eyes from slipping down her cheeks. He sounded as if he hated her. No matter what he said, his kisses didn't feel like he wanted her to go away. Confusion muddled her mind.

Just then Snowflake lowered her head and pushed Matt toward her. He stumbled, then caught himself before he touched her. "You've definitely made friends with that horse."

"I guess—"

"I have to go out and check the herd grazing in the south pasture. If I'm not back, don't wait supper for me."

"I'll keep it warm for you."

He headed for the barn door and stopped beside the plate of food, hesitating before picking it up. He looked back as Eliza patted Snowflake's nose, then left the stall and closed the gate behind her.

He rubbed the back of his hand across his mouth, then stomped out of the barn without taking the food she'd brought.

Eliza watched his broad back as he walked away from her across the empty yard toward the house. She seemed to be able to make friends with everyone. Everyone except the man who had lured her to Wyoming with the memory of his charming ways and the slow grin that melted her insides like butter. So far she hadn't seen much of that man. If he had his way, she would be gone before she could find him again.

Eliza made up her mind to see that didn't happen. Somehow she had found the grit to face her fear of horses dead on. Although he was twice as ornery, Matt wasn't nearly so big. Surely she could get through to him.

9

Standing on the back porch, Matt took off his wet slicker and shook the drops of water from it. Rain dripped from his hat. He was cold and hungry and in the worst mood he could remember. Memories of kissing Eliza pricked him like thorns on a rosebush. All day he'd tried to freeze them out; all day he'd failed miserably.

He stared at the door, longing to be by the fire he knew would be in the hearth, yearning for the warmth he knew waited for him inside the house. He almost convinced himself it had nothing to do with Eliza. Then laughter drifted to him from the kitchen and he heard more than one voice. When he'd put his horse in the barn, he had seen a wagon out front and wondered who had stopped.

Matt opened the back door and walked inside. Wiley was dozing in the rocking chair by the fire, his injured leg propped up on a crate. Across the trestle table from Eliza he saw Hildie Arnold with her baby daughter in her arms. The blond, blue-eyed woman bounced the child on her knee. Her husband, John, a big, bearded, dark-haired man sat beside her cradling a cup of coffee in his hands and smiling at his wife and baby.

A stab of pain cut through Matt for what might have been. He turned away to shut the door. When he looked back, three pairs of eyes studied him. The baby was too busy playing with her fingers.

Before he could hang up his wet slicker, Eliza jumped up and rushed over to him. She stood on tiptoe and threw her arms around his neck.

"Welcome home, sweetheart," she said, then kissed him full on the mouth.

He pulled away from her. "Eliza!" He removed her arms from around his neck. "We have company."

"Hildie and John understand that we're newlyweds. Why, they've only been married a little over a year themselves." When she backed away, the bodice of her dress showed dark spots where the rain on him had soaked through. He could almost see her soft curves and had trouble tearing his gaze away.

She hung his slicker on the peg. "Let me have your hat," she said, just a little breathlessly.

He stared at her for a second. There was a glint in her eye that he sure didn't understand and definitely couldn't trust. He remembered that look from her days of following him around and knew she was up to no good. He just wasn't sure what it was.

"I'll do it," he said, putting the hat beside his coat. He turned back to the group. "John, what are you doing in my neck of the woods?"

John stood and the two men shook hands. "We're headed back from Silver Springs. Heard you got married and decided to stop in person to offer our congratulations."

"Thank you."

Matt glanced at Eliza beside him. The smile she gave him was far too innocent for his liking.

"How long have you been here?" Matt asked his friend.

"Most of the afternoon. Eliza's been telling us all about how the two of you grew up together."

"Has she now?" he said, sliding a glance at her.

"Yes." Hildie brushed blond curls from the baby's forehead, then looked at him. "It's the most romantic story. How she came all the way from Boston to marry you."

Romantic? Eliza had been telling some tall tales. What was between the two of them was a temporary arrangement, nothing more. But this wasn't the time or place to discuss it. Eliza had already made a fuss in town that no one was likely to forget any time soon. He decided the less said the better. There would be time enough when she had gone to deal with explanations.

"We've all eaten supper." Eliza took his arm in an intimate way that sent his heart slamming against his chest. "You must be starving. I kept your dinner warm, just like I promised when we were in the barn earlier." She winked at him, a gesture everyone in that room could see, except Wiley, who was snoring.

"Much obliged, Eliza." Matt held himself rigid, trying not to feel her soft breast rubbing his arm with every breath she took. What the hell kind of game was she playing?

"You'd probably like to get out of your wet clothes first. I put some dry clothes on our bed for you." She emphasized the words *our* and *bed.* He didn't like this, not one little bit.

Matt decided to play along with her, though. No point in adding to the rumors that were no doubt circulating about Matt Decker's contract bride. It had been a week since he'd married Eliza and the talk must still be hot and heavy to make the Arnolds stop by to see them.

"I believe I will put some other clothes on. Would you care to help me in the bedroom, Eliza?" He raised a brow and sent her a look that he knew John would understand, even if Hildie didn't. Two could play this game.

Eliza's smile faltered a little, then she said, "Anything you'd like, sweetheart."

Matt picked up an oil lamp from the shelf and lighted it. Then he put his arm around her waist and, none too gently, urged her down the hall. He gripped her upper arm, tugged her into his bedroom, and slammed the door behind them. On the bed, he saw the nightgown Eliza had worn when they'd been married, and his uneasy feeling grew a lot bigger.

He put the lamp on the dresser, then swung her around and glared down at her. The need to swear built within him, but he managed to tamp it down—for now. He had a sneaking suspicion that before they were through he'd be forced to say more than one word she wouldn't approve of.

"What's going on?" he asked.

"It's pretty obvious. Friends of yours stopped to say hello and I've been getting to know them."

"I'm not talking about that." He picked up her nightgown. "Why is this in here?"

"I thought it would be easier than sleeping in the barn."

Typical Eliza. Start at the tail end of the story and work her way forward. This could take so long, everyone in the other room would think they were doing what newlyweds were supposed to do. "What does your nightgown have to do with sleeping in the barn?"

"I'm trying to tell you."

"And doing a piss-poor job of it, too."

"Matt, your language . . ."

"It's going to get a lot worse it you don't explain what in the he—what's going on."

"The Arnolds stopped by for a visit."

"That much I know." He unbuttoned his wet shirt and pulled his arms out of it. He looked at the dresser and saw her brush and comb and some ribbons and toilet water. His gaze shot back to her. "What are your things doing in here?"

"I've invited our guests to stay the night."

He should have guessed that himself. The weather

wasn't fit for man or beast. No one should be out in it, especially a baby. No doubt John had taken his wife and child to town because he didn't want to leave them alone on the ranch. The rain had come on suddenly and caught them. As much as he hated to admit it, Eliza's common sense was better than her storytelling ability.

That still didn't explain her moving into his room. "What does that have to do with your things being here?"

"This house has three bedrooms," she said, a patient tone to her voice, as if she was speaking to a child. "Wiley has one, you have one, and I have the third. Wiley is still too sick to move back to the bunkhouse, especially in this kind of weather. I've given the Arnolds my room. I thought it best to move my things in here. Unless you'd rather I sleep in the barn?" She raised a questioning brow.

He glanced at the bed, then back at her. She looked sweeter than a spring meadow and twice as soft. The fragrance of flowers clung to her. How in the hell could he sleep with her and not hold her, not kiss her? And . . .

And finish what they'd started earlier in the barn. He'd kissed her in anger and tried to frighten her away. She was trying to fit in. Getting over her fear of horses was her first step. He sensed a stubborn streak of determination and knew she planned to learn everything she could about the ranch. Why couldn't she see that he didn't want her to stay? His kind of life was too dangerous for a woman like her.

There were too many life-and-death decisions to make every day. Look at John and Hildie. John's choices had been to leave his family unprotected while he went for supplies or to take them with him. He'd chosen the latter and now they were caught in weather that could rob them of their health or cause an accident or God knows what.

If Matt had it to do over, he would never have left Carrie alone so close to her time. He didn't ever again want to make a decision that could mean life or death for someone he loved.

He couldn't say why for sure, but he had a feeling Eliza was getting even with him for the way he'd kissed her earlier. And that she wanted not only to fit in on the ranch, but into his bed as well. He wouldn't let her get away with it.

"I'll sleep in the barn," he said.

She looked startled for a second, then she nodded. "All right. So you'll explain to John and Hildie why a man married just a week is leaving his wife alone? Or would you like me to?"

"Just a second—"

"You realize they'll feel bad. And probably offer to sleep in the barn so as not to put anyone out. But it's awfully cold out there for the baby." She paused. "I could offer to keep the baby inside. No, if Jessica was mine, I wouldn't let anyone else have her. I don't think Hildie will take to that idea."

"Eliza, I—"

"The nights are so cold, I don't know if they can keep her warm enough in the barn. Of course, it's better than spending the night on the trail, isn't it?"

"You know, it's—"

She put her hand on the knob. "I'll go tell them."

"Wait."

She turned back and gave him her wide-eyed look. She had him by the short hairs and she damn well knew it.

"Yes?" Her innocent expression mocked him; her full, soft lips tempted him.

Two could play this game. He unbuckled his belt, the satisfaction sweet when he saw the uncertain look that slipped past the bravado in her eyes. "Don't say anything to them."

"If that's what you want, Matt." She started to open the door and he shucked his jeans. Her hand went still.

"You know what I want, Eliza, and you're using it against me." He unbuttoned his woolen underwear and slipped his arms out. The top of the one-piece garment slid down, catching on his hips and keeping him just this side of modesty. "A good wife would dry her husband's back, Eliza. Don't you want to show our guests what a good wife you are?"

"Y-you're not wet."

"Don't you want to make sure?" He watched her swallow nervously as her gaze darted to his belly and lower to what was barely covered. He knew the double-edged prick of revenge when that part of him sprang to life. She gasped and he knew she knew it, too.

She squared her shoulders and raised her gaze, looking him straight in the eye. "If you need your back dried, I'd be happy to do it. So along with cooking, cleaning, and laundry, my duties include seeing to your comforts?"

"Some of them," he said, turning around to present his back.

He heard the chiffarobe door open, then felt soft towel strokes as Eliza rubbed him. This part of revenge was awful damn nice.

Eliza's heart pounded as she drank in the sight of his wide shoulders and broad back. His slicker had kept him partially dry, and his shirt and union suit had absorbed any rain that had slipped past. He was playing with her as a cat toys with a mouse before devouring it. He'd done the same thing earlier. It was high time he learned she'd come to Wyoming so she wouldn't be pushed around anymore.

She was sick to death of being bullied. All her life, her father had dominated her and given her orders. Whenever she was up to there with it, she'd gotten into some kind of scrape. If she was a docile sort of woman, she would be married to Cornelius Fairbrothers now instead of Matt.

She ran the towel down his spine to the two dimples just above his backside. A blush heated her from head to toe.

He glanced over his shoulder. "Press a little harder, Eliza. That feels mighty good after riding all day. In fact, the part of me that sits in that saddle could sure use a rub-down—"

A small sound escaped her and he chuckled. Then anger took hold. Matt was trying to frighten her again by using her ignorance of what went on between a man and a woman. She had to show him he wouldn't get away with it. Being his wife couldn't be any more difficult than taking a drink in the saloon, dragging a dead bobcat to the side of the road, or making friends with Snowflake. She had tamed her fears; surely she could gentle Matt Decker.

He moved his shoulders and the muscles in his upper back rippled beneath his tanned flesh. It was a sight to behold, and a sight that made her mouth go dry. With two fingers, she reached out and traced the line of his neck, over the peak of his shoulder and down the wide, hard muscle in his upper arm.

"Is that good, Matt?" she asked softly, fascinated by the sight of his masculine body.

"Good," he said, his voice a raspy whisper. Then he went still for a second just before he started to move away.

She put her hand on his waist and he sucked in his breath. When he was a young man, she'd seen him without his shirt once as they'd swum in the river. He'd been broad of shoulder and narrow-hipped then. But now, he was broader and harder, filled out like a man. What would it feel like to touch her lips to his warm skin?

Without another thought, she pressed her mouth to his shoulder and felt a shudder go through him.

"Eliza, don't."

"Why? You're not afraid of me, are you?"

"Of course not—"

She moved her lips to his shoulder blade and he went stock-still. She wished she was tall enough to reach his neck. It was like a drug, this sense of her own power flowing through her.

Matt towered over her. Without his shirt, she could see

his strength. He could snap her in two with one hand, yet, with the lightest touch of her fingers and mouth, she had kept him motionless. If only she had more experience. Matt had said there were things he could show her, and she wished she knew them now.

She started to wrap her arms around his waist and rested her cheek against his back. The shrill cry of a baby from the other room stopped her. Matt removed her arms.

"You'd better go see to our company while I change." His voice was husky, and there was more than a tinge of anger in it.

"I suppose I'd better."

Eliza pulled in a deep breath and let it out slowly. A sprinkling of regret settled over her and she shook it away. After all, Matt would share her bed in a few hours. They had the whole night. Who knew what would happen?

Eliza sat in the rocking chair by the kitchen fire brushing her hair. It was late; the rain had finally stopped. The Arnolds had gone to bed hours before since they were leaving at first light to get home. Matt had followed soon after. He hadn't even looked at her.

The spark of annoyance that had goaded her into playing his wife had sputtered and died, leaving her unsure about what to do now. When she was a child, he would retaliate every time she did something to him. Would he slip back into that now? When she went to his bed, would he repay her for forcing him into the sleeping arrangements? It had been a game when she was a girl. She was a woman now, and she wasn't playing.

"Eliza?" Matt's voice was just above a whisper.

She stopped rocking and her brush stilled for a second before she brought it through the strands of her hair and over her breast.

She glanced at him in the doorway. He was fully

dressed except for boots and belt. She pulled the tie of her dressing gown tighter over her flannel nightdress.

"Are you coming to bed?" he asked.

She stood up and turned toward him. "I washed my hair and wanted to dry it."

The glow of the fire highlighted the angles and hollows of his face. He was the handsomest man she'd ever seen, the only one who'd ever caused her to take more than a moment's interest. Intensity burned in his eyes and made her heart race.

He moved closer and stopped in front of her. For a second he stared down; then he touched the strand of hair draped over her breast. He rubbed it between his thumb and finger and said one word. "Beautiful."

Then he blinked and his eyes were empty as if the last of his feelings had drained from his soul. Eliza longed to find the key to his heart, to free the fun-loving man she'd once known. But she was beginning to think she was the wrong person to do so. Maybe she *should* just go away and let him find a woman who could make him happy again.

"I have to get up early. Let's go to bed."

"You didn't have to wait for me."

"I didn't." He shrugged. "You go on. I'll bank the fire."

"All right."

Eliza walked down the hall and turned into his room. The oil lamp beside the bed outlined the white sheets and turned-down comforter. She swallowed nervously. The only time she'd shared a bed with a man was the night she'd married Matt. And all they'd done was sleep, badly at that.

Since she'd come to Wyoming, she'd been asked how much liquor she'd drunk and how many men she'd kissed. She'd told the truth about her kissing and fibbed outrageously about the whiskey. Thank goodness Matt hadn't asked her about her experiences with a man in the privacy of the bedroom. But then, he'd know if she wasn't telling the truth. He'd always known.

She heard his footsteps coming closer. Quickly, she removed her dressing gown and jumped into the bed, pulling the covers up to her chin. The sheets were cold and she shivered. The scent of Matt surrounded her and pressed against her chest until she could hardly breathe. As he came into the room, a stirring of air washed over her. Her body grew rigid.

He blew out the lamp, sending the room into pitch-darkness. She couldn't see her hand in front of her face, but she heard plenty—his breathing, the rustle of clothes, his muffled curse when he bumped against the bedside table. How much clothing had he taken off? Everything? A small thrill rippled through her.

She remembered the sight and taste of his bare back and her mouth went dry.

The mattress dipped from his weight and the covers pulled tight across her breasts as he adjusted them for his big body. His heat worked its way over to her and she felt warmer with him beside her. Then he released a huge sigh and the bed went completely still. She could sense the care he took not to touch her, but the tension was so thick she could cut it with a pair of dull sewing scissors.

She knew Matt; he ignored unpleasant things. And he was trying to pretend she wasn't there. She wasn't sure if she was disappointed or relieved. When her anger flared to life, she recognized it instantly. How dare he try to act as if she didn't exist! He'd done it for as long as she could remember and she was sick of it.

She thought back to Boston and the time before Matt had gone away. Memories of the things she'd done to get his attention came flooding back. In the darkness, she started to smile and she shifted her position in the bed.

"I thought you were asleep." The sound of his voice came to her, creaky as a rusty hinge.

"No," she said, giggling.

"What's wrong with you?"

"Nothing." Her body started to shake with laughter. She felt like a girl again, getting the giggles in church and unable to control them. Her father had sent her out once, chastising her in front of the whole congregation. That night she'd gone to bed without supper.

"Something's on your mind." There was a smile in his tone.

"I was thinking about the time you climbed the tree outside my house and sneaked food in for me."

The bed moved and she felt him roll toward her a little. "I remember. I never agreed with starving a child for punishment."

"I'll never forget the look on my father's face when I told him I wasn't hungry the next morning."

Matt chuckled. "I always thought the minister was too hard on you."

She sighed. "Maybe he had reason. I was willful—"

"Was?"

"All right, I *am* willful. Can I help it if I liked climbing trees, skipping stones, and having foot races? He never approved of my going fishing either."

There was silence for a minute, then a snort. "Maybe because you never caught anything."

"I caught you once. Remember when you tried to sneak up on me and push me in the river?"

"How could I forget? You ducked and I fell in."

"And got caught on my hook." She laughed, then covered her mouth with her hand.

"I still have the scars."

She rolled on her side toward him and closed her eyes, picturing a grin on his face. His breath was warm on her forehead. "Where might those scars be?"

"You know good and well they're on my backside. If I recall, you pulled the hook out."

"You made me do it. I told you to see Dr. Caldwell."

"Thanks to you, I had to."

"Did you tell him how it happened?"

She heard him snort again. "Of course not. I told him I did it on a nail in the barn."

Now that she'd started, she couldn't shut off the flood of memories. She chuckled.

"Shh," he said. "You'll wake everyone."

"Sorry." Giggles welled up inside her and she clamped her hand over her mouth. Her whole body shook and she could feel the mattress move.

"Stop it, Eliza." She heard laughter in his deep voice.

"I can't," she managed to say.

"Then tell me what you're thinking about."

"Do you remember when you put glue on my father's buggy seat?"

There was a second of silence, then a bark of laughter. He stifled the noise, but the bed quaked from the convulsive movements caused by his big body as he chuckled without a sound.

"I'd clean forgotten. Didn't he leave his pants behind and preach his sermon wearing Mrs. Willoughby's tablecloth?"

"That's right." She giggled. "And if you didn't look past his waist, you'd never have known. He was dignified as ever. My father never believed I didn't do it."

"I told him it was me."

"I know. He thought you lied to protect me. Is that why you sneaked food to me?" She scooted closer and her shoulder brushed his.

"Maybe." He tensed and shifted away.

The quiet stretched out so long, she thought he'd gone to sleep.

Then he cleared his throat. "I'd like to know who slipped the firecrackers inside the outhouse while I was using it."

Eliza went absolutely motionless for a second. She'd completely forgotten about that. The memory of Matt bursting outside with his union suit around his knees was more than she could handle. She started laughing so hard she couldn't stop. Tears formed in her eyes and she covered her mouth with her hand. Finally she got herself under control and sniffled as she brushed the moisture from her cheeks.

The bed dipped and he raised himself on his elbow above her. "So it *was* you!"

"Why in the world would you think that?" she asked. Her voice trembled from her effort to keep from laughing again.

"Your hysterical laughter was a dead giveaway."

She choked back a chuckle. "It wasn't my idea. Sally Willoughby paid me a nickel."

"I didn't mind that it scared the—water—out of me. And even the outhouse catching fire wasn't so bad. But when I found out that Cassandra Pierce saw the whole thing—"

"You were sweet on her, weren't you?" It wasn't the money that had convinced Eliza to carry out the prank. Even now, jealousy pricked her at the thought of that girl with the golden blond hair and the cornflower blue eyes.

"Yeah. You could say that." He moved his leg and it touched hers. He pulled it away as if she'd burned him.

But not before she'd felt his long woolen underwear. So he wasn't naked. That should have made her relax, but it didn't.

"She was just a snotty little flirt," Eliza said.

"I wouldn't know about that. She never looked at me again without laughing. I can't believe you did that to me." He loomed over her in the darkness. "If I'd known then, I'd have—"

"What? I could always outrun you."

"I'd have done this."

Before Eliza knew what he planned, Matt had her flat on her back and started tickling her under the arms. She squealed and thrashed on the bed, trying to get away.

"Stop," she gasped, out of breath.

"Not when I've waited years for revenge." He knew her most vulnerable place. With thumb and finger, he grabbed her leg, just above the knee.

Eliza shrieked. "Don't, Matt. I give up."

"I don't." He squeezed slightly and she writhed until she went straight into his arms. Her breasts pressed against his chest.

He tensed and the sound of his breathing changed. It was no longer breathless with laughter from their playful wrestling, but ragged from the closeness between a man and a woman. His breath stirred the hair by her temple and his hand lifted from her knee and slipped up her bare thigh. She sensed the battle that raged within him.

She knew he'd surrendered when his lips touched hers. His mouth was soft, gentle, nothing like he'd kissed her in the barn. Her heart slammed against her ribs and her breath caught in her throat. He lifted slightly and brought the upper half his body partly over hers and pulled her more firmly against his length. She wished she could feel his bare chest pressed to her breasts.

He cupped her face in his hand and threaded his fingers through her hair, bringing a strand closer as he breathed in. "Your hair smells so good."

"I'm glad," she whispered.

He slanted his mouth across hers and teased her lips apart. She opened to him instantly and he groaned. He slipped his tongue inside and stroked her, then traced the corner of her mouth before gently capturing her earlobe between his teeth. His labored breathing drowned out any other sounds.

It drowned out everything but the pleasure that shot through her until she thought she could stand no more. Eliza felt the rigid length of his manhood and knew there was more to marriage than kissing, and she wanted to experience it. She wanted to know what it felt like to be a woman and love a man. Instead of shrinking away, she snuggled close. She heard his quick intake of breath.

"I want you, Eliza." He sounded as if every word of that confession had been dragged from him by torture.

"I want you, too." She touched his face, threaded her fingers through his hair, traced his ear with her finger. "You're my husband."

He went still then and stopped kissing her neck. He released her and rolled away onto his back as he struggled to catch his breath.

Her heart cried out against being abandoned. "What is it, Matt? Why—"

"I—We can't do this. It's wrong."

"How can it be when it feels so right?"

"It just is. It's late. Go to sleep, Eliza."

The coldness in his voice froze out any argument she could make. Suddenly she was too tired to try. She turned on her side away from him and pulled her knees up to her chest. She didn't want to touch him accidentally.

10

Matt stomped into the house sometime after seven the next evening. Every muscle and bone in his body ached with exhaustion after hardly getting a lick of sleep the night before. It was pitch-black and freezing cold outside. But the kitchen was warm and smelled of baked bread and stew.

He caught the unmistakable fragrance of Eliza, too. After having her beside him in his bed, he couldn't miss the scent that was hers alone.

"Hello, Matt," she said from where she stood at the stove.

"Evenin'."

He looked around and what he saw made his heart slam in his chest. On one wall, Eliza had strung a clothesline and hanging from it were her chemise, pantaloons, a petticoat, and her woolen stockings. Several of his muslin shirts brushed intimately against her things. The trestle table was covered with a white linen cloth he'd never seen before. She'd draped a length of material over the one window and the glass in the back door. Not curtains yet, but more homey than this place had been for the last two years. He recalled seeing sheets hanging outside earlier as he'd ridden out. Eliza had been busy.

As hard as he'd fought against it, a part of him had been eager to get home tonight. He told himself it had nothing to do with her, and everything to do with the fact that there would be a hot meal waiting for him in a warm kitchen.

He thought back to her first day on the ranch. He'd come looking for her and she'd been gone with Wiley. Since then, he carried fear for her in his gut most of the time, a premonition of danger. He tried to shake it off, but it stuck with him like the last days of winter. He was relieved to find her here and safe.

He couldn't help wondering if Eliza had time to think about him while she bustled around this place. He had trouble keeping his mind on his work. All day, a vision of her face had haunted him. The sound of her contagious gaiety in bed as they had shared memories. He hadn't laughed like that for longer than he could remember. His hands had ached from clenching his fists to keep from pulling her to him. In all of the last two years, it had been the best night—and the worst.

She opened the oven door and peeked inside. The smell of baking biscuits floated to him. "Almost done," she said.

His mouth watered, but he managed to ask, "John and Hildie get off all right?"

"Yes. I hated to see them go. Especially the baby."

Eliza knew he wanted a baby. Was that why she'd maneuvered her way into his bed last night? His lips turned up in a smile. If it was, she had a funny way of seducing him. Remembering firecrackers in the outhouse didn't exactly warm a man's heart. He thought for a minute. Or did it?

A glow wrapped around him that had nothing to do with the fire in the hearth or stew bubbling on the stove. It had everything to do with shared memories, laughter in the dark, and a kiss that had promised passion and plea-sure. The thought had haunted him all day.

He felt like hell.

When he looked at Eliza, she appeared to be as fresh and sweet as spring. How did she manage it after all she'd done today?

He stared at the clothes strung on a line in the corner of the kitchen. "You've been busy."

"Sorry. With the sheets outside, there was nowhere else to hang them." There was something in her eyes he couldn't read. He thought it might be fear. But why would she be afraid of him?

The brutal way he'd kissed her in the barn. The rough manner he'd used to turn away from her last night. He winced as he shrugged out of his jacket, then hung it on the peg beside the door. After the way he'd treated her, he didn't blame her for being gun-shy. She should know he would never hurt her. But she'd been right about him try-ing to scare her. It was the only way he could think of to keep her away from him.

She knew he wanted a son; she could be relentless when she made up her mind to do something. There was only one way to make a baby and he'd promised himself he wouldn't do that with her. She was going back to Boston, and he intended to send her there as pure as the day she'd arrived in Wyoming.

"It smells good," he said. The whole kitchen smelled good. Newly washed feminine things, fresh-baked bread, hot stew. Eliza.

Her touch spread to every corner of the house. There was no place he could hide. If he was going to survive, he'd better send her back soon. His gaze strayed to the open cupboard above the stove, which contained a half-full bottle of whiskey. He hadn't touched a drop in almost two years. Maybe it was time he did.

He walked across the room and stopped beside her.

"I hope you like stew. I made lots. Wiley's appetite has

been amazing for a sick man. And I knew you'd be back for supper when you didn't come in for lunch. I fed Snowflake earlier some oats and an apple. I hope that was all right. She really is a sweetheart. Thank you for helping me get to know her. If you have time, do you think you could help me try riding her?" She stopped and took a deep breath.

"I think I can find time to teach you to ride." Then he wanted to kick himself. Why had he said that?

He took one look at her and knew why. She was pretty as a picture in her long-sleeved green calico dress. The color matched her eyes and reminded him of the endless miles of grazing land he'd just come back from. Her apron showed streaks where she'd wiped her hands while baking. Wisps of brown hair fluttered around her face. Her cheeks were slashed with white flour and there was a dab on her turned-up nose that he wanted to kiss off.

She looked up at him. "I don't want to take you away from anything important, but now that I've begun, I want to keep going. It was such a wonderful feeling, facing down that fear and getting over it. Well, I'm not over it completely, but it's a start. I've been thinking about this a lot, and I decided if I talk to Snowflake and feed her, maybe in two or three days we could try riding."

He studied her more closely. Her cheeks were flushed and her fingers worried the hem of her apron. She was fidgety as a long-tailed cat in a room full of rocking chairs, and she always went on like this when she was nervous about something. Was it him? Was she afraid he'd brutalize her again?

His gaze strayed to the whiskey bottle and he forced his eyes back to her.

"Eliza? About what happened—the other day in the barn—"

"Several things happened in the barn." She looked him straight in the eye. "Do you mean the horse, or the kiss?"

He cleared his throat. "The kiss."

"What about it?"

"I want you to know it won't happen again. You don't have to be afraid."

"I'm not." She tipped her head a little to the side and played with the end of her braid, hanging over her breast. He swallowed and quickly raised his gaze to the freckles on her nose. "But *you're* scared of something," she said.

"That's the dumbest thing I ever heard," he said too loudly.

"Suit yourself."

There was a tray set for supper resting on the work table beside the stove. She picked up the crockery bowl and ladled a steaming portion of stew into it.

"What's that for?" he asked.

She glanced at him over her shoulder. "Wiley. He's still too weak to come to the table."

That meant he and Eliza would be here in the kitchen alone. He didn't think he had the wherewithal to keep his hands to himself if he had to share an intimate supper with her. Sharing a bed with her last night had been hell. Truth to tell, it didn't seem to matter where she followed him—Wyoming, the barn, the bedroom—he couldn't resist her.

He looked around the kitchen. How on God's green earth could he keep his promise to leave her alone with her underwear strung up all over the place giving him ideas? And her beside him at the table smelling as sweet as a meadow full of flowers? The oil lamps seemed awfully dim in here, too, now that he thought about it.

Was she up to something? The cat was out of the bag about his wish for a child. Because he'd kissed her the way he had, did she think that with a little soft light, a string of underwear, and a bowl of hot stew he'd bed her?

She had another think coming.

"That lazy old man can damn well get off his hind end and come into the kitchen if he wants to eat."

She looked up at him, her brows pulled together, puzzled at his angry tone. "But he's not strong enough—"

"Bullshit."

"Matthew Decker, your language. If you don't mind!"

"This *is* a good reason, Eliza. He'll never regain his strength if he doesn't start moving around. Besides, you've done enough fetching and carrying for him. If he wants supper, he can get out of that bed and have it with us."

"I heard ya clear down the hall. No need to get all worked up, boy."

Eliza jumped. She hadn't seen the man in the doorway. He was wearing a worn flannel dressing gown. His pale, spindly calves peeked out from the bottom, and white socks covered his feet. His dark hair, shot with gray, stuck out all over his head from being in bed.

Eliza put her hand over her mouth to stifle a giggle. She coughed, then said, "You're a sight, Mr. Powell. For sore eyes, I mean. I'm so glad to see you moving around."

"Could use some help. Matthew's right, though. It's high time and past for me to be out of that bed for supper."

She hurried over to him, took his left arm, and looped it across her shoulders. After seeing him safely into a chair, she announced, "Dinner's ready."

"I'm starved," Matt said, and started for his seat at the table.

"Not so fast. You haven't washed up yet."

Eliza moved to the stove to serve up the stew. After gripping the wooden spoon, she stirred. She might be in the middle of Wyoming Territory, but that was no reason to lower her standards.

Matt mumbled and grumbled, not a single word of which she could hear.

"What did you say?"

"I'm starving. I washed up outside. Why should I—"

"Do you want supper? Or do you want to be treated like a stubborn child?"

"Who do you think *you* are?"

She pointed the wooden spoon at him. "I think I'm the woman who's going to make you take your manners out and dust them off."

Wiley cackled. "Good for you, Miss Eliza."

Matt glared at him. "I just want supper. I worked hard all day—"

Eliza put her hands on her hips. "You think I've been twiddling my thumbs?" She waved the spoon in a threatening way. "As long as I'm here, a quick lick and a promise on those hands will not suffice. We're having supper, not jerky and hardtack. Those hands need soap." She pointed to the stove. "I have water warming for you."

Matt's eyes widened in surprise as he glanced at the steaming pot. "Hot water?"

Eliza's irritation flickered and sputtered as quick as it had flared. Since losing his wife, Matt hadn't had anyone to greet him, let alone have supper waiting and warm water on the stove for washing. Her heart went out to him.

"Hurry, Matt. It's all ready and the biscuits will turn to rocks if we don't eat soon," she said softly.

"All right." He grabbed the tin washbasin and walked over to the stove. After pouring steaming water into the bowl, he pumped cold into it to take the burn off. "Do you want me to go on the porch?" he asked.

She shook her head and handed him a bar of soap from the shelf next to the window. "It's too cold out there."

He nodded and put the basin down beside the pump. After unbuttoning his shirt, he shrugged out of it, then slid his arms from the top half of his union suit and let it hang around his lean waist. Eliza swallowed hard. The sight of his chest made her insides flutter like a mockingbird's wings. Ever since seeing him the day before, naked from the waist up, she had ached to trace the mat of hair that was wide just below his collarbone and narrowed down to the waistband of his wool trousers.

She remembered the strength and power of his body

when he'd pulled her to him in the barn that day and again last night. He'd said that it would never happen again, that she didn't have to be afraid. But she wanted to kiss him like that again. Her breasts tingled at the thought of pressing herself against him without the barrier of clothing. What a wicked idea. But was it really so bad?

Her father would no doubt think so. Eliza wasn't sure anymore. That's why she'd been so grateful to leave home. She needed to find out how she felt without being told what she *should* feel. That's why she could never go back.

"Miss Eliza, if you wouldn't mind, could I have a portion of that stew?"

Eliza couldn't respond. She was fascinated by the sight of Matt's broad back and the ripple of muscles across his shoulder blades as he splashed water on his face and rubbed a wet, soapy hand over his neck. She felt as if she'd sucked in her breath and couldn't take another deep one. Through a haze, Wiley's voice came to her again.

"A body could starve around here."

"Hmm?" She turned away and blinked several times. "What did you say, Wiley?"

The old man grinned at her, a knowing smile that made her cheeks burn. "A body could work up a powerful appetite waitin' around here."

"I'll bring you your supper right away." She hurried over the tray with his bowl, then opened the oven and pulled out the biscuits. She looked at the dark tops and groaned. "I'm afraid they're a little too well done."

"That's all right, ma'am. Just throw a couple on top of that stew."

She looked at him doubtfully. "Are you sure?"

He nodded emphatically. "Yes'm. Those're just a mite crisp. A little stew gravy'll soften 'em right up. After Matthew's cookin' I don't doubt these'll be right tasty."

"If you say so." She handed him the bowl and he dug in with relish.

Matt slid his arms into the top of his long underwear,

then grabbed one of his shirts from the clothesline. She watched him stare at her chemise. The tendons in his neck pulled tight and he said something under his breath she couldn't hear. She thought it was a profanity. Then he turned back to her and pulled the garment over his head, leaving the buttons by the collar unfastened. She could see the coarse chest hair peeking through. The old man was right. A body could work up a powerful appetite waiting around here.

"What do you mean you're going back to the bunkhouse?" Matt practically shouted the words.

Wiley put a finger to his lips and shushed him. "Keep your voice down, boy. You'll wake her and she's tuckered out. Worked her little fanny off today. Right hard worker, that little girl."

"Forget Eliza. What's all this nonsense about moving out? You've got to get your strength back. You lost a lot of blood and that was a nasty bump on the head you had."

In the guest room, Wiley pulled the quilt up over the pillow and smoothed it. Then he shuffled to the rocking chair and gathered his shirt and brush and the few personal things that had found their way into the house since he'd been there.

"It's high time I was on my own again. You said so yourself. If I don't move around on my own, I'll never get strong again."

"Since when do you listen to me?"

Wiley looked at him with the most suspiciously innocent expression Matt had ever seen. "Always. Just sometimes you make more sense than others."

Why did he have to make such good sense now? If the old man moved out, Matt would be alone in the house with Eliza. He thought for a minute. Maybe it would be all right. She had done the dishes and was in bed already. She had worked hard and she looked exhausted when she'd said good night. She'd stay put. If he didn't see her, he'd be all right.

Besides, this meant he'd be able to take her back to town. He only had to get through one night.

"Are you sure this is what you want? Before—at supper—I didn't mean to make you feel—"

Wiley grinned knowingly. "I expect I have a fair idea how you were feelin'. Goin' back to the bunkhouse is what I want."

Matt glanced through the open door, across the hall, to Eliza's room. He had told her that what he'd done in the barn wouldn't happen again. He meant every word. For her sake, it couldn't happen. But his body betrayed him. He grew hard at the thought of her soft, womanly curves pressed against him.

She was right when she accused him of trying to frighten her. He felt lower than a snake, but she was dead on about that. He wanted her and had counted on her to stop him. But she hadn't. In fact, she'd cornered him into sharing his bed with her. In spite of the apprehension he had seen in her eyes, she'd met him square on and challenged him in every way to show her what it was all about.

Good Lord, he wanted to. He wanted to bury himself in her softness and relieve the pressure building within him. But if he did, it would ruin her. He planned to get Eliza out of this whole mess in the same condition as when she'd arrived. He couldn't keep her himself, and he wouldn't destroy her chances of having a life with another man.

That thought set his temper on edge like a persistent backache.

He remembered the whiskey in the cupboard. A shot, or maybe two, would dull his senses and help him sleep. In the morning he'd be up before the sun and he wouldn't have to see her. He could make it through the next few hours.

He nodded. "I'll see you down to the bunkhouse."

* * *

Matt felt light-headed as he carried the oil lamp down the hall and into his bedroom. Somehow one drink had led to finishing off the half bottle. Eliza couldn't touch him now, he thought with a grin.

The scents of lemon oil and wood soap filtered through the house and his smile faded. It was going on winter, but you'd think it was time for spring cleaning the way she was dusting and polishing everything in sight, including his manners. The sheets she'd washed and hung outside to dry filled his bedroom with the smell of wind and sunshine and flowers.

As Matt started to unbutton his shirt, he remembered the sight of it intimately brushing her pantaloons in the kitchen. He cursed. Why the hell couldn't she just leave things the way they were? He hadn't bothered cleaning before she got here and when she was gone . . .

He turned and looked at the bed and what he saw there stopped him dead. A knitted yellow wool blanket was rolled up at the foot. Carrie had made it for their unborn child. He remembered teasing her about the color, saying she could make it in blue because his baby would be a boy. He'd been right.

Bitter, searing pain crushed his chest until his eyes watered. Eliza was sleeping in what would have been his son's room. She must have found the blanket tucked in the back of the armoire where Carrie had put it away. Matt had never looked in there after he'd come home from that roundup and found his wife and baby dead.

How many times had he wished he'd died, too? Wiley had fought him tooth and nail and refused to let him give up and die. Eliza had called him a hero. He snorted. If she only knew what a coward he truly was, she wouldn't look at him as if he could do no wrong.

He'd done wrong all right. He only hoped he could get her out of here before any of it that still clung to him harmed her.

*   *   *

Eliza heard it again. A man's voice. It wasn't a dream. She knew Wiley had gone back to the bunkhouse, so it had to be Matt.

"No!" He called out again.

Alarm prickled her scalp. Was he having a bad dream? The first night she'd spent in this room he'd warned her about noises. But this was something else. Maybe he was in danger and needed her help.

She sat up and threw the covers back. When her bare feet touched the cold wooden floor, she shivered, but she managed to control her shaking hands enough to light her lamp. She didn't take time to put on her wrapper. She had to get to Matt.

Holding the lamp high, she quickly crossed the hall and listened outside his room. She could hear the sound of thrashing.

She knocked. "Matt?"

There was no response. She tapped again, then opened the door. "Are you all right, Matt?"

She looked at him in the bed. His chest was bare, and the blankets were twisted around his waist so low she was sure he wore nothing at all. She swallowed and a shiver that had nothing to do with cold rocked her from head to toe.

Taking a step forward, her foot touched something soft. She backed up and lifted the lamp high and away so she could see what was on the floor. It was the yellow blanket that earlier in the day she'd folded at the end of his bed. It was torn. She hadn't noticed that before. The nights had been getting steadily colder and she had wanted to make sure he was warm enough. If she'd known he slept in the altogether and threw his covers off, she wouldn't have worried.

She held the lamp high and studied him. He seemed to be quiet at the moment, his face relaxed in sleep. She longed to look at him without seeing the wary, watchful, angry expression he always wore when his gaze touched her. What harm could it do?

Eliza moved farther into the room and set her oil lamp on the bedside table. She frowned when she saw the empty bottle of whiskey there. She'd never known Matt to be a drinker. But a lot of time had passed and a lot had happened to him. A wave of sadness washed over her.

A part of her resented Carrie. She'd been a capable woman, strong, tall, and raised in the territory. He'd loved her so much he would never get over her passing. She'd been something Eliza could never be—his first and only love.

Eliza sat on the bed, carefully, trying not to wake Matt. He lay on his back with his left arm under his pillow. His face was turned toward the light. Stubble darkened his cheeks and jaw. She didn't think he'd shaved since bringing her here. One curl teased his forehead, hanging almost to his brow. She smiled and couldn't resist brushing it away.

He had such a nice face, she thought. His nose was just right, not too big. Her gaze lowered just a fraction to his mouth, and her chest tightened. His lips were well formed, not too full, but not a firm, straight line. He didn't smile much anymore, but when he did, oh, how her heart would beat. She remembered how soft and warm his mouth had felt against her own.

He moaned in his sleep. "No," he mumbled.

It was almost as if he knew she was there and wanted nothing to do with her. Eliza had never been so confused in her life. One minute he kissed her and she thought he would set her on fire. The next he was as cold as if he'd been doused with a bucketful of freezing water from the Double C creek. Last night when she'd lain beside him in this bed, they'd laughed until they cried. Then he'd kissed her until she thought her heart would fly from her chest, it fluttered so hard. He admitted he wanted her, too. It wasn't until she reminded him he was her husband that he'd turned away.

"Why, Matt?" she whispered. "You sent for a wife. Why won't you let me be one to you?"

He mumbled in his sleep and moved restlessly. The covers slipped lower, exposing his manhood. Her breath caught at the sight of him, fully aroused. She knew what happened between a man and a woman, and she wanted to experience it. She wondered exactly how it would feel to have him inside of her. Her heart raced and her cheeks burned.

She'd heard from her married friends that there was some pain the first time. Her father had said a wife must submit to her husband, but that the act was only to be done for the sake of progeny.

She thought of Jenny Evans and the Arnolds' baby. Those sweet little girls were someone's daughters. They were living, breathing children, warm and vital. *Progeny* was such a cold word to describe them. Looking at Matt, so very male, set her on fire from head to toe. She couldn't believe making progeny was nothing more than a duty to be performed.

Matt wanted a son, and Eliza loved children. Why couldn't they make a baby together?

Because Matt couldn't stand the sight of her and wanted her out of his life.

He moaned and started thrashing. "No," he shouted. "Not again!"

"Matt," she said, brushing the hair from his forehead. "Wake up."

"Eliza!" He jerked and moaned.

"It's all right, Matt." She touched the hard muscle in his bare upper arm and shook him. "Wake up."

He pulled away from her hand and rested his knuckles on her knee. Then he opened his eyes. He blinked several times, then turned his hand over and squeezed her leg. "Eliza? Are you—"

She curled her fingers into her palm. "I'm sorry. I didn't mean to bother you. But I heard you shouting. You were having a bad dream."

"Nightmare." His voice was thick. She wasn't sure if it was from sleep or liquor.

She wanted to touch him, comfort him. But she was afraid. Would he reject her? She only wanted to hold him. Was that so bad? "Maybe it would help to tell me about it."

"No." He swallowed hard. "I'm fine. Go back to your room."

"I can't leave you like this." She started to put her arms around him.

"No!" He brushed her hand away. "I can't do this—"

"What? I only want to comfort you."

"You're in way over your head, little girl. If you know what's good for you, you'll get the hell out of here right now."

"This is the last time I'm going to tell you: I'm a woman, not a girl. And swearing at me is not going to make me leave you."

She touched the inside of his forearm and heard his quick intake of breath. He sat up and gripped her upper arms. Half his face was in shadow, the other half in light. She could see anger in his eyes and feel it in his hands. Something was happening between them and it made her heart pound until her chest hurt. Their noses were inches apart, their mouths so close breath intermingled between them.

She waited for what seemed like forever. Then he lowered his mouth to hers. Heat seared her from his hands and his lips. Her breasts tightened expectantly as shivers danced over her skin.

He lifted his head. "Oh, God," he groaned. "I can't fight you anymore."

"Then don't," she said. She rested her palms against the coarse mat of hair on his chest. The tingle in her fingertips grew and spread from her neck clear to her toes.

He tugged her across his thighs and lowered her to the mattress beside him. She felt his arousal as he settled his length next to hers.

The light glowed behind him and his features were in shadow as he loomed over her. She was glad she couldn't see the expression that had made her a little afraid. But she remembered the sight of his nakedness. "Matt—"

She heard the anxiety in her own voice. She wanted so badly to be a woman, his wife, in the most intimate sense. But she couldn't help being nervous and a little scared. Worse than that, what if he rejected her again?

"It's all right," he said in a throaty whisper. "Everything's all right now. Just relax."

His voice was so kind and gentle and caring she wanted to weep from the sweetness of it. When he covered her breast with his hand, she was overcome with fire.

"You're definitely a woman, Eliza."

A smile turned up her mouth. She wasn't afraid anymore. This was Matt, her hero, her heart. She had followed him home.

11

Matt could feel the softness of her breast through the thin material of her nightgown. He ran his finger up her arm, over her shoulder and neck and across her fragile jaw. For once it wasn't lifted stubbornly. In fact, she didn't look defiant at all. She was stiff as a fireplace poker. He wondered why he hadn't forced her to go away.

No. He was sick to death of reasoning.

He didn't care why she had come to him; he was just grateful that she had. When he first saw her, he'd thought she wasn't real. She had haunted his sleep since he'd brought her here. But tonight the dream was different: he'd come home and the woman he found lifeless was Eliza. Now that very body pressed against him. He knew he had to have her, had to prove to himself that she was living and breathing.

He wanted her so bad it hurt. If this was a dream, he never wanted to wake up.

This was the third time he'd had her in his bed. He couldn't think of anything but her, and he was soul-weary, tired of fighting himself. He didn't want to remember that this was wrong. He didn't want to deal with the whys and wherefores. He couldn't deny himself anymore. All he wanted was to find forgetfulness in her feminine curves and her drugging kisses.

He concentrated on the woman in his arms. She was small and smelled like wildflowers. She arched upward, pressing her breast into his hand still resting on it, telling him with her body what she wanted. In his palm, he felt her nipple tighten into a firm bud.

Frustration pulled in his gut, annoyance at the thin barrier that kept him from what he craved. If he didn't touch her soft skin soon, he'd explode from the need.

He brushed his hand down her thigh, searching for the hem of her nightdress. When he found what he wanted, he pushed it upward and felt her shiver. She was flat on her back and the thing caught on her backside. "Lift your hips," he said gruffly.

She obeyed, accidentally pressing herself against his hardness. The contact forced a groan of pleasure from his throat. With a swift, smooth motion, he pulled the garment up and over her head, then threw it behind him and returned his attention to Eliza. Lifting the sheet, he helped her slide beneath the covers. She pulled them up to her neck.

He leaned on his elbow and studied her in the light from the lantern behind him. Her wide eyes were slightly wary.

"Are you afraid, Eliza?"

"No."

He smiled. "You're lying."

"Maybe just a little."

"A little lie, or a little afraid?"

"Both."

"Do you want to stop?"

"No."

The word was uttered firmly, without hesitation. She was telling the truth. He admired her courage. She freely admitted her fear, yet went on in spite of it. He looked at her watchful expression and vowed to make the uneasy look vanish from her eyes.

He lifted the end of her single braid and loosened the tie holding it. Then he ran his fingers through the brown silky strands and spread them free. He'd ached to see her this way since the night he'd married her and slept beside her with his clothes on. He'd yearned to have her like this since the night she'd come to his bed and made him laugh at the memories of the past.

His gaze lowered to her small, perfect breasts. "You're so beautiful."

"So are you," she said solemnly.

He shook his head. "That's not what a man wants to hear from the woman in his bed."

"That doesn't make it any less true. You are the most beautiful man I've ever seen. Have I ever told you how much I love your mouth? No, of course I haven't. But I do, Matt." She lifted a finger and traced it. "I love your smile and the way your eyes light up when you do. You don't smile nearly enough, you know, and—I love your mouth. I like how it feels—"

"When I stop your chatter," he said, lowering his head to silence her with the mouth she seemed to like so much. She picked the damnedest time to go on about him. But he couldn't quite push away the glad feeling that swept over him at her words.

Her contented sigh was trapped in her throat, and he felt more than heard it. The scent of her hair, her body— her fragrance filled his head and pushed out everything but the need to pleasure her.

He moved the lower half of his body closer until they were touching from knee to stomach, but raised himself on an elbow to study her. "You don't know what you're doing to me," he whispered.

She started to cross her arms over her chest to cover herself. "Am I hurting you?" she asked quickly.

"Lord, no. Except I want you so much I ache from it."
He took one of her hands and pressed a kiss into her palm.

"I want you, too. I'm ready," she said, with determination in her voice. Then she went rigid with her arms at her sides, her hands clenched into fists. She scrunched her eyes tightly shut.

Matt blinked and stared at her. "Eliza, what are you doing?"

He could see the apprehension in the one eye she opened. "Isn't it time to submit now?"

"What are you talking about?"

"My father explained about a man's baser, um—urges." She'd opened her other eye, but her lids were lowered shyly now. "He said it's a woman's lot to submit."

Matt stared at her. The only low-down urge he had at the moment was to swear, long, loud, and crudely. He fought it because he didn't want to frighten her more. His mama had taught him the only rule he needed to live by— "Do unto others as you'd have them do unto you." There was a whole lot he wanted to do unto Eliza and teach her how to do unto him, and none of those things required *submitting*.

He saw red six ways to sundown. How could her father tell her that being with a man was a duty? How could he rob her of the greatest pleasure a man and a woman could share?

It made him mad as hell when he remembered the minister trying to bridle her spirit by locking her in her room without supper. No wonder she'd become a tomboy and climbed out the window. The man had dominated her for as long as Matt could remember. Even now, he was running her life. The night she'd spent in jail must have driven him crazy. Matt grinned as he admired her spirit.

He might have found the strength to leave her before, but he couldn't pull back now. She was tense and nervous about bedding a man. She had let him undress her, even helped, and he knew it was because, for God knew what reason, she trusted him. Something told him he was the right man to show her how it should be between a man and a woman. It would be his gift to her, the freedom to enjoy a man's love. He knew her. Once she'd experienced the pleasure, she'd never settle for less with a man. Later he would deal with why that man couldn't be him.

"You listen to me, Eliza. Forget everything your father told you. It's you and me in this bed. No one else."

She nodded a little uncertainly.

"You're not going to submit to anything."

"But Matt, I want to—"

He silenced her with his finger on her mouth. "This is an act between two people. Both of them partake."

"What do you mean?"

"That I'm going to pleasure you and you're going to do the same thing to me."

"I don't know what to do." There was a note of panic in her voice.

"Don't worry." He grinned. "When we kissed in the barn, that was the first time ever for you and me. If I was the one who taught you how, lady, you're one fast learner."

"I couldn't help it. I—"

"That wasn't a criticism."

"Oh." She moved her shoulders nervously. "I just thought, you know, that maybe I did the wrong thing. I have a way of doing that. Father always said I didn't have the good sense the Lord gave a rock. I've caused you enough trouble. So I—"

He kissed her, partly to silence her but mostly because he needed to reassure her and he knew words wouldn't be enough. He lifted his mouth from hers and watched her, waiting, letting the next move be hers. She bit her lip. "What now?"

"Whatever you want."

"I don't know. I've never done this before." She swallowed. "I can't believe we're talking about it."

"Did you think you couldn't say anything?"

"I never thought about it. I've never done this—"

"So you said. You can talk and laugh, scream and yell if you want to."

"Scream and yell?"

Now he'd done it. He hadn't meant to frighten her. "That's not to say you'll have to scream except from pleasure."

She nodded but didn't say anything. He decided to give her a nudge.

"Do you like it when I kiss you?"

"Oh, yes," she said. Her voice was as delicate as a whisper of wind through the grass in the north meadow.

"Then let's start there."

Eliza couldn't see Matt's expression, but she had heard the snap in his voice when he'd told her she was not going to submit. Even now she felt his effort to control his anger and wondered what she'd done to displease him. Would he kiss her if she had done something wrong? She didn't think so. His head lowered and she held her breath. She could hardly wait.

When his lips met hers, the contact was as soft as a cloud. Her breath caught and held as her heart began to race. He nibbled the corner of her mouth, then moved lower to her jaw and still lower to her neck. Every time he moved to a different place, her breathing increased a notch along with the heat he stirred. She most definitely liked kissing.

"Let's see how you like this," he said, lifting up on his elbow to lean over her.

"Really, Matt. You don't have to bother with what I like. I understand—"

He kissed her just below her ear and Eliza tingled from head to toe as her breath caught. "Oh, my—"

"Do you like that, Eliza?"

"As much as kissing," she sighed. He smiled against her neck.

He trailed his mouth over her chest and found the peak

of her breast. With his tongue, he teased the nipple into a taut bud. "What about this?"

"Oh, Matt. It's wonderful." She was beginning to relax.

He moved to her other breast and did the same thing. "And this?"

"Yes," she said, the word hardly more than a long, satisfied sigh. She was hot all over and sincerely hoped the fever never went away. He was driving her out of her mind and he had only touched her with his mouth. This was more than she'd ever expected to feel in a man's arms. Her breasts ached to feel his hand on her bare skin, the way he'd caressed her through her nightgown. And the intimate place between her legs throbbed in time to her pounding heartbeat. What if he touched her there?

He slid closer and she felt the hard ridge of his desire. A man had his needs and she shouldn't make him wait.

"That's enough, Matt. You don't have to bother about me. I—If you can't wait—That is, if you just want to get on with it—"

"I'll worry about me." Intensity burned in his eyes when he looked at her. "By the time I'm finished, you'll be the one who can't wait."

"I don't—"

When he moved to her other breast, she forgot what she'd been about to say. He nipped gently at the peak with his teeth, then suckled. Waves of pleasure pounded through her.

"Lord," she whispered hoarsely.

"Do you like that?"

"Oh, yes."

"What do you want me to do now?"

"I don't know." She angled her body toward him.

"What, Eliza? Tell me. This time is for you."

"What about you?" Her aching breasts felt full and heavy. Instinctively, she arched closer to him.

"Let me worry about that. What do you want me to do? This?" He cupped her breast in his hand. The roughness teased her skin, and warmth crept inside her until desire washed over her and she grew light-headed.

"Oh, yes," she said. "How did you know?"

"I can read your body. Talking isn't the only way to know what pleases a person. Do you still want to get on with it?"

She opened her eyes and saw him grin, his teeth flashing white against the shadows in his face. "Of course. Only . . . Matt?"

"What?"

"Not too fast."

"Your wish is my command." He gave her a courtly nod. With exquisite care, he lavished attention on first one, then the other breast. He kissed and caressed her until she could hardly breathe.

"What is my lady's next pleasure?" he asked, smiling.

"Show me what *you* like."

His smile disappeared instantly and even with his features in shadow, she could read the urgency on his face. It was almost as if he was in pain. He had said he ached from wanting her.

"It's time for me to partake," she said. She liked it so much when he touched her, she decided maybe he'd feel the same. She gently touched his shoulder and he turned onto his back.

It was her turn to lean over him. Eliza reached out a hand and stroked the contour of muscle on his chest, rubbed her palm against the rough mat of hair, and stroked her index finger gently over his nipple. His quick intake of breath told her she was doing what he liked.

She smiled. "I can read your body, too."

"Is it telling you to kiss me?"

"It said that you liked the way I touched you."

"That was no lie." He tapped his mouth. "It's saying touch me here."

She did, then nuzzled him with small kisses on his cheek, above his beard, and on his chin and neck. She recognized his groan as a sound of pleasure rather than pain as she'd thought earlier.

Suddenly their teasing, playful kisses turned hard and hungry. She met his fire without fear and found that her own need mounted steadily. His hand moved lower, over her belly, squeezed at her waist, then slid between her legs. She arched against his touch. It felt as good as she'd hoped and she was grateful to Matt for taking his time with her.

Her body burned from his touches. But when he parted her legs and stroked the nub there, she gasped at the jolt of pleasure that shot through her. The feeling was so intense it was almost painful. Pressure built within her until she thought she'd die of it. There was more, she just knew it. And she wanted to know what it was now.

"Matt?" Her voice was breathless.

"Hm?" He was nuzzling her neck while his finger slowly, seductively moved in and out of her.

Her body was on fire. "I can't stand any more. *Please* let me submit now." She instinctively picked up the rhythm and her hips began to move.

"Are you sure?" His voice was as scratchy as sandpaper.

She nodded. "I wouldn't want you to wait any longer. Oh, my Lord," she breathed as his fingers continued to build the fire hotter inside her. "Men have urges—"

"So do women," he said.

He nudged her legs apart and settled himself between them. He was heavy on top of her, even though he took part of his weight on his arms. The coarse hair on his chest rubbed against the soft skin of her breasts.

"Eliza," he said. His body trembled and she sensed his effort at self-control. "For a woman, the first time is—"

She remembered the magnificence of him when she'd studied him while he was sleeping. The sight of him had made her apprehensive, but the touch of his hands had taken her to heights of sensation she'd never known existed. He'd taught her that being with a man is nothing to fear, but a pleasure to embrace. She couldn't stop now.

"Please show me. I want to know everything," she said breathlessly. "I'm not afraid. Not with you."

"I'll try not to hurt you."

He thrust forward slowly. The barrier of her maidenhead stopped him and he sucked in a deep breath. His arms trembled and she knew the effort he made to keep from hurting her. Then he flexed his hips and eased past the barrier.

There was a moment of tearing pain. She held onto his shoulders and squeezed her eyes more tightly closed.

"I'm sorry, Eliza."

She shook her head. "It's all right. It's better now."

"There's no more pain. I'll make it good for you. I swear."

Slowly, gently, he began moving within her. She felt a glow in the pit of her stomach that spread through her whole body. The glory of this moment, of being one with this man, was the most wondrous thing she'd ever known. Matt had said she wouldn't submit to anything, that this was an act in which two people pleasured each other. Oh, he was right.

He kept moving inside her, building the pressure, fanning the embers into flames, turning her passion into mindless desire. Her breath came in gasps. Suddenly the tension in her burst, sending pulsing pleasure outward to her arms and legs. Behind her eyelids, flashes of red, yellow, and orange exploded and blended into a feeling so exquisite she wanted to float in it forever.

She was just coming down when Matt tensed and went still. His eyes were closed and there was a look of such concentration on his face. He pushed into her once more and groaned. His body stretched and strained and went taut as the corded muscles in his forearms stood out.

"Oh, Lord," he whispered, lowering his face to nuzzle her neck. He stayed that way as tremors shook his body, then eased himself away and collapsed beside her.

Eliza sighed and waited until her breathing returned to normal. A wonderful glow enveloped her, a shield of light all around, as if nothing bad could touch her. She wished she could feel like this forever. She wished Matt would say something.

She rolled to her side and pulled the blanket up, then snuggled against his arm. His other hand was thrown across his eyes.

"What have I done?" he whispered.

Surely he didn't regret something so beautiful, Eliza thought. Besides, she had partaken, too.

"Not you. *We,*" she said. "And I want to thank you."

"For what?" He didn't move and his voice had lost the warm, teasing tone he'd used earlier to soothe her apprehensions.

"For making me a woman."

He winced as if she'd struck him. "Eliza . . ."

"I was a little more frightened than I let on." She was beginning to be a little scared again. Matt was too quiet and that made her nervous. "You were right, everything you said about love being between a husband and wife who both partake. I—I only hope that I was all right. I—I mean, you pleasured me, but I—You said there are more ways to communicate than just with words. And I'd appreciate it if you'd use one of them now. Matt, what—"

He yanked his arm away from his eyes. "I never said anything about a husband and wife."

"Those weren't your exact words, I suppose. But the meaning was clear. Now that we've . . . you know, we're married. I want to stay—"

Matt threw back the quilt. He couldn't get out of the bed fast enough. As soon as he'd pressed the barrier of her virginity, he'd known it was all wrong, but he'd gone too far to turn back. The satisfied, contented tone in her voice made him want her again. He called himself every kind of a damn fool as he grabbed his pants and stepped into them, then shrugged his arms into a flannel shirt.

"Matt?"

"Go to sleep, Eliza." As he started out of the bedroom, his foot touched something soft. Eliza's nightgown. Beside it was the yellow baby blanket. He picked up the fuzzy square and went to the kitchen.

The room was dark except for the glow of the banked embers in the hearth. He stirred them to life. His head pounded from all the whiskey he'd drunk. It was too much not to feel the effects and not enough to have kept him from making the biggest mistake of his life.

He'd bedded Eliza.

How the hell could he have been so stupid? There was no chance of an annulment now, unless they lied to the judge. And Eliza would never tell a falsehood. When it came right down to it, he couldn't either.

How the hell had he gotten into this mess in the first place? His scheming mother and that godawful hat. No doubt she was still in a state of shock from the language in the telegram he'd sent her from town. What in the world had she been thinking to send Eliza to him? He had wanted a mail-order bride. If he'd gotten one, things would have been fine.

He buried his cheek against the soft blanket still in his hand. "Carrie—" His voice floated into the fire and turned to ash and smoke. He'd finally let her go.

"Matt?"

He closed his eyes and gritted his teeth so hard his jaw hurt. Go away, Eliza, he thought. I don't want to hurt you anymore.

He tossed the blanket into the rocker beside him, then hunkered down in front of the fireplace. With the poker, he moved the embers around until they blossomed into flames. The heat burned his face. Behind him the cold air stirred and the fragrance of wildflowers surrounded him. He knew she was close enough to touch. He stood up and tucked his hands beneath his arms as he studied the fire.

"Go back to bed, Eliza."

"Not until you tell me what I did wrong."

"You didn't do anything."

"Then what's bothering you? Now that we—"

"You can't stay, Eliza."

He didn't look at her, couldn't look. But he felt the shudder that went through her.

"But, I—I thought you changed your mind about sending me back. I was sure everything was different now. I—"

"You thought wrong." He braced his hand against the rock fireplace.

"What about the annulment?"

He felt what it cost her to keep her voice even and cursed himself for being the worst kind of bastard. But it was for her sake that he was doing this.

"Leave that to me."

"But we *are* man and wife in—in the physical sense."

"There are more grounds for annulment than just that. I won't let this ruin your life."

Matt looked at her, then wished he hadn't. She stood there in her nightgown, feet bare, with her waist-length hair floating around her like a silk curtain. The glow from the fire outlined the beautiful body he'd just learned so well. His groin tightened against his will. He wanted her again. The guilt, the remorse, his good intentions—none of it meant a tinker's damn. He still wanted Eliza.

When he'd bedded her, he'd let go of Carrie forever. It was time. The only thing standing in his way now was himself, but he wouldn't step aside. He wouldn't let Eliza in; he wouldn't let himself need her.

Her eyes were aflame in anger, but around their edges he could see the hurt. "You're going to send me back to Boston and expect that my life won't be ruined?"

"Eliza, trust me—"

Even as the words came out he knew it was hopeless. He'd promised himself he would send her back untouched, the way she'd come to him. That was impossible now. He could only console himself with the knowledge that he'd taught her something about the beautiful, passionate woman she was. Any man would be proud to have her. She could still make a life, have children.

Children? He went cold inside. Oh, Lord. No. It was only once. Surely . . . there wouldn't be a child to compound his mistake. Not again; never again. He couldn't—wouldn't take a chance with Eliza's safety. After tonight, he would have to make sure he never touched her. "Listen to me—"

"Don't." She curled her fingers into fists and held them up between them as if she was ready to fight him.

She was right. Why should she trust him? He'd promised he wouldn't kiss her again the way he had in the barn. Hell, he'd done a whole lot more than that, and she had every right to hate him. It was for the best that she did. If she couldn't stand the sight of him, she would keep her distance. After tasting her sweetness and being burned by her fire, he sure didn't trust himself to stay away from *her*.

"There's nothing you can say that I want to hear."

He nodded. "Wiley's on his feet and back in the bunkhouse. I'm taking you to Silver Springs in the morning."

"I'll be ready." She turned away to leave the room. In the doorway she stopped. "Just tell me one thing."

"What?" Stupid question. He knew what was coming. "It was the whiskey, Eliza. I was drunk. That's why I took you to my bed."

"I see." She brushed her knuckle across her cheek before turning away again.

He heard her door close softly down the hall and he flinched as if she'd fired a bullet into his gut. He'd never felt so low in his life. And he'd never lied to her before. He only did now because if she knew the truth about why he'd made love to her, she would use it against him. She didn't understand. None of it. The danger, the loneliness, the loss. He couldn't do it again.

Feelings cut through him like a knife. Just as quickly, he turned them off, like drawing a hot poker over an oozing wound to stanch the flow of blood. He'd done enough bleeding in his life. He wouldn't let himself be wounded again.

Somehow he'd find the strength to let her go. Tomorrow.

12

"Matt's taking me to town today."

Eliza looked at Wiley as he squeezed the tin cup of coffee in his hand and considered her words. He was sitting on the brown wool blanket covering his bunk. She hadn't been in the bunkhouse before. After today, she would never see it again.

The oblong wooden building held rows of bunks on the two long walls, with a table and several chairs in the center of the room. The wooden planks that formed the walls didn't fit snugly together in places, letting the cold wind slip inside.

"You're goin' for supplies? I could use some tobacco—"

"No. I've come to tell you good-bye."

"Good-bye? I thought after last night—" His cheeks turned red beneath his gray stubble.

What did he know about last night? She wished she could forget all about it.

She thought Wiley was looking much better. That made her happy. It was one less thing to feel guilty about when she was gone. God knows, she had enough to regret. She had given herself to Matt because she truly believed that he cared about her and wanted her to stay.

She had tried to fit into his world; she had followed him everywhere she could, even to his bed. He had made her his wife in the most intimate sense. He had taken her virginity and taught her about partaking and pleasuring and he still didn't want her.

"What do you know about last night?" she asked.

"I was certain you had—That is to say, Matt and you— What with your underwear hangin' all over the kitchen and all. Then him starin' at you like a hungry hound dog at a bone." He paused and looked at her face. "Ain't none o' my business."

"You were wrong, Wiley. Matt doesn't care about me at all. He says you're well enough to be left alone while he drives me to Silver Springs. I just couldn't leave without saying good-bye to you." She fussed with the strings of her reticule so he wouldn't see the tears in her eyes.

"Guess I *was* wrong—about you. You are a quitter."

Her head snapped up and she met his gaze. "What's that supposed to mean?"

"Where's that spunky little gal who beat the sh—beat that ole bobcat till he didn't know which end was up?"

"She's still here. But I'm not strong enough to stay with a man who despises me."

"He told you that?"

She shook her head. "Not in so many words. But his actions said a mouthful. It's a losing battle. Matt will never get over his wife's death."

"He told you that?"

"He didn't have to. Last night after we—" She looked up quickly as heat flared in her cheeks. "He couldn't sleep and I followed him to the kitchen. I heard him whisper Carrie's name." Her voice trembled.

"That doesn't mean—"

"Don't try to make me feel better. You're wrong.

Matt's mother was wrong. I was wrong." She sighed. "I can't fight the memory of a dead woman. I have to leave."

"You goin' clear back to Boston?"

She shook her head. "I told him I could never go back and I meant it."

"You gonna work for Brad Slicker?"

She swallowed at the mention of the barkeep's name. She'd never forget how that one drink had burned her throat. Her heart caught when she thought about what Matt had said the night before. The only way he could bed her was to get drunk. Tears burned behind her eyelids and she blinked hard. Last night she had cried silently into her pillow until she'd fallen into a fitful sleep. No more. Matt Decker wouldn't make her cry ever again.

"If that's the only place I can find work, then I will work for Mr. Slicker."

"Damnation!"

"Mr. Powell." She put her hands on her hips. "Really, you must work on your language."

"If you hightail it back to Silver Springs, who's gonna keep me and Matt on our toes?"

She tried to smile. "Thank you for trying." She kissed his leathery cheek above his whiskers. "I'll never forget you."

She walked out of the bunkhouse and down the rise toward the main house. The cold wind made her shiver and she pulled her heavy shawl more tightly around her. The horse hooked up to the wagon tossed its head restively, and she heard the jingle of the harness in the early morning air. She squared her shoulders as her shoes tapped on the wooden planks of the back porch. Correction—Carrie's shoes. When she got to Silver Springs she'd get a new pair and give these back to Matt. He could pack them away, along with his heart. She went inside to finish gathering her things.

*   *   *

"Eliza, come quick," Matt said, poking his head in the back door.

She appeared in the kitchen doorway. "What is it?"

"Wiley. I found him in the bunkhouse. Unconscious."

"What? Why, not more than half an hour ago I—"

He grabbed her arm. "Just come and look."

They went out the door into the strong, cold wind. Eliza gasped at its bite and Matt looked down at her. He hadn't given her time to put on a shawl. He shrugged out of his coat and wrapped her in it. Her hair was pushed back off her forehead as she lowered her face to battle forward against the blast of air. He put his arm around her to help and she sidestepped his touch. Guilt stabbed him, but he didn't blame her after the way he'd treated her.

"Was he unconscious when you left him to get me?" she asked.

"No. I put him on his bunk. He was mumbling and asking for you."

"What happened to him?"

"I don't know. Last night he insisted it was time for him to return to the bunkhouse. Said he'd never get his strength back if he didn't start moving around. Maybe it was too soon. He's been saying he was weak."

She glared at him. "You were the one who insisted he get up and come to the table for supper."

"Yeah." The guilt just kept piling up.

"How was his color?"

"Looked all right to me. But what do I know? I'm the one who said he should get up and move around."

She stumbled on a stone and he caught her arm. Even through his sheepskin-lined jacket a shock of awareness cut through him like a sunbeam through a snowbank. Dammit. She could make him forget himself without even trying. If she made up her mind to try, he would be in a lot of trouble. He was right to send her away.

As he turned the knob and pushed the door, the wind took it and banged it open. He put his arm around her and ushered her inside out of the cold. She flinched at his touch and moved away as fast as she could.

The old man lay on his back on his bunk. Outside, the howling wind rattled around the corners of the building and scratched to get inside. When the door shut, Wiley opened one eye.

"Matthew?"

"Yeah. I've got Eliza with me. How do you feel?"

"Like I was kicked in the head by a mule."

"Did you hit yourself when you fell?" Eliza asked as she moved beside him and sat down on the bed. She touched his temple and moved her hand over his head checking for injury. "I don't feel any bumps or lumps." She looked at Matt, puzzlement pulling her delicate brows together.

"Don't know what happened. All of a sudden I got light-headed and then everything went black. Next thing I knew Matthew was helpin' me to lie down."

Eliza studied him. "I don't understand this. Your color looks good. Your strength should be returning. I know you've been eating like a horse."

"Yes, ma'am. Your cookin' goes down real easy. With you leavin', it'll probably take me longer to get back on my feet."

"He looks fine to me," Eliza said. "Maybe he just stood up too quickly or something. As far as I can tell, there's no reason he can't be left alone. I'm anxious to get to town."

"You are?" Matt asked. He stared at the back of Eliza's head. Her hair was slipping from the knot on top. A rush of pleasure stampeded through him, just the same as the night before when he'd loosened that hair from the braid. Her neck was bare to his gaze and he remembered her moan of desire when he'd touched his lips right there beneath her ear. He could understand why she shied away from him, but why the hell was she so eager to get back to town? Now that he'd awakened her woman's passions, was she preparing to try them out on another man? The thought made him mad enough to chew nails.

"He doesn't look fine to me," Matt said.

"What do you know about it?" Eliza asked.

"Not a whole lot. And that's why I can't take the chance."

Wiley was like a father to him. If anything happened to the older man, Matt would have even more on his conscience. Surely a few more days wouldn't make any difference. The weather would probably hold. He'd keep his hands off Eliza. He'd have to, for her sake. When he was certain Wiley could be left for a day or two, then he'd take her back to town.

Matt shook his head. "We're not going anywhere today."

"Now, Matthew, there's no call to change your plans on my account."

"He's right, Matt."

"I am?" Wiley looked surprised. "I mean, of course I am."

"You're fine," she said. "If you just stay in bed, you'll be all right until Matt gets back."

"What do you think, Matthew?"

"A few more days won't matter."

"Fine," Eliza said. "I don't mind living out of a trunk."

"I'm real sorry about this setback, Miss Eliza." The old man sat up in bed with the pillow behind him. He heaved a huge sigh from the effort. It seemed to sap his strength to move around. "I think it'd be all right if you go."

"No." Matt cleared his throat. "Do you want to come back up to the main house where we can keep an eye on you?"

Wiley thought about it, then shook his head. "It's best I stay here and get used to it. I'd be obliged if one or the other of you would come by every now and then . . . just to say howdy."

"I don't suppose you'd turn down a cup of coffee and some sugar cookies?" Eliza said.

He grinned. "No, ma'am."

"Then I'll whip up a batch." She glanced up at Matt, her mouth tightening to an angry line. "They keep disappearing."

"Funny thing about those cookies," he said, looking at the ceiling.

It was strange how quickly he'd taken to her cooking. He would miss it when she was gone. But he'd gotten used to fending for himself once. He would do it again.

Late in the afternoon, Eliza went to the barn, where she scooped a handful of oats from the bucket and walked over to the stall where Snowflake stood contentedly watching her. She held out her open hand with the food in it. "Here you are, pretty girl."

The horse nibbled at her palm until every last bit was gone, then sniffed and looked up, her big brown eyes pleading for more. Eliza rubbed the horse's ears, then rested her cheek against Snowflake's nose. "I only have a few more days here, little girl. If I'm going to learn to ride you, it had best be now."

When she'd told Matt she wanted to conquer her fear of horses, that was the God's honest truth. She'd only left out the part about learning to ride so that she could follow him around the way she had in Boston. Last night had changed everything. She had handed him her heart and soul and body. That wasn't enough for him. *She* wasn't enough. He would never want her and there was nothing she could do to change his mind.

She had to survive on her own, and she would do that in Silver Springs. But before she did, she needed to learn as much as she could. Starting with riding a horse. She'd conquered her fear of being around them. It was time to learn to get on one.

She had watched Matt saddle Buck and tried to remember all the steps. First the bridle. She saw one hanging in Snowflake's stall. After she unlatched the gate, it swung wide with a rusty groan. She stepped inside and patted the horse's back as she passed. "Good girl. I hope you've done this before, because I sure haven't."

The metal on the bridle clinked as she pulled it off the nail on the wall. She looked at the tangle of leather straps and held it up, picturing the bit in the horse's mouth and trying to figure out where her ears fit into the thing. She put it in front of Snowflake, who obediently opened her mouth while Eliza slipped the metal between her teeth. Then she stood on tiptoe to fasten the straps that held the bridle in place. The long leather reins dragged on the ground.

Eliza surveyed her work and nodded with satisfaction. "Not bad. If I do say so myself." She rubbed the horse's snout. "And you. You're such a good girl." Thank goodness. She'd never have had the courage to try this with another horse.

The next step was the saddle. Eliza remembered Matt throwing a blanket on his horse's back first. Hanging over the rail of the stall she saw what she was looking for. She grabbed the coarse, heavy square and settled it on Snowflake. After arranging it to her satisfaction, she said, "This is much easier than I thought it would be. Now for the saddle."

It was resting on the railing beside the spot where the blanket had been. Before pulling it down, Eliza studied the thick straps hanging down. She'd watched Matt fasten them beneath his horse's belly. She noted the metal buckle where the belt fastened to keep the saddle in place. She nodded, satisfied that she knew how it worked.

"I can't imagine why I've been so afraid of this."

She reached up and grabbed the horn and the back part of the seat and slid it off the fence rail. The weight of the thing took her by surprise. It was too heavy to hold and it fell, bringing her to her knees. Dust stirred up and with it, the odor of hay. Her nose tickled and she rubbed it thoughtfully as she studied the heavy pile of leather in front of her.

She had to get it on Snowflake somehow. The horse tossed her head, then studied Eliza with her big, gentle brown eyes. "I know, little girl. I'm not sure either."

She tried to pick up the saddle and managed to lift it.

Her breath came in gasps from her efforts. The thing must weigh more than fifty pounds. Matt made it look so easy. Even if she could lift that pile of leather and straps past her knees, there was no way on God's green earth that she had the strength to put it on Snowflake's back. What if she asked Matt for help?

She shook her head. He'd agreed to teach her to ride, but she couldn't ask him for anything now. When she was on her own in Silver Springs, she couldn't be running to anyone for help. She might as well start learning to do things by herself right now.

Did she need the saddle to ride? When she'd been in town, she'd seen Ethel Buchanan's youngest boy, Walter, Jr., riding bareback. He'd raced all up and down Main Street as easy as you please. If he could do it, so could she.

She looked ruefully at the saddle at her feet and then up at the railing where it had come from. She wanted to put it back, but if she couldn't lift it onto Snowflake, there was no way she had the muscle to replace it.

A vision of Matt's broad back flashed through her mind, the ripple of muscles when he easily saddled Buck. With it came a rush of breathlessness.

One by one the memories of the night before came back even as she tried with all her might to push them away. She couldn't forget the feel of the restrained power in his arms as he'd loved her. Or the softness of his lips when he'd kissed her. The feeling of him inside her, of being one with him. Or the wondrous explosion of pleasure that had left her weak all over.

She'd never forget the look on his face when he'd told her she had to leave. Tears stung her eyes again and she stomped her foot. Snowflake snorted and tossed her head, rattling the bridle. Eliza patted her back.

"Sorry, sweet girl. Didn't mean to startle you. It's nothing important—just men."

Eliza removed the horse blanket, then gathered up the reins and led the horse from the stall. Hay on the barn floor muffled her clopping hooves. Late afternoon sunlight filtered in from the door.

"I'm going to get on you now. Be a good girl and I have a treat for you." She pulled the two long straps into one hand and rested it on Snowflake's back, then jumped. It didn't take her long to see that she needed something to stand on.

The stall gate would work. She closed it, then aligned the horse parallel. Eliza stood between the animal and the fence. She climbed halfway up the slats, then turned and tried to swing one leg, with skirt and petticoats, over the horse's back. The animal sidled away and Eliza lost her balance and jumped off the gate. Dust rose and made her sneeze.

"Let's try this again, sweet girl." Eliza heard the note of irritation in her voice and watched the horse blink her eyes. She held the bridle and stared at Snowflake as she talked. "You have to help me. Hold very still this time."

Eliza climbed up on the fence, turned sideways, and hooked the heel of her shoe on a slat. She lifted her other leg and swung it on the horse's back. Snowflake sidestepped and Eliza landed on her backside in the hay.

She picked herself up, brushed herself off, and stomped over to talk to the animal face-to-face. She pointed her finger. "Listen here, Snowflake. You're not helping. I'll make a deal with you. You hold still or you don't get that treat. Don't move a hair and I'll give you an apple. What do you say?" Snowflake tossed her head and nickered softly.

Eliza nodded. "All right then. Let's try this again."

She positioned the horse in front of the fence and climbed up on the slats. This time, instead of swinging her leg over, Eliza decided to put her arms over Snowflake and hang on. If she could stay put, then she could swing her ankle over and sit astride. Before she could do that, the horse sidled away from the stall and left Eliza hanging with her hands and feet dangling and her abdomen resting on the horse's back.

A tall, wide shadow blocked out the sunlight in the doorway.

"What in the world are you doing?"

Matt's hands were on his hips and Eliza couldn't see his expression. But she could picture the disgusted look on his face. She shut her eyes for a second, then looked heavenward and whispered, "Why me?"

"What was that?" he asked.

"I said I'm riding Snowflake." It wasn't easy to talk in her present position, but Eliza was afraid to let go.

"Good Lord, you're going to kill yourself."

Snowflake shuffled restlessly. Eliza had an image of herself slipping beneath the horse's hooves. Her stomach knotted with fear.

He was beside her in a heartbeat and she felt his hands at her waist, easily lifting her down. Violent trembling shook her. He turned her and pulled her against him, then wrapped his arms around her. She thought he touched his mouth to her hair in a fleeting kiss, but she knew she must have been mistaken.

His heart pounded against her cheek, a match for her own. Was he frightened for her? Why would he be? She was nothing but a thorn in his side that he couldn't wait to pluck out and throw away.

The smell of horses and leather and sunshine clung to him. He was strong and competent and she wanted to let herself pull comfort from him, just for a minute. She wanted to encircle his waist with her arms and snuggle a little closer to his solid warmth. But he wasn't safe for her. Every time she got close to him, he hurt her.

She put her hands on his chest and pushed with all her strength until he let her go.

"What's wrong with you?" he asked.

She glared at him as her fingers curled into a fist. "If I were bigger, I'd punch you right in the nose."

"Because I pulled you off that horse?"

"Because you treated me like a saloon girl last night."

"You were trying to *be* a saloon girl when I carried you out of the Silver Slipper."

She'd pinched him for that and it had felt pretty good.

Eliza looked him in the eye and knew that target was too far away. She made a fist and slugged him in the stomach as hard as she could. He doubled over and the air whooshed from his lungs.

He straightened up and croaked, "What was that for?"

"For treating me like a loose woman."

"I never thought of you that way—"

She pulled her arm back and prepared to haul off and let him have it again. He grabbed her wrist with one hand and wrapped his other arm around her waist, yanking her hard against him. His grip was like iron.

"Why, you—" She tried to get free.

"You don't think I'd be stupid enough to let you do that again, do you?"

"I think if you know what's good for you, you'll unhand me."

A slow half smile turned up the corners of his mouth. In spite of the fact that she wanted to throttle him, in spite of the fact he'd used her body and stomped on her feelings, in spite of the fact that she was anxious to get away from him before he broke her spirit, that grin nearly stopped her heart. Maybe because she didn't see him smile very much anymore.

She stopped struggling, partly because there was no way she could fight the power in his wide chest and muscular arms, but mostly because she couldn't trust herself *not* to surrender to his charm. That was the last thing she wanted to do. She wouldn't leave herself open to his hurtful words a second time.

"Let me go, Matt," she said quietly. "I won't hit you again."

His eyes narrowed and he watched her warily. "You pack a pretty good wallop."

Finally, he released her and she stepped away from him. He picked up Snowflake's reins and led her back into the stall, then shut the door.

"Why did you try this alone?" he asked her. "I told you I'd help you learn to ride." His deep voice and gentle tone wrapped around her like a warm, wool blanket and sent goosebumps up and down her arms.

The feeling was the same as if he'd touched her bare skin with his sure, strong hands or pulled her into the safety of his arms. She swayed toward him, wanting to know those sensations again. In a rush she remembered that she couldn't trust anything he offered and pulled back.

"I don't need your assistance in order to ride, thank you."

He looked startled for a second, then his expression became shuttered. He glanced inside the stall and raised one brow when he saw the saddle in the hay on the floor. "No?"

She lifted her chin. "I'm going to ride bareback."

Something about the way the muscle in his cheek moved told her she'd just said the wrong thing. She remembered the silent deal she had made with herself for Wiley's life. This didn't count as arguing. She was merely telling him what she planned to do.

"First you have to get on. It's easier with a saddle." He rested one booted foot on the lower slat of the gate. "You want me to lift it for you?"

"No." She raised her chin another notch. "I'm going to do it by myself."

He eyed the hay covering the back of her skirt. "You're doing a fine job of it."

"Don't concern yourself about me."

"I am concerned."

"Why?"

"I care about you."

"You've never lied to me before, Matt. Please don't start now."

In this very spot, Matt remembered telling her he'd never kiss her again. When he took her in his bed, he'd made himself a liar in more ways than one. Even worse, he still wanted her.

He'd lied again when he'd said liquor had made him bed

her. Whiskey had nothing to do with it. He'd been stone-cold sober when he'd taken her, and he'd wanted her more than he'd wanted to keep his promise to send her back to Boston untouched. He was the worst kind of fool and a liar to boot.

When he'd told her nothing had changed, it was another bald-faced lie. Everything had changed. He'd let Carrie go forever when he'd made love to Eliza. He knew Eliza thought he was still in love with his dead wife. If he told her the truth, he would open doors he didn't want to look behind. Instead, he rubbed salt in her wound by letting her believe he mourned for Carrie.

The shattered look still hovered in her eyes, and he regretted it more than he could say. But as sure as he knew Wyoming was a hard land, he knew he would do the same thing again if it meant protecting her. He just had to make sure he never made love to her again, not ever. He prayed she wasn't pregnant from that one time.

He prayed for the strength to keep his distance from her. It would be so easy to slip back into the easy give-and-take they'd shared years ago. That's why he'd told her she couldn't stay.

But the suspicion he saw in her green eyes sliced clear to his soul. Eliza had never looked at him that way before, and he hadn't known how much the loss of trust would hurt.

"You have no reason to believe me, but I do care about you. Let me help you before you hurt yourself."

The horse nickered softly as she *clip-clop*ped over to Eliza and stuck her face over the fence.

As she stroked Snowflake's shiny brown coat, Eliza frowned. She was thinking very hard about something and that made him nervous. Her eyes glittered suddenly with a determined look.

"All right, Matt. There is something you can do."

"Anything. Name it."

"I want you to teach me how to ride and use a gun."

He'd expected the first part, but the second took him completely by surprise. "Absolutely not!"

"You said *anything*." She turned away from him. "Lie number two."

It was more than that, but he'd lost count. "Eliza, be reasonable. You have no use for a gun in Boston."

She whirled around. "I'm not going back there."

"But—"

"You keep telling me that's what I'm going to do. I've got news for you, Matt. I'm never going back there. I can't."

"Why the hell not? What happened to doing whatever I say without a word of argument?"

"I'm doing my best to honor that promise. But things happened before I left home."

"What things?"

"My father told me if I married you I was dead to him."

Matt felt as if she'd punched him again. He'd had no idea. He knew her father hadn't liked him much, especially after that business with Emily O'Leary, but all Eliza had ever said was that she wasn't going back. When she accepted his marriage contract, she had truly turned away from her old life. She'd given up her only family for him. But why?

As soon as the thought was there, he turned away from the answer. He didn't want to know.

"I'm sure your father didn't mean it."

"Oh, he meant it, all right."

"What does that have to do with me teaching you to use a gun?"

"I'm going to stay in Silver Springs. I think I should know how to ride and handle a gun. Don't you?"

"No. I think you should go back to Boston."

"And just where would I go when I got there?"

"To my mother."

She laughed mirthlessly. "Your mother thought we should be married. I can't go back and tell her that it didn't work out. And I won't ask her for charity."

"But she owes you. After the trick she pulled—"

Eliza shook her head. "I don't want anything from anyone. I'm going to make my own way. Here in Wyoming."

He gritted his teeth. "Don't count on any help from me."

"Lie number three.

"What?"

"You just said any help I wanted, you'd give me. This is exactly what I'd expect from you *now*. Don't give it another thought, Matt. I'll teach myself how to shoot."

"The hell you will. You'll handle a gun by yourself over my dead body."

She nodded emphatically. "When I learn how, I can arrange that."

"That's what I'm afraid of."

He would do anything to remove the mistrust clouding her eyes—anything but tell her that life was stirring inside him for the first time since he lost Carrie. He was afraid Eliza would find out that he was coming alive again. If she knew, she would make him admit that it was because of her. If he put that into words, then it would be real. He didn't want to feel anything for her. Emptiness was better than pain.

"I take your silence to mean that you don't intend to teach me." Determination gathered on her small face, pulling her mouth into a straight line.

That made him nervous. Was she planning to handle a gun on her own, the way she had the horse?

"The last time you decided to do something on your own, Wiley wound up a scratching post for a bobcat."

She flinched as if he'd slapped her. He knew Eliza. He knew she felt bad enough about what had happened, so he deliberately threwn it in her face. If that was the only way he could change her mind, by God he'd do it. For her sake. Didn't she understand that everything she wanted to do was dangerous?

"I feel awful about Wiley." She lifted her chin and looked him in the eye. "But I can't ride a horse and if you hadn't found us—If I'm going to stay in Silver Springs, I have to be able to take care of myself. I promised I wouldn't give you any argument, and I'll keep my word. You don't want me to ride or shoot by myself, so I won't."

He studied her obstinate expression. "I know that look. What are you planning to do?"

"I thought when I get to Silver Springs, I'd ask Mr. Whitaker or Mr. Slicker to teach me."

Rage boiled up inside him. Either one of those two-bit, whoring bastards would use any excuse to get close to a lady like Eliza. The thought of her, in the arms of another man, *any man,* made Matt so mad he couldn't see straight.

"You don't hear very well, do you? I told you once that Ed Whitaker is the biggest skirt-chaser I know. And Brad Slicker was trying to get you drunk because he wanted to—"

"At least I've been warned about them. No one told me about you."

She had him there. He'd vowed to keep her safe and he hadn't. Now she wanted to learn to ride and shoot a gun so that she could get away from him.

"I'm responsible for you. If any harm comes to you because of Whitaker or Slicker—"

"Nothing will change my mind, Matt. I will find someone to teach me what I need to know."

He knew she would. And he didn't trust anyone but himself. Matt had no choice and he knew it.

"You win. Meet me here tomorrow morning at sunup. I'll teach you to ride."

She nodded. "I'll be here."

"Do you have clothes fit for sitting astride a horse?"

"Don't worry about me. I'll manage."

"I'll see what I can find for you. Do you have a warm coat? It's cold."

"Boston was cold, too."

He nodded. "I'll see you here in the morning. Unless you're smart and change your mind."

"Not likely," she said, raising her chin.

In spite of himself, he couldn't hold back the tide of anticipation as he found himself looking forward to the morning and her lesson.

13

"*She's so big.*" Eliza stood with her back against the corral fence, staring wide-eyed at Snowflake. The horse waited patiently two steps away from her, saddled, with the reins wrapped around the top rail. "She didn't seem so big in the barn."

"There's nothing to be afraid of," Matt said. He held the bridle and patted the horse's nose as he looked across her brown back. Eliza's breath was coming out in little white clouds in the cold morning air as her fear grew.

Beneath her jacket, she wore a white cotton blouse of her own and the split skirt he'd found in Carrie's trunk. The latter was far too big and was gathered at the waist with a belt. It was meant to hit the top of a woman's boots, but on Eliza the heavy skirt dragged on the ground and gathered dust. Matt had expected it would bother him to see her in the old clothes. The only thing that disturbed him was being reminded again how small and delicate Eliza was. The last time he remembered seeing Carrie wear the skirt was just before she'd told him she was going to have his child.

He glanced at Eliza's flat stomach, nearly obscured by the abundance of material, and prayed to God that he hadn't given her a baby. He wanted one of his own so much he'd been willing to marry a stranger, but the thought of Eliza carrying his baby weighed on his mind and pulled tight in his chest.

This overwhelming feeling of protectiveness for Eliza was something he hadn't counted on when he'd agreed to teach her to ride. She turned up the collar of her coat. He tried to forget there was no sheepskin to keep the cold out. He watched her pull tight the knot under her chin that held the woolen scarf over her ears. His own were beginning to hurt from the frigid wind. He hoped she would give up this foolish notion before they both froze or caught their death.

Best hurry her along and get it over with.

"Okay, hold on to the pommel and put your left foot in the stirrup. Lift yourself up and swing your right leg over her rump and sit. I'll adjust the length of the stirrups when you're settled."

She nodded and white puffs floated in front of her face as she let out a long breath of air. Her green eyes glittered with resolve, but he saw the lurking fear when she clenched her teeth together and lifted a shaking hand.

Matt moved behind her. He took her wrist and placed her palm on the saddle horn. She did as he'd directed with her foot and he encircled her waist with his hands and helped her mount.

She sat in the saddle and looked down at him, swallowing hard. "It—it's very high."

Her whole body shook and he wasn't sure if it was from cold wind or cold feet. God, why was she putting herself through this? he wondered. If she'd just go back to Boston where she belonged, there'd be no reason for her to get near a horse.

He shortened the stirrups for her and tucked her riding skirt out of the way so her feet fit securely, trying not to notice her slender ankles and the glimpse of shapely calf. He ignored his own body's response to that split-second sight, pushing away the thought of her legs wrapped around him in bed. It was dangerous to think of her that way.

"You're gonna be fine, Eliza. I'm going to lead you around the corral so you can see how it feels. All right?"

She nodded. "Matt?"

"Yeah?"

"Slowly. Please?" she whispered.

"Don't worry," he said, turning toward the fence to untie the reins.

The leather saddle creaked, telling him she was moving around. He glanced at her from the corner of his eye and saw her hands tighten on the horn until her knuckles turned white.

She leaned over the horse's neck. "I'll make a deal with you, Snowflake," she whispered. "I won't kick you or whack you with the reins to make you go faster if you promise to be a good girl and not let me fall off."

As if she'd heard and approved, Snowflake tossed her head and her halter rattled.

Matt walked her around the corral slowly, letting her get used to the horse's gait. "You all right?" he called over his shoulder.

"Yes," she said breathlessly.

He stopped her by the fence where they'd started. "Now you need to learn to use the reins."

"Does that mean I have to let go of the saddle horn?" Her eyes opened wider and Snowflake shifted restlessly, as if she sensed Eliza's unease.

"There's no other way. Do you want to forget it?" She shook her head. "You were going to do it by yourself yesterday."

"That was different."

"How?"

"It just was. Inside the barn I could just sit on her."

She was terrified. In spite of that, she was pushing herself to do this. Once again, he was humbled by her courage.

"Here. Take the reins."

She looked at the leather straps, then at her hands gripping the saddle horn. "How will I keep from falling off?"

"Grab hold with your knees and inner thighs."

She nodded and he watched her press her legs tighter to the horse's flanks. But she made no move to take the reins.

"Eliza, you have to let go."

She nodded, and he could see her struggle to try and release her grip. "I can't," she whispered.

"Let's try this." He pulled her foot from the stirrup, placed his boot in it and swung up behind her. As much as he wanted her to give up, he couldn't stand to see her so frightened. Besides, something in him admired the hell out of her determination to conquer her fear.

He settled himself behind her and she nestled her little body into his. She was soft and warm and female, and it was enough to drive him out of his mind. If he'd known it would come to this, he never would have volunteered to help her.

"Let go of the horn, Eliza," he said gruffly. Reluctantly, he put his arms around her. "I'm here. You're safe. All right?"

"Yes," she said. "It's just that I—"

"I'll make a deal with you. If you swear not to pinch me or punch me, I promise I won't let you fall."

She gave a short, nervous laugh. "I promise."

She hesitated only a second before releasing her grip. After flexing her stiff, gloved fingers, she took the leather strips. He put his right hand over hers and showed her how to move the rein to guide the animal and let Snowflake know which way to go.

"With the bit in her mouth, does it hurt her when I do that?"

"No. But you don't have to pull hard. It doesn't take a lot of movement. Snowflake has a sensitive mouth. She'll get the idea."

He repeated the same motions with her other hand.

"Put your feet back in the stirrups," he said. When she obeyed, he continued, "When you're ready to move forward, just give her a kick with your heels."

"I promised I wouldn't kick her—"

"You don't really have to kick. Gentle pressure. It won't hurt her, I swear."

Matt showed her what he meant, then let his legs hang down as they moved forward. He rested his hands on his thighs, ready to take over if Eliza panicked, but letting her see that she could do it by herself. Snowflake walked slowly around the corral and he felt Eliza begin to relax.

They circled again and she turned her head to talk to him. "I think I'm getting the hang of this."

"I'll slide off and you can do it by yourself."

"No! I—I mean, not yet. Please?"

Eliza prayed he wouldn't leave her high up on a horse all alone. She wasn't ready yet to give up the warm, strong, secure feeling of his presence. His thighs cushioning her behind and his broad chest at her back were reassuring. Her belief that no harm would come to her while he was there was complete and unshakable. After all these years, he was still her hero. She knew he didn't want her as a woman, but that was different from his ability to keep her safe.

"Just one more circle around the corral," she pleaded. As much as she hated to admit it, she wanted him near her for the little thrill of pleasure she got from being close to him as much as for his encouraging presence.

He slid closer to her. "All right. Let's trot her." She put her heels against Snowflake's sides and pressed. "Is that how it's done?"

The horse increased her pace.

"There's your answer. You're in control, Eliza. She'll do what you tell her."

Eliza wasn't so sure she liked trading a slow, steady pace for the bouncing as the animal moved faster. "How do I make her stop?"

"Pull back on the reins like this," he said. He put his arms around her and covered her hands with his own. Her chest felt tight and her breath came faster, but this time it had nothing to do with fear.

But Matt Decker didn't want her as his wife, she reminded herself. She had forced him to help her learn to ride. She couldn't expect anything more. If only it didn't feel so good when he held her in his arms. When she settled in Silver Springs, the memory of her time here on the ranch would have to be enough to sustain her through the long, cold winter, and all the winters of her life.

Her recollection of a night spent in his arms was all she would ever have of him. Her breath caught when a tight little pain slammed her in the chest.

"You all right? You tensed up again."

"I'm fine." She sighed and pulled back on the reins the way he'd shown her. Snowflake slowed to a walk, then stopped. "I think I should try it by myself now."

Matt's hands lingered a few moments around her. Then he squeezed her waist reassuringly before removing his arms and sliding off the horse.

"You won't go away?" She wanted to do this; she just needed to know he was close by until she was confident on her own.

"I'm just going to sit on the top rail," he said nodding toward the white rail fence. A grin turned up the corners of his mouth suddenly. "At this rate, you'll be a cowboy in no time."

"Do you really think so, Matt?" She was afraid to believe anything good that he said. She was sure she would never be able to measure up to Carrie.

"A week ago you wouldn't even go near a horse. Now look at you." She thought there was a light of admiration in his blue eyes, and her heart soared at his praise. She wanted to see that look, but not for sitting a horse. In another time and another place, she wanted to see an expression that would tell her she was his woman. But there was little chance of that.

"Can I go with you to the north meadow tomorrow?" she asked.

"How did you know about that?"

"I overheard you telling Wiley it was past time to go out there and check the herd."

"It's a long ride. You're not ready for it."

"I don't have a lot of time to practice, Matt. I'll be moving to Silver Springs any day now. When I do, I want to be comfortable on a horse. The only way I can do that is a long ride."

"No, I don't think that's a good idea." His mouth tightened and he pulled his hat down low over his eyes. Once again she'd managed to snuff out the glow of admiration.

"Whatever you say, Matt. But would you mind saddling Snowflake for me before you go? I'll just take her for a short ride around the ranch."

He shook his head. "Until I'm sure you know what you're doing, I don't want you riding without me."

She rested her elbow on the saddle horn and stared down at him from the horse's great height. She was accustomed to looking up at almost everyone. This was the first time she had looked down at Matt. Being on a horse had its advantages. "Then take me with you," she said.

"I don't have time to nursemaid a tenderfoot—or any other parts of you that aren't used to a saddle."

"You won't have to take care of me. I promise. I'll keep up, Matt."

He snorted. "You don't have any idea how hard that ride is."

"I'm sure I can do it. You said yourself I was practically a cowboy."

A strange look crept into his eyes. "You're going to do it anyway if I don't take you with me. Aren't you?"

"Why would you think—"

He held up his hand. "Save your breath. I'm only going to say this once. If you insist on going, I promise you'll regret it."

"No, I won't."

"Then you still want to go?"

"Yes."

He nodded. "It's your butt." He patted Snowflake's neck. "We leave first thing in the morning. Pack some food. We'll most likely be gone until sundown."

"Will you teach me how to shoot?"

"You don't give up, do you?"

"Not when it's important."

"And you think this is?"

"I certainly do."

"If you can still stand up when we get where we're going, I'll show you how to load a gun without shooting yourself."

She smiled at him. "I'll hold you to that."

"Quit bouncing, Eliza."

"I can't help it."

She gritted her teeth to keep from saying a string of those words he always said when he was provoked. If he told her one more time to use her knees and go with the motion of the horse, she'd skip practicing gun handling and just shoot him.

She drew air into her lungs, then let it out in a sigh. A cover of gray clouds blocked out the sun, making it cold enough to see her breath even though it was getting close to noon. She was hungry and tired, and it had been almost two hours since she'd had any feeling in her feet. Every bone in her body ached, as well as the softer parts of her that had no bones.

The first hour had been wonderful. Eliza hadn't realized how cooped up she'd felt in the house, nursing Wiley, cooking, washing, and dusting. The clear, cold Wyoming air had blown the cobwebs from her head and invigorated her spirit. Staying in this wonderful young land where she had the freedom to be herself had been the right decision. There was no doubt in her mind.

Three hours later she was ready to admit she might have been a little hasty. But she'd rather face an angry bobcat than tell Matt as much.

"You still with me, Eliza?" He spoke without looking at her. He had been doing that all morning.

"Yes." As hard as she tried, she couldn't keep the cross, cranky tone out of her voice—not even for that one word.

"We'll stop to rest the horses when we get there."

Rest the horses? What about her? She glared at his broad back. That heavy sheepskin jacket gave his already masculine bearing a boost that made her insides clench as much as her thighs were from gripping the horse as she tried not to bounce. And the worst of it was she didn't want to be attracted to him.

When she didn't say anything, he glanced over his shoulder. "You all right?"

It took every ounce of her willpower not to wince, and she even managed a sweet smile. "Perfect," she said.

"Good." He turned around and clucked to his horse. Buck instantly surged into a trot. Snowflake followed suit, but, instead of the fluid, graceful motion Matt seemed to achieve with his horse, Eliza started bouncing faster. Her teeth clicked together and every time her backside smacked the leather saddle, she wanted to cry out in pain. She clamped her jaw shut, not only to keep from crying out, but to keep from biting her tongue. Her head throbbed and she was worn out. But she would rather walk barefoot on open coals than let Matt know she was the least bit uncomfortable.

He stopped and waited for her. When she pulled up beside him, he pointed. "Just over that rise is a spring. We'll stop there."

"Can't be too soon for me," she muttered under her breath.

"What?"

"I said, do we have to stop so soon?"

Surprise chased away the smug expression on his face. "If we don't, there won't be any place to water the horses."

She nodded.

"Hah!" he hollered. Buck took off.

"Oh, Lord," she said as Snowflake trailed behind.

Matt pulled his horse to a stop near a bubbling spring. Snowflake trotted obediently after and came to a halt beside Matt. He swung gracefully from the saddle while she groaned inwardly. He made it look so easy. In a matter of seconds, he'd unsaddled Buck, slapped the horse's rear end, and sent him to the stream to drink.

Eliza prepared to dismount. She grabbed the saddle horn and put her weight on her left leg in the stirrup while she swung her other over Snowflake's hind end. When she had both feet on the ground, her knees nearly buckled. She looked around for Matt to see if he'd noticed. He was busy gathering small pieces of wood. Relieved, she let out her breath and held on until she trusted her legs to hold her up.

"Unsaddle Snowflake, Eliza." He was squatting beside the small fire he'd just started.

"Now?" More than anything she wanted to sit beside the warmth and hold out her frozen hands and feet.

"The animals always get taken care of first." He shot her a look and seemed to make his own assessment. "Do you want me to do it for you?"

"No. I'll take care of my horse."

She bent to unbuckle the cinch and almost cried out at the muscles that tightened painfully in her back. She took a deep cleansing breath.

"Did you say something?" he asked.

"Not a thing." She unfastened the strap and took hold of the pommel and the seat of the saddle, then let it slide

down and fall to the ground. She nearly went down with
it, but gathered all her strength to stay upright. Then she
slapped Snowflake's hind end and the horse moved to
drink beside Buck.

Matt untied a blanket from behind his saddle and
spread it on the ground beside the fire. She felt him
watching her as she walked toward the warmth of the
crackling flames. Eliza tried to move normally, but her
legs were wobbly and she felt as if the horse was still
between them. A light-headed sensation swept over her,
making her dizzy. She stopped and closed her eyes until
the feeling passed.

"Don't you dare faint." There was a hard edge to
Matt's voice. "Sit down before you fall down."

He came up beside her and put his arm around her
waist to guide her to the blanket. As he helped her sit, dull
pain shot from her lower back all the way to her ankles.
Her buttocks felt hot and cold at the same time. She
couldn't stifle the moan that formed in her throat.

"Sore?" he asked.

"No."

"You're not a good liar."

"Unlike some people I could name," she said, spearing
him with a look, "I haven't made a habit of it."

He hunkered down beside her and they were so close
she could see the dark ring of blue that circled the irises of
his eyes. Sunlight glinted off the whiskers covering the
lower half of his face. He'd been almost clean shaven
when she had married him in Silver Springs. In the weeks
she'd been at the ranch, she didn't think he'd shaved even
once. He had a thick, full beard. It was shot with brown,
red, and gold, just like his hair, but darker.

He'd never had a beard in Boston and she decided she
liked it. It gave him a rugged male look that made her
insides flutter like a flock of geese heading south for the
winter.

She hated that she could be mad as a wet hen at him

one minute and weak in the knees the next. The sooner she was away from him, the better.

He lifted his hat and ran splayed fingers through his shoulder-length hair. Then he turned his ice blue gaze on her. "Why don't you just admit that your backside hurts like hell?"

A huge sigh escaped her. She didn't have the strength to reprimand him for swearing. "Why should I?"

"Because then I won't have to show you how to use a gun."

Matt watched her as that sank in. He studied her carefully, looking for the signs that would tell him how she really felt. It didn't take a genius to see she was about done in. He was almost glad she'd insisted on coming with him so he could prove to her she didn't belong here. Maybe she'd see that Wyoming was no place for an impulsive female.

Then again, he was afraid maybe he'd pushed too hard. He wanted her to confess she was hurting so he could back off.

"Admit it, Eliza."

She shook her head and raised her chin. "I'm fine," she insisted, settling her split skirt around her. She took off the gloves he'd given her and stretched her hands toward the fire. "Just let me rest a minute and then I'll be able to stand. You promised if I could, you'd show me how to handle a gun."

"I haven't forgotten."

"You haven't made any secret of the fact that you'd like to forget it."

"Guns are dangerous."

"So are bobcats. If I'd known how to shoot, Wiley wouldn't have been so badly hurt."

She was right about that. If Wiley was back on his feet and not too weak to be left alone, she wouldn't be here with him now. He didn't like the idea of her living in town alone.

He hadn't thought she was really serious about staying in Silver Springs, but with her determination to ride, he was beginning to wonder. She wouldn't give up. That was something else about her that hadn't changed in the last eight years.

The wind blew and he turned up the collar of his sheepskin jacket.

"Are you cold?" he asked.

When she nodded, he threw another few pieces of wood on the fire. "Eliza, you stay here and rest. I'm going to quickly check the herd and when I get back, we'll head to the ranch."

"What about the gun?"

"Another time. You're in no condition to handle a weapon."

"Is that lie number three or four?"

"I'm just thinking about what's best for you."

"Horsefeathers."

His brows went up.

"Before you say anything, that's as close to swearing as you'll hear me come. And it's only when I'm severely provoked. Besides, my language is not the issue. You promised if I could still stand, you'd teach me—"

"You're not standing."

"A technicality."

"Damn it, Eliza." How did she manage to make him want to protect and pamper her one minute and paddle her sore backside the next? She was the most stubborn, exasperating female he had ever had the misfortune to know. "Now is not the time to learn about guns."

"All right." She held her hands toward the flames and was quiet for a while.

Matt went over to his saddle and untied the burlap bag of food she had packed. He brought it to her by the fire. Every day she worked her way more under his skin. He couldn't let that happen. If necessary, he'd drag Wiley from his sickbed and take him to town, too.

Why the hell hadn't he thought of that before? Surely that tough old man was strong enough to survive the trip to town. Matt just didn't want to leave him alone. Besides, they could have the doctor in town look at him and see why it was taking so damned long for him to heal.

He took out some of the biscuits and smoked ham. When he turned to offer some to Eliza, he saw that she was dozing. He went over to Snowflake's saddle and pulled off the other blanket, then covered her. On impulse, he brushed his mouth against her temple. She stirred a little and mumbled something.

"Sleep, Eliza. You've earned it. I can't leave you here alone. I'll check the herd another time."

He watched her, memorizing the delicate arch of her brow, her pointed chin, every freckle on her small nose. Soon the loneliness was all he'd have to contend with, not an ornery, headstrong female who didn't have the common sense God gave a rock. But the closer the time came to sending Eliza away, the more ill-tempered he felt. He wondered if it was already too late for him to close his heart to her.

14

Matt sat up in bed when he heard the scrape of a chair in the kitchen. It was past midnight and pitch-black in his room. Eliza had been asleep for hours. By the time they got back to the ranch, she had been exhausted, even after her short nap. He'd fixed beans and biscuits that were hard as rocks, and she had hobbled into her bedroom, still insisting she was fine.

Something crashed in the other room. He jumped out of bed, grabbed his pants, and pulled them on. He took his pistol from the dresser, then opened the door and looked into the hall. At the end of it, he saw flickering and knew someone was stirring the fire in the kitchen hearth. Eliza's door was open, and when he checked, he saw that her bed was empty. He put his gun back, then moved toward the flickering glow. Something had to be wrong to get her up in the middle of the night after the grueling day she'd had.

He'd pushed her hard, almost as hard as he drove his cowboys during roundup. But unlike them, she was a beginner on a horse. Still, she hadn't uttered one word of complaint.

He walked into the kitchen and saw her in front of the fireplace. She wasn't wearing her wrapper, just the muslin nightgown she'd worn the night she married him. Her long hair hung to her waist, and her feet were bare. Every muscle in his body tensed at the tempting sight of her. His hands clenched as he closed his eyes for a moment to shut out the slender beauty of the body he'd explored so thoroughly, visible now through the thin gown.

When she stooped to lift the piece of wood she'd dropped, he heard a strangled groan.

"Eliza?"

She half turned at the sound of his voice and he saw her wince in pain. He hurried over to her.

Bending down, he took the log she was trying to lift, then put it on the glowing embers. Soon the dry wood caught and crackled. In the flickering firelight he saw the strain on her face as she tried to stand.

"What's wrong, Eliza?"

She met his gaze and tried to smile. "I suppose you wouldn't believe me if I said nothing."

He shook his head and held out his hands to help her up. "You're obviously hurting."

As she put her slender fingers into his bigger palms, she sighed. "I'm sorry I disturbed you. I'm really fine. It's late and you have to get up early. Please go back to bed."

"I told you not to bounce."

Her eyes opened wide when she realized he knew exactly where and why she hurt. "I couldn't seem to stop. I gripped with my knees and thighs like you said, but I just kept on bouncing."

Guilt carved a path from his gut to his chest. This was all his fault, because he had wanted to show her that she didn't belong here. Wyoming was hard and wild, and it was difficult to survive even if you were born to it. Eliza had been raised in relative comfort in the East.

They had shared a special friendship once, even though more often than not he had wanted to throttle her. He almost smiled. He felt that way now and if she wasn't already sore . . .

He was the one who should be horsewhipped. It was his fault she was in Wyoming and had been disowned by her father. He knew how that felt. And because of him, everything was worse. After promising himself he wouldn't, he'd taken her virginity. Now she couldn't go to another man untouched. Instead of regretting that, he couldn't suppress the primal pleasure that raced through him. He couldn't stand the idea of her with another man.

Matt knew if he had any decency, he would let Eliza into the place she was trying so hard to fill. But he wasn't decent, and he wouldn't condemn her to his way of life. He wouldn't see her suffer the same fate as Carrie.

Eliza was a very special woman. He couldn't let her stay and take a chance with her life.

He watched her walk slowly to the stove. "What are you doing?"

"I'm going to heat some water. I thought if I soaked, it might ease some of the soreness."

"I have something better."

"Don't bother about me, Matt. This is my own darn fault." She stooped to lift a bucket and sucked in her breath. When she looked at him tears of pain glittered in her eyes. "You warned me, but I wouldn't listen."

Matt knew he was just as much to blame. He could have made it easier on her. He didn't have to take her all the way to the north range. He could have turned back anytime, but he hadn't. He was trying to teach her a lesson. Something told him he was the one who was going to learn a thing or two, though.

"Quit being stubborn, Eliza. That will only make a bad situation worse." He walked to the cupboard beside her, opened the door, and pulled out a bottle.

"What's that?"

"Liniment."

"What's it for?"

He looked at her and couldn't help grinning. "A green-horn tenderfoot who doesn't know when to quit."

She looked up at him with a small smile that told him she was laughing at herself. "I have news for you. It's not my foot that's tender, and there's no part of my body that feels green." She pressed her hands to her thighs. "Red would be my guess."

He swallowed hard as she pressed the muslin gown against her body, outlining the shapely curves. He was the worst kind of bastard to even think that way while she was in this condition, but his body seemed to have a mind of its own. He couldn't help it: he wanted her.

But he'd walk naked in a snowstorm before he took her in her present condition.

"Wait here by the fire," he said. "I'll get a blanket and you can lie on it while I rub you down with this stuff."

She held out her hand. "I can put it on by myself."

If only she could. He shook his head. "You can't reach. Besides, you have to work it into the muscle and I don't think you have the strength to right now."

He left her and went to the guest room for the quilt on the bed. In the hall, he paused by her door and thought about bringing her wrapper. A corner of his mouth turned up slightly. That was something like shutting the barn door after the horse was long gone. Besides, in the shape she was in, she was safe from him.

He went back to the kitchen and spread the quilt on the floor in front of the hearth. "Lie down there on your stomach."

She did as he instructed and a pained groan escaped her.

Matt took a deep breath and let it out. He pushed Eliza's nightgown up to her knees, baring her slender calves to his gaze. A groan built inside him, but he didn't dare let it out or she'd know what he was feeling. He couldn't let that happen. Instead, he uncorked the bottle and poured some of the strong-smelling liquid into his palm and rubbed it between his hands.

She lay quietly, her cheek pillowed on her forearms. Her brown hair spread over her shoulders and down her back like a silk shawl. If his hands hadn't been covered with liniment, Matt was sure he would have buried his fingers in the long, thick strands. "I'm going to rub this into your muscles. It'll probably hurt some, but after a while you'll feel better."

She nodded. "Thank you, Matt. I don't deserve your kindness."

After what I've done I can never make it up to you.

He started at her ankle and in a rolling motion worked up her calf to her thigh. His wrist brushed her gown up higher and he felt her leg tense beneath his touch. She shivered.

"Does that hurt?" he asked.

"A little."

In the firelight he caught sight of her buttocks and the black-and-blue bruises there. He gritted his teeth before he blurted out one of those words she was always giving him hell for saying. No wonder she hadn't been able to sleep.

Then he went hot and cold at the same time. He was going to have to rub liniment *there.* God was punishing him; there was no question about it. He wished he could make a bargain like Eliza had. He would take his chances in hell if only he didn't have to see her, touch her, and resist her. This time the groan slipped out.

Eliza heard him make a funny, strangled sound and lifted her head to glance at him over her shoulder. "Are you all right, Matt?"

"Fine," he said gruffly. There was something in his tone, in just that one word, and she knew he was not very happy about this.

"You don't have to do any more. I'm feeling better—"

"Lift up your hips," he said harshly. "I need to push your nightgown out of the way."

Eliza wasn't sure if she should feel humiliated or delighted. She decided humiliation was probably the right emotion. After all, the man was rubbing her backside because she was a complete failure on a horse. Still, his hands felt wonderful, magical. With his thumb, he pushed against the knots in her muscles and the sensation caught her somewhere between pain and pleasure. Then he moved to her buttocks and put his palm on the place where she hurt the most.

A sound built, then caught in her throat before slipping out. His hands made her feel wonderful. It was very close to the way he'd made her feel when he took her in his bed. Her cheeks flamed. Her breathing increased.

"What's wrong? Do you want me to stop?"

"No. It feels so good." She shook her head and shifted her hips slightly to glance at him.

He wore jeans with his long underwear. At his neck, his chest hair poked out the vee opening. The sleeves were pushed up to his elbow, revealing wide, strong forearms. Her gaze lifted to his face. His mouth was practically a straight line and furrows slashed a path between his brows.

He wanted to stop. She'd heard the annoyance in his voice, and she saw the proof in his eyes and his set features.

"On second thought, I do want you to stop." She pulled her nightdress down, then rolled to her side and raised up to a sitting position, leaning on her hip—the part that hadn't smacked against Snowflake's back.

She took in a deep breath before pushing herself to her knees, then her feet. Matt's gaze burned over her from her bosom to her bare toes and its heat stole the air from her lungs.

He stood up and replaced the cork in the bottle, then wiped his hands on a towel.

"I'm sure I'll be able to sleep now," she said.

That was a bald-faced lie. Apparently, she had picked

up his habit. After the way his hands had made her feel, she'd be lucky to catch a wink of sleep, but she couldn't stay near him a second longer knowing he didn't want her.

She turned her back on him and started to slowly walk toward the hall. More than anything, she wanted to look dignified when she left. Her halting steps were a dismal failure. She heard his bare feet slap against the wood floor, then his palm cupping her shoulder stopped her.

He put a hand around her waist and the other beneath her knees and lifted her in his arms before she could protest.

"Put me down. I can walk."

"Barely," he said gruffly.

Her breast, naked under her nightgown, rubbed against his chest and she felt the vibration of his deep voice clear down to her toes. A shiver started in her chest and rippled through her abdomen, her thighs, calves, and feet.

"Are you cold?" he asked.

She shook her head and put her arms around his neck. Their faces were inches apart and the dancing flames in the hearth highlighted the desire that flickered in the depths of his eyes. He still hadn't shaved since bringing her to the ranch. His beard was longer now than when he'd kissed her in the barn or later when he'd loved her so thoroughly. His hair, just brushing his shoulders, was brown shot with gold. But the whiskers covering the lower half of his face were more reddish. What would that beard feel like against her cheek? His mouth, so finely shaped, so clearly defined, showed through the beard, and she wanted to press her lips to his.

She leaned her head closer to him and felt his chest move as his breath came out in a rush.

"You're a witch, Eliza. And you've put a spell on me. I can't get you out of my mind," he muttered just before his mouth touched hers.

The contact flowed over Eliza like warm honey, sweet and seductive. All her resolutions to stay away from him

flew out the window. She burned all over, and not from
the liniment.

When he lifted his mouth, she heard his ragged breathing and stared into his eyes.

She knew that look from the night of passion she'd
tucked away in her heart. She wanted to know another
night exactly like it. But her greatest fear was that he'd
turn away from her again. She could bear almost anything, except that.

"I'm not a witch, and you'd better forget about me,
Matt. Either put me down so that I can walk under my
own power or take me to my room. I'm very tired."

His gaze burned into hers for a moment before he
nodded.

"All right." He started down the hall with her in his
arms.

He stopped in front of her door and started to go in,
then hesitated. He stared at the bed, then at her, and took
his arm from beneath her knees.

Eliza shivered as the cold inside the house wrapped
around her the way his body heat had. She wished with
all her heart that things could be different and she could
show him how she felt. He'd closed himself off and
wouldn't let her inside. There was nothing more she
could do.

"Good night," she said. "Thanks for the liniment. I feel
much better now." Her voice caught on a sob and she
closed the door before she let him see her foolishness.

Matt knocked on the bunkhouse door. He waited in the
cold morning air, watching his breath form little white
clouds.

He pounded again, once. "Wiley? You in there, old
man?"

From inside came a scraping sound, then footsteps.
Matt pulled his hat lower over his brows. What was going

on in there? He and Eliza had left the old man alone for most of the previous day when they had gone riding. When they came back to the Double C, Wiley had been fine. What was taking him so long to answer the door? Had he fallen again and not told them?

Matt had raised his hand to rap again when a voice called out.

"Get your skinny butt in here before you freeze it off."

Matt opened the door and stepped inside. Wiley lay in his bunk with the covers pulled up to his neck. He had a funny look on his face.

"How're you feeling?" Matt pulled one of the wooden chairs to the side of the bunk and sat down, then tucked his cold hands under his arms.

"A little better. Still weak."

"But you didn't have any more dizzy spells while Eliza and I were gone yesterday?"

"Nope. How far'd you take her?"

"To the north meadow." He watched the old man's gray brows go up.

"Helluva long ride for her. What got into you, boy?"

"Had work to do. She insisted on coming along." He shrugged, but the probing questions made him uncomfortable. He'd asked himself the same thing.

"Can she still walk?"

"Hardly. She couldn't sleep last night. I had to use the liniment on her."

Matt couldn't suppress the rush of pleasure the memory of being with Eliza brought. He wished it hadn't made her sore, but he couldn't forget how good it felt to have her company on the ride, then, later, to touch her soft skin as he'd rubbed liniment over her legs and backside. The sadness in her eyes bothered him a lot. When she'd asked him to take her to her room, it was as if he'd snuffed out a spark inside her.

He'd deliberately hurt her after bedding her so that she would stay away from him. His plan had worked better than he could have hoped. He'd expected to feel relief, but instead he felt like horse manure. Maybe his father had been right about him all along.

"Somethin' wrong, Matthew?"

He met the older man's gaze and shook his head. "So you stayed in bed yesterday?"

"Yup. 'Cept when we had a visitor."

"Who was it?"

"That Evans fella came by askin' for Eliza."

A man was asking for her? The intense jealousy that tightened inside him took Matt by surprise.

"I don't remember any Evans."

"He came by here lookin' for a job just before you got Eliza from the stage in Silver Springs."

Matt thought for a minute, then remembered the cowboy. He recalled little Jenny, and Eliza using the last of her money to buy her a coat, and the man drunk in Brad Slicker's place when he'd carried Eliza out of there.

"Why was he here? And why was he asking for Eliza?" He heard the leashed anger in his own voice and wasn't surprised when Wiley's brows shot up again.

"Don't know. Just said to tell her thanks for everything. And that Jenny liked her a whole lot." Deep lines appeared in his forehead. "Who's Jenny?"

"His daughter. Eliza took a shine to her, too."

"He didn't stay long. Looked mighty peaked and coughed somethin' fierce. Then he left."

Matt nodded. "I suppose there's no reason to be concerned. Evans seemed pretty harmless."

"Yeah. Can't say the same for you, takin' Eliza all the way to the north meadow." He shifted in the bed. "That's a far piece for a new rider."

Disapproval rang loud and clear in the old man's look and voice. Wiley wouldn't understand that Matt had pushed her that hard for her own good, that he was trying to discourage her from staying in Wyoming. That he wanted her to go back to Boston where she'd be safe.

"I already told you—she insisted on going with me."

"You didn't hafta take her all that way."

"The herd needed checking."

"Horseshit. Could've waited. You had somethin' up your sleeve."

"Watch your language. Words like that might slip out around Eliza."

"So you're gonna keep her around?" Wiley's pale blue eyes speared him with a look.

Matt shook his head. "Soon as you're strong enough to travel, I'm taking you to see the doc in town. I plan on takin' Eliza, too, and leaving her for good."

"You're still set on it?"

Matt nodded, but the emptiness inside him got a lot bigger. "I'm going to check on the horses."

Eliza walked into the barn and tried to control the shivers racking her from head to toe. It was colder today. Or did it just feel that way because she was black-and-blue all over? She didn't feel as bad as she had the night before, thanks to Matt's liniment and his wonderful, big, gentle hands. Too bad there wasn't some kind of medicine she could rub on her heart the way he had on her body. She sighed. Thinking that way didn't do her any good at all.

She opened the door to Snowflake's stall and stepped inside. The horse whinnied a welcome and *clip-clop*ped toward Eliza. She stroked the velvety nose and felt the animal's heat. The cold didn't bother her quite as much here.

"How are you, pretty girl? Are you sore, too?" She went to the side of the stall and picked up the brush she'd used to stroke Snowflake once.

That was the day Matt had kissed her when the horse had nudged her into his arms.

"Should I be angry with you?" Eliza asked as she brushed the shiny brown coat. "Did you know what you were doing?"

The boards in the loft overhead creaked and Eliza stopped brushing to listen. Was it the wind? She hadn't noticed any on her walk from the house. In fact, it was more still outside than she'd seen it the whole time she'd been here.

She scratched Snowflake's ears, then went to the bucket of oats and grabbed a handful. She walked back into the stall with her palm open. The horse nickered softly, then nibbled the grain.

"I'm sorry it's not an apple, sweet girl. Next time I'll bring you something better than these boring old oats. If I have any apples left after making pies, I'll give you one."

Just then, a shuffling from the loft above her sent bits of dirt and hay down into her hair. Eliza went still as fingers of fear prickled over her neck and scalp. Someone was up there. She wished Matt had taught her to use a gun yesterday. Looking around she realized that wouldn't do her any good because she didn't have a pistol. Should she get Matt?

It was probably just her imagination, and he'd laugh at her and say that's why she should go back to town.

The pitchfork caught her eye. She picked it up, surprised at the heavy weight. She stood listening for a long time, waiting for another sound.

Boots rang on the barn floor behind her. Before she could swing around with the pitchfork, she felt a hand on her shoulder and screamed.

Matt took the long sharp tool from her shaking hands. "What are you doing?"

She pointed toward the ceiling. "I think there's someone up there," she whispered.

He glanced upward, then back at her. Instead of the skeptical, mocking look she'd expected, his eyes sparked angrily. "Why didn't you come for me?" He hefted the pitchfork. "And what the hell were you planning to do with this?"

"Whatever I had to," she said, lifting her chin. "If you had taught me how to use a gun—"

"We can argue about that later," he said, taking her arm and leading her from the stall. He pulled her over by the barn door. He put his mouth close to her ear and spoke very softly. "You're right. Someone's up there. I'm going to check it out. You go to the bunkhouse and wait with Wiley."

She shook her head.

"Eliza, don't argue with me. I want you out of here and safe."

"What if you need help?"

"I won't. Besides, what are you going to do? Stab him with a pitchfork?"

"If I have to."

"Eliza—" The scuffling noise stopped him. He sent her a withering look as he pointed to the bunkhouse.

She shook her head, and he turned and walked toward the ladder, then climbed into the loft.

Eliza clasped her hands together and bit the corner of her lip as she waited. She heard his boots when he stepped on bare boards. Then the hay rustled and she heard a high-pitched squeal.

"What are you doing up here?" Matt said.

"Who is it, Matt?" Eliza called. Something about his tone told her he knew whoever it was and there was no reason to be afraid.

"See for yourself." He appeared at the top of the loft and in his grasp he held a white-haired little girl.

"Jenny!" Eliza rushed to the foot of the ladder. "Come down here right now."

"I'll bring her." Matt picked the child up in his arms, turned, and took each step very carefully.

He set her on the floor and Eliza bent and opened her arms. The little girl flung herself into them so hard, the two of them almost fell over backward. Eliza noticed she wore the blue coat she had given her.

She held Jenny away from her. Blond bangs caught on golden lashes framing her warm brown eyes. Her thin face was pale and her lips almost colorless.

"What are you doing here?" Eliza asked. "How long have you been up there? Are you hungry? Well, of course you must be." She took a breath and looked at Matt, lifting her brows questioningly. He shrugged. "Where's your father, sweetheart? Did he leave you here alone?"

"Is he coming back?" Matt asked.

Jenny reached into the pocket of her coat. "I have a note."

When Eliza took the piece of paper from the girl's hand, she noticed her fingers were cold as ice. She glanced up again. "She's freezing, Matt. Can we take her down to the house?"

He nodded. "Is that all right with you, Jenny?"

"Yes, sir. I'm pretty cold." She looked quickly at Eliza. "This coat is real warm though, ma'am. Didn't mean to sound ungrateful—"

Eliza put one finger over the child's mouth to shush her. "I never thought that for a second. For pity's sake, you don't even have mittens. Matt?"

He picked up the child. "We'll have you warm in no time." With long confident strides, he walked out of the barn.

Eliza watched his broad back as she followed him. Jenny's small arm and hand rested on his strong shoulder. Something pulled tight in her chest; the sight was too sweet for words. He was so good with children, and she knew he wanted one of his own. He had planned to marry a stranger and have an heir. But he had married her by mistake and then had had to drink whiskey before he could bear to touch her.

She squeezed her hand into a fist, crushing the piece of paper. Someone he'd never laid eyes on was preferable to her. Tears burned her eyes. She pressed her lips together and shook her head. This would never do. She had to stop feeling sorry for herself and take care of that child.

Eliza followed Matt into the kitchen and watched him set Jenny down in front of the hearth. He stirred the embers into life and put several logs on top. Before long, a roaring blaze radiated warmth into every corner of the kitchen. Jenny watched his every move with huge, solemn blue eyes.

"Let's take off your coat now, sweetheart." Eliza handed the crumpled note to Matt and knelt down to unbutton the garment.

"What do you make of this?" he said, handing the paper to Eliza as she hung the coat on a peg beside the back door.

She read the badly misspelled words, then looked at him. "All it says is that because I was kind to her in town, he knew we would take care of her as if she was our own."

"That's right, ma'am."

Eliza walked back to the child. "Why does he want us to take you?"

"Pa's real sick, Eliza. He said he needs time to get well so he can work and put together a little nest egg for us. He said if he knew I was taken care of by good, decent folk, he could do that."

"And why did you stay in the barn so long?"

"Pa told me to. Said I should stay put as quiet as a mouse so's he could get far enough away so Mr. Decker couldn't find him." The child turned her backside to the fire to warm it. "I stayed as quiet as I could, Eliza. Then I heard you talkin' about givin' apples to that horse and my mouth started waterin' somethin' fierce."

"Good Lord, of course you're hungry. I'll fix you something to eat." Eliza stirred the fire in the iron stove, then took a skillet and placed it on the heat. "Eggs and biscuits should be good for starters."

"Yes, ma'am." Jenny nodded eagerly and turned to warm her front by the fire.

Eliza looked at Matt and with her head motioned him toward her, out of the girl's earshot. "What are we going to do?" she whispered.

He leaned back against her worktable beside the stove and crossed his arms over his wide chest. "First time he came by here looking for work, he had a rickety old wagon. Wiley said he was here yesterday morning. He can't have gotten too far in that thing. I'm surprised he made it to town in it, let alone back again."

Eliza nodded. "That note sounded like he meant for us to keep her permanently, like he wasn't coming back." She stirred the eggs in the pan. "He asked me to make sure she turned into a fine woman, like me."

Matt's mouth pulled into a straight line. "I'll ride out and see if I can track him. We can't keep her. You're not staying and I can't take care of a child."

Eliza glanced at Jenny, her worn, patched dress, and the long, straight white-blond hair hanging down her back. Her heart ached for the poor child, but what Matt said was true. Eliza couldn't stay with him; he'd made it clear he didn't want her. But she wouldn't abandon Jenny. When she left the Double C, she'd take the child with her and somehow find a way to support them both.

15

Matt sat down at the kitchen table and wrapped his cold hands around the cup of coffee Eliza had handed him the moment he'd walked in. He'd been out looking for Jenny's father since sunup. It was late afternoon and he was sick of eating jerky and cold clear through to his bones.

"Did you see any sign of him?" Eliza asked. She sat down in the chair across from him and started peeling potatoes.

"I remember the wagon he had when he first came looking for a job." He took a sip and shook his head. "I was sure it would be easy to track."

"Maybe he wasn't in the wagon. Did you ask Jenny?"

"No." He looked up at her. "It doesn't matter whether he was driving a wagon, riding a horse, or walking barefoot. There was no sign of the man. He's just disappeared."

"Maybe that's what he planned."

His mouth thinned to a straight line. "I don't think he ever planned on coming back."

"Then we'll take care of Jenny."

"Where is she now?"

"She went down to the bunkhouse to keep Wiley company." She stopped peeling and stared at him. "First thing we need to do is find clothes for her. Poor thing. She has so few belongings, Matt. Hardly a decent dress to her name."

"I know."

"Is there anything I could use to make her some clothes? It won't take much, she's such a tiny little thing. An old tablecloth? Some of your old shirts that I could piece together?"

"There's a trunk out in the barn with all of Carrie's clothes. You can cut those down."

Eliza shook her head. "You don't have to give those up. I've already used enough of her things. I don't want to disturb anything else."

He studied her and knew it was already too late to keep things the way they were. Things were disturbed, starting with him. And the way she looked right now wasn't helping to calm him down any. Her brown hair was pulled on top of her head without the usual braid and the mass of curls floated around her small face. Her eyes, so big and green he could get lost in them the way he did on his own fine grazing land, looked back at him. Innocent, trusting, caring. A window to her heart, which he knew was as big as the territory of Wyoming. No, it was way too late to keep her from disturbing him.

She was in his thoughts during the day, and the vision of her haunted his dreams at night. Every day that passed with Eliza in it sent Carrie's memory further away into a small warm place. He'd never forget her, but she couldn't hurt him anymore. He wasn't bothered about that.

The thought of Eliza becoming a part of his heart disturbed him a lot. On top of that, now there was the problem of what to do with Jenny Evans.

"Carrie's things aren't doing anyone any good tucked

away in that trunk. You learn fast out here not to waste anything. Use whatever you can find."

Eliza continued to look at him. "What else is on your mind?"

He blew on his coffee, then took another sip. "What are we going to do with her? We can't keep her."

Her chin lifted a little. "Why not?"

"You know why."

That look marched into her eyes, the one that let him know he wasn't her hero anymore. He hated that expression, but he wouldn't take on another female who had no place to go.

"I won't abandon her, Matt. Her mother died when she was three years old, and her father just left her here." Her eyes narrowed as she fixed her gaze on him. "I think he knew what he was doing. The man was obviously ill. Maybe even dying. From what Wiley and Jenny said, I think his cough was worse. He picked out the best home he could for his child."

"Would've been nice if he'd talked it over with us first before leaving her."

"I'm not surprised he didn't. What would you have said?"

"No, of course."

"See? He knew I'd bought her a coat, and you're a successful rancher. He probably decided to overlook the fact that you carried me out of the saloon."

"If I'm so bad, why did he leave her?"

"He was counting on *me* to take care of her. And I plan to do just that."

"She can't stay on the Double C." That would be too much like being a family. He couldn't even think about that.

"When I go back to town, I'm taking Jenny with me."

"You still won't consider going back to Boston?"

She looked into his eyes and he could read the irony there. "My father disowned me. Do you think he'd take *me* back, let alone an abandoned child? Think about it, Matt. This is my father we're talking about."

Eliza was so generous and giving, he figured she must take after her mother. He had never met the woman, as she had died before he'd saved Eliza from that stampeding horse. But knowing her tightfisted father the way he did, Matt knew Eliza wasn't like *him*. There was no way on God's green earth Eliza would walk away from Jenny Evans or turn her back on anyone she loved. She had taken the child into her heart, lock, stock, and barrel.

Truth be told, he liked the girl. She was a sweet little thing, eager to please and not a bit of trouble. But he couldn't take on the responsibility.

"I know you don't want to go to my mother, but she'd love Jenny—"

Eliza shot him a look fit to kill.

"So . . . Boston is out of the question." He ran his fingers through his hair. "She can't stay here. I can't take care—"

"I understand that. I already told you: When you take me to Silver Springs, Jenny's coming with me."

"Speaking of that, how is Wiley today?" He almost dreaded hearing her answer. If he was well enough to be left for any length of time, Matt would have to take Eliza and Jenny into town. A part of him rebelled at the idea. The wiser part of him argued back that if Eliza didn't go soon, he might not be able to let her go at all. "It's been four weeks since the accident. If he's not strong enough, I think we'll go to town anyway and he should see the doc."

"I haven't talked to him all day. I sent Jenny down to check, but that was a long time ago. Maybe I should go see what the two of them are up to." She put down her knife and stood up.

"I'll go with you."

Matt pulled her heavy shawl off the peg by the door and settled it around her shoulders. He lifted her hair which was caught underneath the thick wool. In doing so he was rewarded with a tempting look at the slender column of her neck. Without thinking he started to move closer.

"Is something wrong, Matt?"

He stopped just in time and cleared his throat. "Nothing. It's just cold as a witch's—I mean, it's real cold outside. Probably get snow before long. We won't be able to travel once that happens. I hope that old man has recuperated so I can get you and Jenny to town."

"Not any more than I do."

He couldn't see her face, but he heard the steel in her voice. If there had ever been a chance that she would find a place in her heart for him, it was too late now. She couldn't stand him. He'd let her down too many times. He wasn't the man she'd thought he was, the one she had followed after as a young girl.

He regretted that life in Wyoming had changed him into a man different from the one she'd expected to marry. Someday he hoped she would understand that he'd never meant to hurt her. Everything he'd done had been for her own good, because letting her go sure as hell wasn't going to be easy for him.

They went outside and walked up the rise to the bunkhouse. He wanted to put his hand on her elbow and assist her, but after his slip in the kitchen he knew touching her at all would be a mistake.

When they reached the bunkhouse Matt knocked on the door. There was no answer.

He rapped again as he opened the door. The room was empty.

"Where do you suppose they are?" Eliza asked.

"I'd guess the barn. Too cold to be anywhere else."

"Wiley must be feeling a lot better."

The same thought had crossed his mind. It irritated him that she sounded so cheerful about it. He frowned suspiciously. Yesterday the man was bedridden with the covers pulled up to his neck. Today he wasn't even inside.

Matt was beginning to smell a rat, a big one with pale eyes and gray-streaked black hair.

They walked into the barn and saw Jenny standing beside the open gate to a stall while Wiley bent over to tighten the cinch on Snowflake's saddle. When he finished, he motioned the little girl forward. She came instantly, and, with no visible effort or strain, he lifted her onto the animal's back.

Matt's gut tightened with anger. That old faker! He'd been pretending to be an invalid while Matt did the work of two men. Not to mention all the fetching and carrying Eliza had done for him. Why had he pretended to be ill? That wasn't like him. Did Eliza know anything about this?

He glanced at her and watched her face change from astonishment to annoyance as she realized that they'd been tricked. She clearly hadn't had the least notion what Wiley Powell was up to.

Matt moved forward and stopped just outside the horse's stall. Tension and anger coiled tightly in his belly. Eliza could have been back in Silver Springs, before he had . . . before they'd . . . If she was carrying a child, Matt knew he would never forgive that meddling old man.

With an effort, he controlled the tumbling emotions within him. He didn't want to startle the horse, not with Jenny on her back.

"You deceitful old polecat," he said. His voice was low and tight with anger. Snowflake stood quietly, but Jenny looked startled. Wiley whirled around.

He looked surprised at first, but buried it pretty quickly. "Matthew. Eliza. Didn't see you two there."

"No, I don't suppose you did." Matt sucked in a big breath of air. "How long have you been back on your feet? Since the first night you went back to the bunkhouse?"

The old man scratched his whiskered chin as he thought for a minute. "Pretty near."

"That was three weeks ago! Why?"

"Had to be done."

Matt glanced at Eliza as her eyes widened. "Do you have any idea what he's talking about?" he asked.

She shook her head and pulled her shawl tight across her bosom as she folded her arms in a good imitation of an outraged schoolmarm. "I'm as anxious for an explanation as you are."

Wiley glanced at the wide-eyed, confused child atop the horse. "This little gal said she wanted to ride Snowflake."

"That's not what I'm talking about and you know it, you old—"

"Careful, Matt," Eliza said, putting her hand on his arm. Her soft touch burned him clear through the sheepskin. "I heartily agree that this is a very good reason to swear, but there's a child present."

The leather saddle creaked as Jenny shifted her slight form. "Don't worry, Mr. Decker. I've heard those words before."

In spite of his anger, Matt couldn't help feeling sorry for Jenny. No little girl should be exposed to what she had been. But come to think of it, Eliza had grown up just the opposite. Her father had kept her sheltered from the real world, even tried to tell her what went on between a man and wife in the privacy of the marriage bed was wrong and merely something to be endured. She had turned out sweet and open and damned spunky. Jenny's exposure to the lower side of life hadn't stifled her basically sweet nature. No wonder Eliza had taken to her so readily.

Whether he swore or not, Matt needed to know why the person he trusted most in this world had played him false.

"Why did you lie to me, Wiley?"

"It wasn't a falsehood. Not exactly."

"I'm afraid I have to disagree with you there, Mr. Powell," Eliza said.

Matt saw the old man wince at her formal tone.

"Your behavior is reprehensible and worthy of reproach."

"Ma'am, if you're sayin' I'm a scalawag and deserve to be horsewhipped, I don't agree." He put his hands up. "Hear me out, both of you."

Matt and Eliza stood side by side with arms crossed over their chests, and stared at the old man.

"You two needed time to work things out between you. Matthew, you're always goin' off half-cocked and gettin' yourself into a fix. You make up your mind and you're stubborn as a mule."

"But this is between Matt and me, Mr. Powell."

"And *you*, missy." He waved a finger at her. "I thought you had more backbone than to let him tell you what to do without a word to say in your own defense."

Eliza looked at the hay as she shifted her feet, as if his words hit her too close to home. "It's because—"

He waved a hand in annoyance. "Don't matter why. Point is, you two needed time to see you're plumb crazy about each other."

"Horsefeathers!"

"Horsesh—manure," Matt said, looking at Jenny.

She grinned at him. "It's all right. I've heard that one, too."

Matt clenched his hands into fists. "You had no right to interfere."

"I heartily agree with Matt."

Wiley smiled indulgently at the two of them. "See? I knew sooner or later the two of you would agree about something."

Eliza looked at Matt as he returned her gaze. If it hadn't been so tragic, it would be funny. She thought about Wiley cooped up for all these weeks, pretending to be ill. She couldn't stay angry at him. He'd been trying to help.

Besides, the idea of what he'd gone through to fool them and how easy it had been . . .

Her mouth started to twitch in amusement. She saw Matt's lips turn up at the corners, too. They burst out laughing at the same time. Wiley cackled along with them and even Jenny giggled, though she didn't fully understand what was going on.

Matt stopped chuckling suddenly and his expression sobered. "This doesn't change anything. It just makes everything easier. Tomorrow at first light, I'm taking Eliza and Jenny to Silver Springs."

The following morning, Matt stared out the window in the top part of the kitchen door. The yard was covered with what looked to be a foot of snow and it was still coming down in huge flakes. As far as he could tell, it didn't look like there was a chance of it stopping real soon.

He heard Eliza's bedroom door open and her slow steps as she came down the hall. She wore a green wool traveling suit and carried her carpetbag in her hand.

She stopped in the doorway and looked at him. "Good morning."

He nodded.

She set her bag down just inside the doorway. "My trunk is packed and I'm all ready. I want to let Jenny sleep as long as possible. She has so few things that I can throw them together in practically no time whenever you're ready to leave. I'll make coffee and you just let me know when you want to go." She stopped for a breath.

Matt was vaguely annoyed that she seemed so anxious to leave. He supposed he shouldn't look a gift horse in the mouth, but it didn't really matter whether or not she was chomping at the bit to go. He figured this was as good a time as any to break the news to her.

"You might as well let Jenny sleep and unpack your things. We're not going to Silver Springs."

She had started to cross the kitchen. At his words she went still. Standing less than a foot from him, she slowly turned back toward him. He flinched at the angry look in her eyes. For a sweet-looking woman, she could sure turn on a man. There was no doubt about what she was feeling. She'd never been a good liar—in fact, the night he married her she pointed out that if she had been, he never would have left Boston. Every emotion she felt reflected clearly in her expression.

"Why are we *not* going to town this time?"

"It's snowing like a son of a—gun out there."

Her mouth dropped open and she went to the window beside the pump. Standing on tiptoe, she looked out at the yard. "I wondered why it was so quiet." She sighed. "It's so beautiful."

"Yeah, beautiful. But we can't travel in it."

Her shoulders tensed just before she set her heels on the floor and rounded on him. "Why not? What's a little snow?"

"A little snow? It shows every sign of being as bad or worse than the blizzard we had the night Snowflake was foaled." The muscle in his right cheek contracted as he studied her. Why was she so all-fired eager to leave?

"This is getting ridiculous, Matt. Pack and unpack. Going back, not going back. I'm sick to death of the whole thing. I want to be done with it."

And me? Do you want to be done with me? he thought. "Maybe so, but it won't be today or any time soon. We'll just have to make the best of it."

"I can't do that anymore. If you don't want to take me, then I'll go by myself."

"That would be a stupid way to die, Eliza." He moved between her and the door as if he expected her to make a run for it. He wouldn't put anything past her after she'd jumped out of the wagon the way she had.

"I don't intend to die. I'll take every precaution. I've been through snowstorms."

"Not a Wyoming blizzard."

"Fiddlesticks. Snow is snow."

"There's no way a wagon can get through that. You can barely ride a horse. Convince me that you can make it safely to Silver Springs and I'll saddle Snowflake for you."

"Well, I'll just—"

"What about Jenny? Risking your own neck is one thing. Would you endanger her with your foolishness, too?"

"It's not—"

"Or would you leave her like her father did?"

She stared at him for several seconds, then blinked. When she lifted her gaze to his, he saw surrender. He'd chosen the right way to beat her, and it didn't bother him in the least that he'd used Jenny to keep Eliza from doing something so dangerous.

"You win, Matt. I couldn't abandon her." She turned toward the doorway and picked up her carpetbag. "I'll go unpack my things."

He moved forward and took her bag. Their fingers brushed and he saw a flicker of confusion in her eyes. "I'll carry this to your room for you."

"Don't be nice to me, Matt. It's all so much more difficult then."

"I'm not being nice. Just practicing my manners." She studied him for a minute and almost smiled.

"Well, as long as you're not being nice, I'd appreciate the help."

He picked up her carpetbag and took it down the hall to her room. The darkness in his soul battled the small ray of sunshine her presence brought him. She had enough heart and soul and spirit to . . . why, possibly, to survive this wild, untamed territory. If he knew that for sure, he would let her stay and be his wife. But he couldn't know that. She had to go where there were people, where it wasn't so isolated as at the Double C. Still, he couldn't deny that he was glad she had to stay just a little longer.

* * *

"How come you and Eliza don't sleep in the same room, Mr. Decker?" Jenny stared at Matt with big, curious eyes. "I thought married folk slept in the same bed."

The three of them had just finished supper and were by themselves since Wiley fixed his meals in the bunkhouse now. The little girl sat at the kitchen table with pencil and paper while Eliza washed up the dishes. She had decided if they were going to be cooped up for an indefinite length of time, Jenny should do some lessons. No point in wasting time.

Jenny's expression looked innocent enough, but something told Matt that she wasn't keen on book-learning and the question was her way of putting off the inevitable. Still, her straightforward inquiry made him uncomfortable. What should he tell her? How much did she know about what went on between a husband and wife in the bed they shared? And how in the hell would he ever explain to the girl that he and Eliza couldn't sleep in the same bed even though he *had* already claimed her as his own?

Eliza glanced over her shoulder. "Jenny's waiting for an answer, Matt."

He glared at her. The smile on her face might fool the child, but the gleam in her eye told him there was wicked intent behind it. She was enjoying this. She was getting even because he wouldn't let her go to town in the middle of a blizzard. She was punishing him for doing the right thing.

He stared at her. Two could play this game. "Eliza could probably explain it better than I could, Jenny. You should ask her why she sleeps in her own room."

Eliza's fingers squeezed the water from her dishrag until her knuckles turned white. She sent him a look fit to kill. That expression of hers was getting mighty familiar.

She thought for a minute, then smiled. "Actually, sweetheart," she said, looking at the child, "it was Mr. Decker's idea for me to have my own room. I'm sure he could explain it far better than I could."

Jenny's gaze bounced from Eliza back to him. "So why don't you want Eliza to sleep with you?"

Matt gritted his teeth. If he ever found this child's father, he'd throttle him within an inch of his life. "I get up very early, Jenny. I don't want to disturb her. That's why she has her own room."

The child nodded solemnly, quiet for a long time. "Then how are you ever going to make a baby?"

The plate in Eliza's hand slipped and shattered on the floor. Matt nearly choked on his coffee. When he controlled his fit of coughing, his gaze locked with Eliza's.

"We aren't going to have babies," he said.

"Why not?" Jenny pushed the straight blond bangs from her eyes and looked up at him as she waited for his answer.

"We don't want to have children," Matt said.

Eliza cleared her throat. "How many falsehoods is that now, Matt? I've lost count."

Jenny looked confused. "Falsehood? Is that something you wear to keep the snow off your hair, Eliza?"

"No, sweetheart. It's something else."

Worry replaced the bewilderment on Jenny's face. "If you don't want children, then I guess Pa was mistaken. I'll have to leave." She stood up.

Eliza gasped and started toward her. "That's not true, Jenny. Of course we want you."

Matt could have kicked himself for what he'd said. He hadn't even thought about how Jenny would take it.

He went down on one knee before the child. "You have a home here on the Double C as long as you want it." He took her small hands into his, pencil and all. "Just because Eliza and I don't want children of our own doesn't mean you have to leave."

"He's right, sweetheart."

"Eliza, are you sorry we couldn't go back to town today?" Jenny asked.

Eliza glanced from the child to Matt and he watched

the war of emotions charge across her face. He hadn't thought about it, but now that Jenny had asked he was mighty curious to hear the answer to that question himself. Was she sorry? She had been ready to take on a Wyoming blizzard to get away from him.

Eliza shook her head. "No, I'm not sorry we couldn't go to town." She sat down beside Jenny. "Let's do some more reading."

Her voice was too high and her movements were jerky, unnatural. She was lying through her teeth so Jenny would feel secure with them. Hell, how could the child feel that way when Eliza didn't feel settled? She kept packing and unpacking. Even God was against them, using the weather to keep her here. If Wiley hadn't played them false all these weeks, he would have been able to take her back before the snow. Now it was anybody's guess how long she would have to stay against her will.

He'd deliberately pushed her away and had done a better job of it than he could have hoped. If only he'd done it sooner.

Matt looked at the two of them with their heads bent over the book. The oil lamp on the table beside them illuminated straight blond hair and Eliza's brown braid shot with strands of red and gold. Her mouth curved around the tip of a pencil, and the urge to touch her was almost more than he could stand. Light kissed the soft contour of her cheek and his gut ached as he fought the urge to take her to his bed. If Jenny hadn't been there, he wasn't sure he could have resisted Eliza's pull at him.

But watching the two of them brought its own brand of pain. He pushed away the need to fill the hole inside his soul and be a part of them.

This was like being a family, and the sweetness of it tore at him. He couldn't let it go on. He glanced outside and watched the snow still falling, even harder now. And he couldn't stop it.

16

After taking care of Buck, Matt fastened the barn door. Moonlight shone on the snow in the yard, making it almost as bright as day. He could see his breath; he was cold clear through after rounding up strays all day. Near as he could figure, he'd gotten them all, except for the ones that wouldn't be found until the spring thaw. The herd seemed content in the south meadow. He couldn't wait to go home.

It had been three weeks since Jenny had been left with them. Matt went to work before they got up in the morning, and got back at sundown, but he knew from what Eliza said that the child was eager to help around the house. He saw only their nighttime routine, when supper chores were finished and Jenny's lessons completed, and Eliza sat by the fire in the kitchen mending.

Matt knew he was on dangerous ground, that he shouldn't count on this comforting domestic scene every night, but he couldn't help himself.

He stomped the snow off his boots, then went through the back door into the kitchen. The warmth made his eyes water after the cold outside. When he saw Jenny standing by herself at the stove stirring something, he had a bad feeling.

"Where's Eliza?"

Jenny glanced over her shoulder and smiled. "Evenin', Mr. Decker. Strays all rounded up?"

"Yeah. Where's Eliza?"

The child turned back to her pot. "She was real tired. Ever since she lost her breakfast this morning. Oh, horsefeathers!" she said, looking angry with herself. Her shoulders tensed, then she met his gaze. "Don't tell her I told you. She didn't want you to know."

Matt's bad feeling grew. "Where is she now?"

"Resting. She told me to wake her so she could fix supper, but she felt poorly all day. I didn't have the heart. I'm heating up last night's stew and she lets me make biscuits every night. I can do that all by myself."

"That's fine, Jenny." Matt smiled at her eagerness to please, even as anger toward her father knotted his insides. How could a man abandon his own flesh and blood? He was just glad that the child had been left with Eliza, someone who would make sure she'd be all right.

Eliza. Worry caught hold of him and held on like a cowboy breaking a stubborn bronc.

"Jenny, I'm going to look in on Eliza. Are you all right here?"

"Yes, sir."

"Good girl." He nodded with satisfaction and walked down the hall to the room across from his.

It was dark when he entered it. He smelled the scent of flowers and knew he could find his way to Eliza even without a lamp. Moonlight peeking around the curtains guided him to the oil lantern on her dresser. He lit the wick because he wanted to see for himself that she was all right. Eliza lay on the bed with the quilt over her legs. He checked the steady rise and fall of her chest and sighed with relief.

Her long hair was free of its usual braid and flowed over her pillow, tempting him to touch it. The light flickered over her features, highlighting the hollows beneath her eyes and her pale cheeks. Jenny had said she lost her breakfast. He'd noticed for the last week or so that she'd eaten hardly anything. He almost hoped she was sick with something that only lasted a day or two instead of what he feared.

Matt sat on the bed. The mattress dipped beneath his weight and Eliza stirred. Her lids fluttered before she opened her eyes. After blinking several times, she smiled her ever-ready smile. She'd never looked more beautiful to him than she did right then.

"You're home," she said, the warmth of being glad to see him in her voice.

"Yeah."

She sat up quickly. "What time is it? I didn't mean to sleep so long. I told Jenny to wake me."

"She didn't want to disturb you. What's wrong? Do you have a fever?" He put his palm to her forehead.

She shrugged away from his touch. "I'm fine, Matt. Just let me get up so I can fix dinner."

"Jenny's warming stew and biscuits. I want to know—"

"She's such a lovely child. I don't understand how her father could have just left her. Unless there was something more we don't know about. He did have that terrible cough. I'll bet he did it because he knew it was best for her. Do you think he'll really come back—"

"Have you had your monthly since you've been here?" he blurted out.

She stared at him as if he'd sprouted wings. "What are you talking about?"

"Your monthly. You know—"

She shifted self-consciously on the bed. "I know what it is. Why do you want to know?"

"For the last week or so you haven't been eating enough to keep a bird alive."

"I just haven't had much appetite—"

"Jenny said you were sick after breakfast."

"Yes, but—"

"She said you've been tired."

"A little. The rest helped."

"It's not like you to sleep in the afternoon. Jenny said—"

"Jenny said an awful lot." Irritation clipped her words.

"She's worried about you."

"There's no reason. I'm perfectly fine."

"You didn't answer my question. Have you had your monthly in the seven weeks you've been here?"

"I don't know why you're going on so about this."

"I need to know. I'm worried—"

"For pity's sake, what's wrong with you? I already told you there's no reason." She threw the quilt aside and tried to slip past him off the bed.

He took her upper arm to stop her. "Have you had it?"

"I don't think that's any of your business and I won't discuss this with you."

He tightened his grip enough to keep her there but stopped squeezing just short of hurting her. "Dammit, Eliza. This is important. Now tell me whether or not you've had—"

"No."

"You're late?"

"Yes."

"Are you always late?"

He felt her embarrassment when she wouldn't look at him or answer him. This was too important. He shook her gently. "Don't get missish on me now. I need to know."

"No. I'm never late."

"Oh, Lord."

"But I've heard things can happen. God knows I've been through a lot of changes, between traveling on the train and the stage and the fall out of the wagon."

"You jumped."

She ignored him and went on. "The sprained ankle, and what happened to Wiley. This is probably not unusual."

"What about getting sick?"

"Maybe I ate something bad."

"What did Jenny eat?"

She thought for a minute. "Same thing I did."

"Did she get sick?"

"No." She looked at her hands. "What's wrong, Matt? Why are you going on about this? I'm sure there's nothing to worry about—"

"The hell there isn't. You're pregnant, Eliza."

She raised her gaze to his then, and her eyes grew wide in shock. She'd had no idea. He didn't know why that should surprise him. Her father had kept her ignorant of what a man and woman could share in the marriage bed. What he'd shared that night with her was heaven. Finding out she was carrying a child was his hell to pay.

"But we only—I mean, it was just—"

"It only takes once."

"A baby?" He watched different emotions cross her face. Shock. Wonder. Joy. Then a glow took over and just stayed there. "I can't believe it. I'm going to have a baby?" she asked, pressing her palms over her still-flat abdomen.

"Looks like it," he said grimly.

She swung her knees toward him and pressed her palms against his chest. He glanced down and saw that when she'd slid to the side of the bed, her dress had caught and now he could see her calf and knee and a little thigh. His groin tightened at the sight and he hated himself even more. This was his worst nightmare come true and he still wanted her. If she was smart, she'd run far and fast away from him. Her eyes glowed with happiness and she was looking at him as if he was some kind of hero. He couldn't be that for her—not ever again.

"Oh, my. I don't know what to say. I had no idea. I was sure it was some sort of sickness. This is—"

"The worst possible thing that could have happened."

"I thought you wanted a baby."

"I did. I do. Just not—"

"Just not with me." Hurt instantly gathered in her eyes.

He wanted to explain, but he just didn't know how to make her understand. "Eliza, let me try—"

"No." She pulled out of his hold and slid off the bed. "I'm sick of trying. You've made no secret of the fact that you don't want me here, you can't wait to be rid of me, you can't get over what happened in Boston eight years ago."

"Boston? You mean what you told your father?"

"Yes. You can't forgive me for it."

"That's not true. Everything I've done has been for you,"

She held up her hands. "Hold it right there, Matthew James Decker. Don't you dare blame this on me."

"I'm not—"

"Yes, you are. But I don't care what you think. I'm happy about this baby. When it's safe to go back to Silver Springs, I'm taking Jenny and we'll make a life in town. I'll have my baby and raise both children by myself." She clenched her hands into fists as her whole body shook with anger. Her eyes spat fire and she practically hissed the last words at him.

"I've only ever cared about keeping you from harm, Eliza."

"Then you should have let me go back to town when I jumped out of the wagon. I've come to more harm at your hands than I ever would have there." She turned away and left the room.

He wanted to take her in his arms and soothe her. He wanted to hold her and tell her everything would be all right. But he couldn't. He wanted to tell her there was no reason to go back to town now. Nothing could protect her from what lay ahead of her. She was right. He'd harmed her in the worst possible way.

Eliza tried to remain calm as she walked through the kitchen and out the back door. She didn't want to upset Jenny and until she could get herself under control, she knew she'd do just that.

She didn't realize where she was headed until she

stopped in front of the bunkhouse. By the time she got there, she was shaking from cold, not anger.

She knocked once as hard as she could.

"Come in."

She opened the door and marched inside. With hands on her hips, she stood and glared at Wiley. "I'm going to have a baby and it's all your fault."

He set the pistol he was cleaning on the table. "Somethin' tells me yore startin' someplace in the middle of what's got you riled. Take it easy. We'll sort this out. First off, I ain't never laid a hand on you, so there must be somethin' else I'm accountable for."

Wiley's expression never changed, but that was the most sentences Eliza had ever heard him string together. She must have upset him.

"If you hadn't played possum, I wouldn't be having a baby."

"That there makes it all 'bout as clear as mud. How do you know you're in the family way?"

"Matt told me."

"How did he know?"

"Jenny told him I lost my breakfast."

"It's all getting clearer by the minute." He stood up, walked around the table, and pulled out a chair. "Sit down, Eliza."

She shook her head. "I don't want—"

"Sit!"

She blinked once, then did as he ordered.

"Now then. Tell me what's goin' on, startin' at the beginning. And I already know about the baby part. Why are you all fired up?"

"You told me Matt wants a child."

"That's the truth." He rolled his eyes and sighed deeply.

"He told me the same thing just a few minutes ago."

"Then I don't get—"

"But he said having a baby with me is the worst possible thing that could happen."

"Do tell?"

"And it's all your fault. If you hadn't pretended to be sick, I'd have gone back to Silver Springs before I—That is, before Matt—I mean, before we—"

"What you're saying is you and Matt bedded down together. I thought as much." He grinned at her like a doting uncle.

Her cheeks burned, but she couldn't deny the truth of his words. "Stop laughing at me."

"Yes, ma'am." But his expression never changed.

"What are you smiling about?"

"Matthew's gonna be a father."

"No, he's not."

His gray-and-black brows shot up. "You're not sayin'—"

"No! He's the only man I've ever—Never mind. What I'm saying is he doesn't want this baby because it's mine."

"Hold it right there, missy. You're wrong about that."

"He came right out and told me—"

"Don't believe everything he says. He wants a baby, all right. That's why he wanted a mail-order bride in the first place."

"Then why—"

"You're not gonna get it less'n I spell it out, are ya?" He leaned his elbows on the table and met her gaze. "He wanted to marry a stranger so he wouldn't care about her. He's tryin' so hard to get you off the Double C, I reckon he cares about you somethin' fierce."

"That doesn't make any sense."

"You're tellin' me," he said, scratching his head. "Jehoshaphat."

"Let me see if I understand this. Matt's trying to get rid of me because he *does* have feelings for me and he doesn't want to?"

"That's the way I see it. He knew straight off he was in trouble when he found out who you were. He's had ties to you for a lot of years and that scared him more than a little."

"Then why didn't he let me stay in town when I wanted to?"

"'Cause that's not his way. He feels responsible for you and I got the feelin' it ain't just 'cause his ma sent you here."

"He saved my life once."

He nodded as if that explained everything. "So, when he found out who he'd married, he already had feelin's for you. That like to scared the sh—I mean the stuffing out of him."

"So you played sick hoping to keep us together long enough for him to come to his senses?"

"Now you're gettin' it, Missy."

"But don't you see? When Carrie died, she took Matt's heart to the grave with her. He'll never love me."

"He already loves you. How do you feel about him?"

"What?" His words took her by surprise and her head snapped up as she met his gaze to see if he was joking. She could tell he wasn't. "He doesn't love me."

"Let's leave that question for now. What about you?"

"I'm so angry at him—"

"That's not what I asked. You knew who you were hitchin' up to and you still came all the way from Boston. Now I want to know why. Do you love him?"

She stared at the old man and the mud cleared and she knew he was right, at least about her. "Yes. I love him. I've always loved him. Since I was twelve years old and he saved me from that stampeding horse." Good Lord, but it felt good to say that out loud.

"Thought so."

Then her exhilaration plummeted. "Don't look so pleased. It just makes everything worse. He doesn't want me or this baby."

"Wrong again, Eliza. He's afraid."

She snorted. "Matt's not afraid of anything."

"Yeah, he is. He's afraid of losin' you."

"So he won't even try to make this marriage work? He keeps pushing me away."

He nodded.

"That's just about the dumbest thing I ever heard."

"Never said he was the smartest fella in Wyoming."

"So you think I should keep trying to get through to him?"

"If you love him like you say? Yes, ma'am, I surely do. You can't give up. And now ya got that young 'un to consider. Matthew's hardheaded, but awfully dang softhearted. He'll want t'be a part of his son's life."

"You think it's a boy?" She smiled as she rested her palm over her stomach.

"Yes'm, I do."

She nodded slowly. "I'll think about what you had to say."

"Can't ask for more than that." He grinned. "You still mad at me?"

She thought for a minute, then shook her head. "You were only trying to help, like Matt's mother. Did the two of you cook this up together?"

"No, ma'am."

"You decided all on your own to play sick and keep me here?"

"Yes, ma'am."

"You are a puzzle, Mr. Powell."

He shook his head. "I just care about Matthew, like he was my own son. If he loses you, he'll lose the best thing he ever had."

"What about Carrie?" She had to know. "He already lost the best thing in his life."

"He loved her. No question about that." He rubbed his whiskered chin. "But he buried his feelings for her long before he bedded down with you. Else he never woulda done it."

She wasn't so sure. But she had her child to think about and plan for. And Jenny, too. Maybe Wiley was right and Matt cared for her a little. If he did, Eliza only had one choice. She had to stay. Then she could be his bride and make a happy, loving home for all of them.

17

Matt poured himself a cup of coffee and sat down at the kitchen table with Eliza and Jenny. It had been a week since he'd found out about Eliza's condition. He felt as if he was walking around in the middle of a dark cloud, day and night. The bad dreams had come back worse than ever.

He had tried to get Eliza to stay in bed, but since he wouldn't tell her why he wanted her to, she would have none of it. Jenny had given him funny looks, since he'd been spending more time in the house with the two of them. Eliza had tried to get him to go about his work, but he couldn't. If someone needed to ride out and check on the herd, he sent Wiley.

Eliza's day started with cleaning up breakfast things and she had even insisted if he was going to be underfoot, he could help, too. Jenny had giggled when Eliza had tied an apron around him that hardly covered his front.

After kitchen chores, Eliza and Jenny would bend their heads over primers and paper. The child was bright but restless. Matt had the feeling she'd rather be outside running around than sitting in one place. But Eliza insisted morning light was best for her eyes so that was when they did lessons. Only when the girl absolutely couldn't sit still did Eliza send her out to use up some energy. More often than not, they finished up after supper.

"Are you a teacher, Eliza?" Jenny asked.

Eliza sent the child a look that said she knew what she was up to. "I've already told you I went to school to get my credential."

That was the first Matt had heard of it.

"What about you, Mr. Decker?" Jenny asked Matt.

"I'm not a teacher." He suspected she was trying to distract both of them from the lesson.

He saw the smile in Eliza's eyes when she looked at him. She knew it, too. Jenny fiddled with the paper spread out in front of her.

"How did you happen to bring all these school things with you all the way from Boston?" Jenny asked.

Matt knew from the little girl's tone that she wished they had been lost on the train or stolen by stagecoach robbers or fallen into Indian hands. He was more curious about why Eliza never mentioned teaching when she lived in Boston. Had she lost her job when she'd landed in jail after the rally?

Eliza brushed the straight bangs from Jenny's eyes. "I brought them with me because I wanted to have children and I knew they'd need learning. So I packed all this in my trunk."

"Didn't you have linens or dishes or other stuff that isn't something to read or write on to put in your hope chest?"

"No." Eliza laughed. She glanced at Matt and he couldn't help grinning back.

"Did you teach in Boston?" he asked.

She shook her head. "My father thought it best for me to stay at home and take care of the house."

Matt saw the shadows that chased away the light in her eyes. He'd known her father was a stern disciplinarian, but he hadn't been aware of how domineering he was until now. Matt would never understand the man turning his back on her because she'd decided to come to Wyoming to marry him, but he didn't doubt that Reverend Jones meant exactly what he'd said. She could never go back to Boston, at least not to her father. She had given up an awful lot to marry him. His heart caught. She'd given up everything.

Jenny heaved a huge sigh. "Even though you're a teacher, I bet you'd rather ride Snowflake than do lessons. Right, Eliza?"

Eliza's mouth twitched for a second and she caught the corner between her teeth to keep from laughing. But Matt saw. Her gaiety glowed like a sky full of twinkling stars.

"Yes, I'd rather ride Snowflake. But this is important, too. One more page, sweetheart. Then you can take a break and finish up after supper. Wiley said something about taking you for a ride to gather pinecones."

"Really?"

Eliza nodded. "You finish this first. Then you can take the rest of the day to play with Mr. Powell."

Jenny nodded and grinned, then bent over her book when Eliza pointed to it. As the little girl painstakingly read each word out loud, Eliza picked up a pencil and absently stuck the end in her mouth. From time to time she would patiently correct a word and her sweet voice washed over Matt. The house was warm and cozy, just from her presence, and he wasn't anxious to go outside when several feet of snow still covered the ground.

The fullness of her lips and her cheerful patience pulled at a core of tenderness within him that had been untouched for a long time. It was like something had broken apart inside him and the pain was bittersweet.

The last time he'd tasted her lips was right here in this room before a blazing fire. He recalled the smell of liniment, the scent of flowers floating from Eliza's skin, and the satin feel of her flesh beneath his hands. He shifted uncomfortably in the chair.

Ever since the night he'd bedded Eliza, he hadn't been able to get her out of his mind. she was spunky and spirited and had proven more than once that she had the grit she needed to take on Wyoming Territory. But even her steel backbone and stubborn streak wouldn't necessarily save her from the child that grew in her womb. The thought chilled him in places the cold outside couldn't reach.

Jenny slammed her book shut. "I'm done."

"You're finished," Eliza corrected her. "You were done when God made you."

"I thought Ma and Pa made me," she said.

Matt groaned inwardly. This child seemed unnaturally preoccupied with babies.

"That was just a figure of speech." Eliza smiled, then stood and stretched muscles that were cramped from sitting in one place too long.

Matt remembered a restless girl not much older than Jenny who'd had trouble sitting still for lessons. Eliza had changed in more ways than one. Her calico dress pulled across her soft, womanly bosom, and he recalled how perfectly her breasts had fit into the palms of his hands.

He was suddenly hot all over and the thought of all that snow outside seemed mighty appealing. He needed to find something to do away from the house—but not too far away and just for a little while.

"I think I'll go to the tack room," he said.

Jenny jumped up. "I want to go find Wiley."

"Yes, but put on your coat and hat."

"I know, and my mittens. You say that every time I go out."

Eliza tapped Jenny's nose. "That's because I don't want you to catch your death. It's very cold out there."

"Yes'm." Jenny pulled all her warm clothes from the pegs by the door and one by one put them on. Then she was gone.

Matt followed her lead and pulled on his sheepskin jacket. He went out the door and headed for the barn.

Eliza wandered around the kitchen until the restlessness was too much. She'd felt a little peaked that morning and hadn't been able to shake the fluttery sensation in her stomach. Maybe some fresh air would help. She grabbed her shawl and a basket for gathering eggs and went out the door after the other two.

A cold, crisp breeze slammed her in the face as she stepped off the back porch. Everything was covered with white, but the sky was cloudless and as blue as Matt's eyes. Her breath caught as a vision of him came to her.

"'Bye, Eliza." Jenny waved to her from Snowflake's back as she rode by.

"'Bye, missy." Wiley lifted a hand. "We're not goin' far. But don't you fret if we're not back till supper. I'll take good care of her."

"I know you will," Eliza said, waving.

She stood there and looked at the land and mountains in the distance. Wyoming had been beautiful before, but covered with snow it was breathtaking. Several storms had added to the snow accumulation since the day Matt had told her the bad weather would prevent her from going back to town for a while. The last four weeks had flown and, with every day that passed, she grew more attached to Jenny and Matt. The new baby would make everything perfect.

Matt had stopped to say good-bye to Wiley and Jenny, and watch them ride away. Now he trudged through the snow to the barn.

Her gaze went from the soft powder at her feet to his wide shoulders. She grinned as she thought what a very large target he was. Stooping down, she gathered a handful of snow and formed it into a ball about the size of her palm. Then she hurried after him until she was within striking distance. After drawing her arm back, she let the snowball fly. With a healthy splat, it landed right at his collar. She nodded with satisfaction, hoping some of the cold would trickle down his neck.

He stopped and turned slowly with a frown on his face. "It's too cold out here for you."

He was beginning to get on her nerves with all this serious protectiveness. "You're just afraid I'll show you up the way I used to."

"Only because you cheated and had help."

"I don't have anyone with me now," she said.

A slow half smile tugged at the corner of his mouth and Eliza forgot all about being cold.

"You shouldn't have started this," he said.

"Why not?" She put a hand on her hip.

He quickly bent and grabbed a handful of snow. "Because I plan to finish it real quick and take you back inside."

"Unless your aim has improved, I won't be going inside any time soon."

Eliza stood her ground rather than turn her back on him; she wanted to see the snowball coming. When it did, she ducked to the side.

"You missed me," she taunted. "You're out of practice, Matt. You never used to miss."

He picked up more snow and Eliza did the same, molding it between her hands into the right shape. Matt moved closer, like a predator stalking his prey. A deadly gleam in his sky blue eyes told her he wouldn't stop until he was avenged. She backed up several steps, but he kept coming.

"Don't you want to surrender now?" she asked.

"Why? Did you put rocks inside the way you did last time?" he asked, pointing to the snow in her hand.

"That wasn't my idea."

"Who threw it?"

She grinned. "They made me. I had the strongest arm."

He shook his head and snow flew from his hair. "Your aim is still pretty good."

"Are you sure you don't want to give up?" she asked, hefting her snowball.

He shook his head. "*You* might want to consider it

though." He was three strides away and took a threatening step forward, never taking his gaze from hers.

She pulled her arm back and let the snow fly. With cat-like quickness, he moved to the side and the snow flew harmlessly by him.

He grinned, a smile that sent shivers down her back. Not because she was afraid of him. And not because she was cold. She wanted him.

Just when she thought she had her feelings for him tucked away in a place where they couldn't hurt her, he'd look at her—or smile as he was doing now—and melt her insides like snow in a warm kitchen. She just couldn't stand it.

She turned away and tried to run, but her feet sank in the drifts. A pile of snow hit her right between the shoulder blades. She shook off her heavy shawl and turned.

"Now you're in trouble," she said.

He merely smiled and lifted one brow. His look made her stomach all quivery and that made her mad. Ignoring the cold that made her hands ache, she dropped to her knees and started scooping snow and hurling it at him as fast as she could. Just as quickly, he would toss it back. Realizing she was getting the worst of it, she stood up and started laughing.

"I know when I'm licked," she said. "I think I'll go gather my eggs now."

"Go on back to the house. I'll gather them for you," he said, picking up the basket she'd dropped. "Now that I've proven who is the superior snowball fighter." He turned away then.

Big mistake, Eliza thought. He was just a step away. She gathered enough snow to hold in two hands and shovel-tossed it at his back. This time she knew some went down inside his jacket since he lifted his shoulders and pulled at his collar.

He turned slowly. "That was low, Eliza." There was a wickedness in his expression. "You really did it that time."

He moved toward her and lifted a handful of snow. He

could hold more snow in one of his hands than she could hold in both of hers. There was a time to fight and a time to run. This was definitely the time to run. She squealed once and whirled around. The deep snow sucked at the shoes that were too big for her and she couldn't move fast enough. He caught her in one stride and grabbed her around the waist.

The movement threw both of them off balance and they toppled to the ground. He managed to turn so that his back hit the snow first and she fell on top of him. She was breathing hard from the exertion. Matt shifted to the side and then she had her back in the snow, with him rubbing more of it in her face.

She started laughing and tried to still his hand. He was far too strong. "Matt! Stop!"

He grinned down at her, his teeth white against the brown, gold, and red lights of his beard. "You started this when you broke the truce. I'm gonna finish it."

He picked up more snow. She put up a hand to block him. "Mercy."

Matt stopped laughing as he stared down at her. On his side, he had one arm beneath her, cushioning her back from the cold. The icy wet snow slipped from his other hand as he studied her rosy cheeks and bright happy face. Her eyes sparkled and the breath caught in his chest. Before he could stop himself, he lowered his mouth to hers.

Her lips were cold against his own and her dress was wet. But where his jacket was open, their chests touched and the skin beneath the soaked material burned. Slowly he moved his mouth over hers, savoring the softness, memorizing the texture, pulling her heat into himself, melting his cold core.

Her warm, sweet breath fanned his face as it grew faster, shallower, a perfect match for his own. Clouds of white puffed up between them. She nestled closer to him and he groaned as the small, seductive movement sent the blood roaring through his veins.

"I'm the one who needs mercy," he whispered. But he knew no one could save him.

Somewhere between the kitchen and the snowball fight, all his good intentions had gone to hell.

He sat up and pulled her with him. All he wanted was to carry her into the house, to his bed, and love her until they were warm and breathless from it. He needed to love her until he could forget all the pain that was to come.

She started to shiver as a frigid breeze blew over her wet clothes. He remembered Eliza telling Jenny to wear warm things so she wouldn't catch her death. Dread cut through him. How could he have been so stupid?

"You've got to get out of those wet things," he said. He jumped up quickly and held a hand down to her. She took it and he noticed her bare hands were blotchy red from the cold. Damn. He knew better than this, but her fun-loving nature and ready smile had sent his common sense to hell.

Matt grabbed her arm and tried to move her forward toward the house. She stumbled and he helped her stand. Shivers shook her from head to toe. He quickly lifted her into his arms.

"For goodness' sake, Matt. Put me down. I can walk to the house."

He ignored her and carried her onto the porch and inside the warm kitchen.

He set her down before the hearth. When she started to walk toward her room, he stopped her. "Stay here by the fire." Her hands looked stiff and shaky with cold. "I'm going to help you out of your clothes, but first let me get a blanket to wrap around you."

"Good heavens," she said. "What's gotten into you? You're t-treating me like a china doll. I won't b-break."

Brave words, but he heard her teeth chattering. "You're going to have a baby. That snowball fight was a stupid thing to do."

"I'm not an invalid, M-Matt."

"Quit arguing. Stay there while I get a blanket."

He quickly shrugged his jacket off, then went to her room and grabbed the quilt from her bed. He hurried back to the kitchen. In spite of her protests, she had stayed where he'd left her, still shivering.

He pulled the rocker close to the fireplace and sat her down to take off her shoes and stockings. Then he stood her up and came up behind her to unfasten the buttons on her dress. It was sopping wet. His own hands were slow from the cold and he cursed his own stupidity. Out here, far from town and doctors, a chill could be deadly, especially in her condition. It didn't matter that she had started it, or that the snow glistening in her thick dark lashes and clinging to her clothes had made him think of other things. He should have known better.

"I'll have you warm in no time, Eliza."

"I feel b-better already," she said, trying to smile through chattering teeth.

She was really something. He was kicking himself from here to kingdom come and she was downright cheerful about the whole thing. But that was because she couldn't see into the future like he could.

Matt pushed her dress down and helped her step out of it. The wet snow had soaked through to her petticoat, so he untied it and lifted it over her head. Her chemise and pantalettes were wet, too, and he knew he couldn't take any chances. Quickly he stripped her down to nothing. He couldn't help seeing and responding to her beautiful body, but he tried not to think about that as he dragged the blanket around her.

He put another log on the fire and poked the embers into life until it was crackling with warmth. He made sure the rocker was close to it, but not so she'd be burned. "Sit down, Eliza."

With stiff movements, she obeyed. He went down on one knee in front of her, then picked up her feet and placed them on his thigh and put his hands over them. He started to massage some warmth back into them. When he was satisfied that the blood was circulating heat there, he returned his attention to her face. Her cheeks were pink, her hair a mass of tangled silk coming loose from her braid, her mouth full and soft. He stood up and backed away before he could lose control and kiss her.

"Wh-where are y-you going?"

"To change into dry things."

When he came back, she was still shivering and he knew he had to hold her to warm her up. It was his own fault for not walking away when she threw that first goddamn snowball. He took her upper arms and stood her up.

"Wh-what now? I f-feel much better."

"We have to share our body heat. It's the only way to get you warm fast."

He sat down and tugged her onto his lap. She pulled the blanket tight and curled against his chest as trustingly as a child, as if she had complete faith in him. Tightness clutched at his throat. Didn't she see that believing in him was a mistake? He hadn't been able to take care of Carrie. What if he couldn't do anything to save Eliza?

He wrapped his arms around her and slowly her trembling subsided. She felt so good curled in his arms. He wished they could stay that way forever.

She lifted her cheek from his chest and looked at him with soft, heavy-lidded eyes. "Matt?" Her voice was hardly more than a whisper and felt like a caress.

"What?"

"Kiss me."

He blinked. "What?"

"I want you to kiss me. I told you I like it when you do. The way you did outside in the snow." She snuggled close. "Or, better yet, the way you did the last time we were alone in this room. Make me feel that way again."

How could he not kiss her? He wanted to give her anything that would make her happy. Besides, it was killing him to have her this close and not taste her lips.

He lowered his mouth to hers and the softness was so

wonderful it made his chest hurt. Forever wouldn't be long enough to kiss her.

She pulled her mouth from his and drew in a ragged breath.

"Matt, do you remember all the things you showed me? How to partake and how to pleasure? And how to submit?" she asked in a whisper. When he slowly nodded, she continued, "Let me submit again."

"No!"

Anger surged through him. He was furious at her for making him feel again. He didn't want to feel anything, and he'd been running from it since he'd found out who he married. Eliza Jones was the only woman on earth who could have cracked the wall he'd built around his heart. Her innocent passion was a wonderful gift and a terrible curse. Her tenderness was like salt water washing over the wound festering inside him. The thought of life without her loomed ahead of him like a never-ending void.

He felt her surprise at the force of his answer and tried to gentle his tone. "I don't think that would—"

"I think," she said with her mouth against his neck, "that you think," she said after she stopped nibbling his earlobe, "far too much."

She wiggled her little butt in his lap and he couldn't stop his groan of pleasure.

"We can't." He leaned his head back to give her more freedom. "The baby."

"We won't hurt the baby. What have you got to lose?"

You. The thought sucked the air from his lungs and he held his breath as long as he could. If he could hold it forever, maybe he'd never have to feel the pain.

But she was right. The damage was already done. Why shouldn't he give her what she wanted? Anything she wanted. He shared her need. He would give her so much pleasure; he would make everything up to her. He would make memories to carry him through the winters without her.

"Are you sure about this, Eliza?" He stared into green eyes smoky with desire and had his answer.

He stood with her in his arms and quickly carried her to his room and kicked the door shut behind them. In three strides, he was beside the bed, where he gently set her on the mattress. The quilt fell away, baring the beauty of her body to his starving sight. He drank in the grace of her feminine curves, her perfect breasts, her slender waist. Suddenly he knew he would die unless he could bury himself inside her and feel her legs wrapped around him.

When she held her arms out to him, he knew there was no longer a choice. He had to have her. Quickly he shed his clothes. He joined her on the bed. She encircled his neck with her arms and fervently clutched him against her. She embraced him the way she did everything in life, eagerly and without restraint. He soon grew rigid with need.

"Matt?" she whispered as she snuggled closer to him.

"What?"

Her hand slid over his shoulder, across his chest, and down his side, stopping at his waist. "I want to touch you."

He sucked in his breath.

"That's considered partaking, isn't it?" she asked.

"Oh, yeah. I just didn't think you'd want—"

"I do."

He hadn't expected that. But it was typical of Eliza. Running when she'd just learned to walk, singing when she'd just learned to talk. Barely overcoming her fear of horses before asking to ride. She threw herself whole-heartedly into whatever she wanted. He thanked God that she wanted him. He wanted her so much he ached, and he prayed for the patience to make this perfect for her.

When he took her hand, his own shook as he guided hers down. Her cool fingers closed around him and his eyes slipped shut as he savored the pleasure of her touch.

"You're so smooth and—full," she said, wonder mixing with shyness in her voice.

"Because I want you." Huskiness laced his own words.

"Do you?"

"Lord, yes."

"I'm ready to submit any time," she said a little breathlessly.

"Let me make sure."

He moved his hand to cup her breast and smiled when her nipple tightened at the barest touch of his thumb. Sliding further down, he spread the lips hiding her feminine secrets and slipped his finger inside her. Moist warmth enfolded him and he groaned as his groin throbbed painfully in response.

"You're ready."

"I told you."

She parted her legs for him and he smiled. "Not so fast."

"Why?"

"Because there's more I intend to show you."

He kissed her breast as his finger primed her for his entry. At the same time, he rubbed his thumb over her nub.

She gasped. "Matt, what are you do—"

He moved faster and heard her breathing grow rapid and shallow. She arched against his hand and her hips took up an instinctive rhythm. When she tensed, he moved his hand faster. She tightened around him and buried her forehead against his chest as shudders of pleasure began within her. When the shivers from her release subsided, she smiled contentedly.

She looked at him. "I didn't have any idea."

"I know."

"Matt?"

"What?"

"Is it wicked to do this in the middle of the afternoon?"

A smile turned up the corners of his mouth just before his deep laugh filled the room.

She started to pull out of his arms. "I didn't mean to be funny."

"I know. I'm sorry." He swallowed the last chuckle. "It's just that I never know what to expect from you." He brushed the hair from her face, then buried his fingers in the silky strands. "It's never wicked to do this."

She smiled. "Good. Because I want to submit again. Women have urges, you know."

"I do now. I need you so much it hurts."

Eliza had never been so happy in her life. The gladness filled her up until she thought she'd burst from it. He hadn't come right out and said he loved her, but needing her was about as close as he could get. Wasn't it?

"I need you, too, Matt."

He kissed her as he gently spread her legs. When he knelt between them and poised himself to enter her, Eliza lifted her hips. She eagerly waited to feel inside her the powerful length of him that she'd held in her hand. Never to have known this exquisite joy in the arms of the man she loved was just about the saddest thing she could imagine. Thank God she hadn't been turned away.

With one push he slid inside her and she welcomed him. She met his thrusts until his heat became her own, until she rose with him to the peak of ecstasy. Together, they slipped down the other side.

As she lay in his arms, the need rose in her to put her emotions into words. She couldn't hold it back any more than she could have stopped an avalanche of snow from the top of the Laramie Mountains.

"I love you, Matt."

Her whisper hung between them, coming to life and charging the air.

He tensed, then rolled away from her without responding to her confession. She knew he'd heard it. A feeling of uneasiness swept over her, but she told herself he was tired, too tired to say anything. Lord knows she didn't have any strength left in her limbs.

Eliza convinced herself it was all right that he didn't say what she wanted to hear. Actions spoke louder than words. And everything he'd done had told her that he loved her, too.

18

"*Do you want more coffee, Matt?*" Eliza asked as they finished supper later.

"I wouldn't mind a little more." Wiley held out his cup. "It was mighty cold out there today. Right, little missy?"

Jenny nodded and tried to find her mouth with her fork at the same time. The peas rolled off and plopped in her mashed potatoes. "Did you see all the pinecones we found, Eliza?"

"I certainly did. We can burn some of them in the fire and the pine scent will go all through the house," she said. "You've had quite a day." She met Matt's gaze and smiled, a secret little smile that told him she was thinking about spending the afternoon in his bed. Her expression said she was a satisfied woman and it wouldn't take much coaxing to get her to do the same things that night.

She grinned at Wiley. "I'd say you both deserve another cup of coffee," she said, pushing her chair back.

"Don't get up!" Matt said. Three pairs of eyes turned in his direction to stare at him. "I mean, I can get it."

He stood up and walked over to the iron stove and

grabbed the handle on the coffeepot. The metal burned him instantly and he dropped it. "Damnation!" he swore, shaking his hand.

Eliza jumped up and pumped water into a bowl, then brought it to him. She plunged his hand in the ice-cold liquid. He sucked in his breath and tried to pull it out.

"Leave it in there," she said firmly.

"My fingers are starting to ache."

"It's no more than you deserve for lifting it barehanded."

She lifted his wrist from the bowl and turned his palm up, holding it in both of her hands. The smell of baking bread and flowers drifted from her skin and mixed with the scent of the love they had shared that afternoon.

Love.

She had told him she loved him. The pain twisted in him again. Why had she said it now, when he might lose her? It changed everything.

"Matt, are you listening to me? You were gathering enough wool to make us all sweaters for the winter."

He blinked and looked down into her green eyes. A cloud blocked their usual sparkle. He tried to put aside his dark thoughts.

"I'm sorry. What did you say?"

"I said, is your hand hurting now?"

He nodded. "Like the devil."

She traced the red mark between his thumb and index finger, then bent her head and kissed it, the way she did when Jenny hurt herself.

Eliza glanced up at him while still cradling his big hand between her two small ones. "Put it back in the water. When your fingers ache from cold, take it out until you feel it burning. Keep doing that until you can leave it out of the water without pain." There was a mischievous twinkle in her eyes. "Whatever would you do without me, Matt?"

"That there's a good question." Wiley's brows pulled

together. "The roads are passable since after that last storm. Haven't heard you say nothin' about takin' Eliza and Jenny back to Silver Springs."

Matt sat down at the table and jammed his hand in the water. "No need now."

Jenny clapped her hands together. "Ya mean we get to stay here with you and Wiley?" She turned her big blue eyes and her sweet smile on Matt.

"Would you like that, Jenny?" he asked.

"More than anything."

He studied the little girl sitting to his right, and with his uninjured, dry hand, he tapped her freckled, turned-up nose. She reminded him of Eliza as a girl. "You know, Jenny, you have a home here on the Double C always. No matter what happens, we want you to stay. Right, Wiley?"

Eliza refilled his coffee cup and shot him a puzzled look.

"Since when do I get a say-so about what goes on around here?" the old man asked.

Matt ignored him and looked at Jenny. "That means he wants you to stay as much as I do."

"Even if my pa comes back, Mr. Decker?" she asked.

"If he comes back, it's up to you."

Jenny jumped up from her chair and threw her arms around Matt's neck and buried her cheek against his shoulder. He couldn't deny his tender feelings for this child. As he patted her back, he heard sniffling on his left and looked over in time to see Wiley Powell brush a knuckle beneath his nose.

"That's about the sweetest thing I ever did hear," he said.

"You goin' soft on me, old man?"

"Nope. It's this dang cold weather. Makes my nose run."

"Mine, too," Eliza said, brushing her thumbs across her moist eyes.

Jenny pulled away from Matt and went to Eliza, who was standing by the stove. She hugged her around the waist, then looked up. "Before I help with chores, is it all right if I go tell Snowflake we get to stay?"

"Of course, sweetheart."

Wiley took a last swallow of his coffee and stood up. "I b'lieve I'll go with her."

"You're trying to get out of chores, too," Eliza said, a teasing glint in her eyes.

"Dang. I'd hate to come up against you in a poker game."

"You two run along. I guess I'll have to clean this up alone since Matt already has his excuse with that burned hand." She put her hands on her hips. "You bundle up now."

"We will, Eliza," Jenny said as she grabbed her coat from the peg and followed Wiley out the door.

Matt stood up, took his hand out of the water, and wiped it on his napkin. The need to escape was dragging him under. This would never work. He couldn't stay in this house with her and make believe day after day that everything was all right. Sooner or later, Eliza would see through him and he'd have to tell her about his fears for her. He couldn't do it.

Without a word, he went down the hall to his room. The sight of his tangled sheets and twisted blankets brought its own brand of pain. When he pulled his clothes out of his dresser and threw them on the bed, the faint fragrance of Eliza drifted to him. Could he ever again sit in a field of wildflowers and not think of her? He damn well intended to try, and he planned to start now. He was getting the hell out of this house.

"What are you doing, Matt?"

He turned to see her standing in the doorway. "Moving into the bunkhouse."

"Why? After what you just said . . ." It was a whisper, but he winced as if she'd screamed. "After this afternoon . . . Well, I thought—"

"I won't share a bed with you."

"I'm not asking to share your bed." The words were clear, but the hurt in them told him that was exactly what she wanted. She had told him she loved him. "Why are you moving out of the house, Matt?"

"It's better that way. For both of us."

She clasped her trembling hands together, then looked up at him and swallowed. "All right. I guess I have to accept the fact that you don't want *me*. But what about the baby?"

"I don't want the baby either." He couldn't let himself want the baby.

Her eyes widened and she backed up as if he'd struck her. Then she turned away and started to leave the room.

She usually fought tooth and nail for what she wanted; he'd been prepared for that. He hadn't been ready for her to walk away without a word.

"Eliza?"

She turned back. "What?"

"Don't you have anything to say?"

"You don't want to hear it."

"Tell me anyway."

She dragged air into her lungs, then met his gaze. Her eyes were so full of hurt and disillusionment, he almost went to her and pulled her into his arms. He almost told her he was a fool and that it was all a mistake. But he couldn't.

"You're not the man I always thought you were." She stopped and bit the corner of her lip as she stared at the ceiling for several moments. "I've been so wrong about you all these years." Her voice cracked then, and she reached out to him in a completely helpless gesture. When he stood his ground, she fled the room.

Matt felt as if she'd plunged a knife in his gut. If he just held still, maybe he wouldn't bleed or feel more pain. Everything had been so much easier before Eliza had made him feel again. He hadn't known it would hurt so much to stop being her hero.

*   *   *

"I have to go away, Jenny." In the guest room, Eliza tucked the little girl in bed. She pulled the thick quilt up to the child's neck and brushed the stick-straight blond hair from her forehead.

Jenny caught her hand and held it in a surprisingly strong grip. "Why are you going away? Mr. Decker said we have a home here as long as we want it."

"He said *you* do, love. I can't stay."

"I don't understand." Tears filled the blue eyes. "I want to be with you."

Eliza just couldn't stay there any longer with a man who didn't want her. She knew she couldn't leave until morning and had agonized whether to tell Jenny at bedtime or not to say anything at all. But she couldn't leave without explaining. The poor thing had been through so much and she wanted her to know they wouldn't be separated long.

"It's all very complicated, but all you have to think about is that we'll be together soon. I'm going to Silver Springs and when I get settled there, I'll send for you."

"But I want to stay with Mr. Decker, too. He wants us here. I know he does."

"He doesn't want me here. If you'd be happier here—"

Jenny sat up and threw her arms around Eliza's neck. She felt the child's warm, wet tears soak through her high-necked cotton blouse. "I thought I finally had a ma *and* a pa," she whispered between sobs.

Eliza's already chipped heart broke completely and shattered into pieces. Hot tears burned her own eyes. Was it wrong to run?

She wasn't sure. She only knew that since Matt said he didn't want her or her baby, there would never be anything for her on the Double C. She'd been fighting a war she never had any hope of winning. Matt would never get over losing Carrie.

Eliza knew he could never love her.

So her mind was made up. Wiley had said the roads were passable. She had to get away before another storm trapped her there with the man who had moved out of the house because he couldn't stand the sight of her.

Jenny's sobs shook her slender little body, and Eliza brushed away the tears that had started to trickle down the child's cheeks.

"Don't cry, love. It's just for a little while. I'm going to go to Mrs. Buchanan's boardinghouse and I'm certain she'll help me."

Jenny blinked at her. "Mrs. Buchanan's?"

Eliza nodded. "Maybe she'll have a room for us. Would you like that?"

The corner of Jenny's mouth lifted a little. "I would. But I don't think Walter, Jr., likes me very much."

"Why do you say that?"

"I followed him around a lot when Pa and I stayed there after Mr. Decker gave me that money. He called me a pain in the—"

"Mr. Decker called you that?" Eliza couldn't help being shocked.

"No. Walter, Jr."

"He used that kind of language to you?"

"Yes'm. But—"

"There's no excuse for that. I'll talk to Mrs. Buchanan and Walter, and I promise you he won't speak to you that way ever again."

"What if Mrs. Buchanan won't let us stay with her after you talk to her?"

Eliza tugged Jenny close and pressed the girl's cheek to her chest. "We'll find somewhere else. But I *will* take care of you. Do you believe me?"

Jenny pulled out of her embrace and looked up solemnly. She studied Eliza for several long moments. Finally she sighed deeply. "Yes'm."

Eliza sensed there was still something Jenny wasn't saying. "What's troubling you, love?"

"I'm gonna miss you something fierce, Eliza. Don't let it be too long."

"I won't. I swear."

All she had now was her baby and Jenny. Matt was lost to her. Except it was hard to lose someone you'd never had in the first place. She vowed that she would stop looking back. Forward—that was where she'd go. Wyoming wasn't exactly the perfect place she'd thought it would be, but she still wasn't sorry she'd come. She'd found Jenny, and she had a baby on the way.

She wished she had her girlish dreams of Matt, though. She wished she'd never had to face just how much he despised her. After giving Jenny a quick kiss she left and ran to her own room. She didn't want the child to see her so upset or hear her cry for the very last time over Matt Decker.

"Jenny told me you were leavin'."

Eliza whirled around and dropped her carpetbag in the hay covering the barn floor. "I didn't hear you come in."

"Figured that." Wiley leaned his weight on the leg the bobcat had clawed, then put his hands on his hips. The look he sent her was purely disapproving.

"Don't you try to talk me out of this, Wiley. I've made up my mind."

"Why would I try to talk you out of it?"

"Because you always do. And it's worked. Twice. But not this time."

"Why won't it work?"

"Because you're wrong."

"Ain't said nothin' yet. How can I be wrong?"

"Did Matt move into the bunkhouse?"

"Yup."

"Didn't you wonder why?"

"Yup." He shifted his position and waited for her to go on.

"Matt doesn't want the baby," she blurted out. She pulled her borrowed coat up around her neck. It was cold and she wasn't looking forward to the long ride to Silver Springs, but that was better than facing the coldness in Matt's blue eyes. She could bear his lack of interest for herself but not for her baby.

Wiley frowned. "Did he tell you that?"

She nodded. "His exact words were that he didn't want the baby *either.*"

"Meanin'?"

"That he doesn't want me. He can't even bear to be in the same house with me. That's why he moved into the bunkhouse with you."

"You're the one who's wrong, Eliza."

She felt like hitting him. "There's nothing wrong with my ears. I know what I heard."

"That's 'cause you were listening with your ears and not with your heart." He rubbed a hand across his whiskered jaw. "I thought you had a heart as big as that pretty smile of yours."

"Flattery will not work. I've made up my mind and I'm going. And for your information, I have no heart left. Matt broke it into a million pieces."

"He didn't mean to. Fear makes a man do foolish things."

"Matt's *afraid*? Of what? Surely not of me? I'd never hurt him. In spite of everything he's done, I can't help loving him. That's why I have to go. It's too hard to see him day after day and know he doesn't feel the same about me."

"He already knows how hard it is to lose someone he cares about. That's why he's pushing you away."

"If he'd just met me halfway, if he'd given me just one ray of hope that we could make it . . ."

"He couldn't. He thinks he's going to lose you the way he did Carrie and her baby."

Shock slammed her in the chest and she took a step backward. "You mean he thinks I'm going to die?"

He nodded. "And the baby, too."

She shook her head. "Women have babies all the time without any problem."

"That's clear thinking. He's not able to do that."

"Matt's an intelligent man. I can't believe he thinks that. Why, I know lots of women back home who have come through childbirth without complications. You're just trying to talk me into staying. It won't work."

"Matt's smart as a whip when it comes to ranchin', but female things are clean over his head. He lost Carrie and his baby and he thinks he's gonna lose you, too. Ain't common sense, it's gut feelin'."

"I don't believe you."

She walked over to Snowflake's stall and the animal nickered softly. Eliza opened the gate and stepped inside. She pulled an apple from her pocket and offered it to Snowflake, who lowered her head and took the food. While the horse munched and tossed her head, Eliza looked up again at Wiley.

"Where's Matt now?"

"Left early this mornin' to check the herd."

"Good."

She pulled the bridle from the peg on the wall and put it in the animal's mouth.

"Why 'good'?"

"Because I never want to see him again."

"Liar."

Her gaze flew to his. "I've never told a lie in my life."

"You're lyin' to yourself. That's the worst kind of false-hood."

"What are you talking about?"

"You're crazy in love with that man."

"I never de—"

He held up his hand to stop her. "Don't interrupt me. You're crazy in love with Matthew. And he loves you back. You're runnin' away so's he'll have to come after you. You want to see him again, all right, and you're lyin' to yourself if you think you don't."

She absently patted Snowflake's neck. "Why, Mr. Powell, you're mighty eloquent."

"Don't rightly know what that means, but—"

It was her turn to hold up her hand to interrupt him. "I wasn't finished yet. Those are pretty words, but you're wrong. I don't want him to come after me."

"Suit yourself."

"Thank you. There is something you could do for me, if you would?"

"'Course I'll take you to town, seein's you got your heart set on it. I'd never forgive myself if somethin' happened to you or that there young 'un," he said, pointing to her abdomen.

She looked down and blushed. "That's not what I was going to ask. But thank you." She lifted the horse blanket and threw it over Snowflake. "I was going to ask if you'd bring Jenny to Silver Springs after I get settled."

"If she wants to go, I surely will," he said. When Eliza started to lift the saddle, he quickly moved beside her. He grasped her upper arms and moved her out of the way. "If you try stunts like that, you're gonna lose that little one and Matthew won't look so stupid, will he?" he asked, glaring at her.

Guilt shot through her. He was right. She had to think about the baby. "I'll be more careful."

He nodded sternly. "See that you are."

He lifted her carpetbag from the hay. "I'll hitch up the wagon."

She nodded. "Do you think Jenny will be all right here by herself?"

"That little girl has spent plenty of time by her lonesome. She'll be fine. But I'll hurry on back."

"Thank you, Mr. Powell."

"I'm not so sure you should be thankin' me."

"I'll miss you." She threw her arms around him and stifled a sob.

He sniffled. "Dang cold weather makes my nose run."

"Mine, too," she said, wiping a tear from the corner of her eye.

He left her then to get the wagon ready. She stifled any guilt she felt about not saying good-bye to Matt. Her leaving was best for both of them. It was her way of thanking him for saving her life.

Now they were even.

19

It was way past sundown when Matt went to the bunkhouse looking for Wiley. When he couldn't find him there, he checked the barn. He found it empty and walked down to the main house, steeling himself to see Eliza.

In the kitchen, the older man was stirring a pot of something on the stove.

"Where's Eliza? And Jenny?" he asked.

"Something came up." There was a clipped, angry edge to Wiley's voice that told Matt he wasn't going to like the answer to the question he had to ask.

"What came up?"

"I had to take Eliza to Silver Springs."

"You what? To town and back? That's too hard on a woman in her condition. What the hell were you thinking of, man?"

"She didn't come back with me."

When the words sank in, the pain took Matt's breath away. "She stayed in town?"

Wiley nodded. "Said it was best for everyone."

"You took her? How could you do—"

Wiley held up a hand to stop him, but the look in his pale blue eyes would have been enough. "Wasn't my first choice. She was so all-fired eager to get away from you, she was goin' on her own. Hog-tyin' her was the only way to stop her and I wouldn't do that to a lady. 'Course it mighta been better than what you did to her."

"Moving into the bunkhouse, you mean." It wasn't a question.

"That was part of it. Mostly it was what you said about not wantin' her and the young 'un she's carryin'."

"She doesn't understand. Just because I saved her life once, she thinks I can keep her safe. I can't. Not from this." Matt jammed his hands in the pockets of his sheepskin jacket and looked at his old friend, hoping he'd understand.

"You don't have to explain to me. I was with you when you found Carrie and the baby."

"If only I'd been here. Maybe I *could* have done something—"

"We've been through this. Ain't nothin' anyone coulda done. Carrie was too narrow-hipped to bear children."

Matt looked up and the fire inside him burned his chest. "You were right. I did want to marry someone I didn't know. I wanted to have a child without having to worry about feeling anything for the mother. It was wrong. And I'm being punished. Eliza is carrying my child and it's going to kill her."

"You love her, don't ya?"

The question stopped him cold. Matt had always been drawn to Eliza. Since he'd brought her to the ranch, he'd been trying to ignore the feelings she stirred inside him. But as soon as Wiley said it, he knew it was the Lord's honest truth. He couldn't lie about it anymore. He did love her, more than his own life—and even more, he realized now, than he'd ever loved Carrie.

"Of course I love her. But what difference does that make?"

"It makes all the difference in the world. You gotta go after her."

"No."

"Knothead! What the hell are you thinking of?"

"Eliza."

"In a pig's eye."

Matt gritted his teeth. "I'd only hurt her. She needs something I can't give her."

"Matthew—"

"There's nothing you can say to make me change my mind. She's better off in town with more people around her." He turned away and started to the door.

"People like Ed Whitaker?"

Matt whirled around. "He was hangin' around her?"

A gleam stole into Wiley's expression. "Darn tootin' he was chasin' after her. She's a fine-lookin' woman."

"She's my wife. She's carrying my child."

"You told her you don't want her. And Ed Whitaker can't see yet that she's in the family way. Probably wouldn't care neither."

"Goddammit to hell!" Matt set his hat on the back of his head and thrust his chin out. "I told her to stay away from him."

"Has she ever done what you told her to?"

Matt thought for a minute and the answer didn't bring him any comfort. "No."

"So what d'you intend t'do about it?"

He tucked his hands beneath his arms as he looked at the ceiling. He had no right to interfere in her life.

"Nothing."

"You're a lot of things, Matthew. But I never counted *fool* among them."

"'Bout time you did," Matt said, and stalked down the hall and into his bedroom.

The fragrance of wildflowers drifted to him. Pain squeezed his heart before he could stop it. She wasn't here; she was in town with Ed Whitaker sniffing after her.

He realized he hadn't seen Jenny. Had Eliza taken her, too? He wasn't sure he could stand any more.

He walked down the hall to the child's room. He opened her door and relaxed when he found her sound asleep. On the table beside her bed sat the hideous hat Eliza had worn when she had spoken vows with him.

He remembered Reverend Wilson's words about marriage being serious and not to be entered into lightly. He had taken Eliza to be his lawfully wedded wife. He loved her so fiercely he ached from it. Why had his own mother done this to him?

He left the room as silently as he'd entered and went back to the kitchen. It smelled of wildflowers and biscuits and he expected Eliza to walk in any second. He knew she was gone, was never coming back. But all the little changes she'd made were still there. Curtains over the window, a tablecloth on the trestle table, not a dirty dish or pot anywhere to be seen, not even on the back porch. Worst of all were the changes she'd made inside him. He could feel again. He wished to God he couldn't, because then being without her wouldn't hurt so much.

His gaze went to the cupboard above the stove. Without hesitating he opened the door and pulled out a full bottle of whiskey. That should be enough to make him feel nothing as he had before Eliza had come back into his life.

Matt's eyelids fluttered, but he resisted opening them. His sour stomach complained, his head hurt, and he was lying on the most uncomfortable pillow . . .

The strong smell of coffee filled his nostrils and turned his guts inside out. He managed to open his eyes and found himself looking at the kitchen table. His forehead rested on his crossed forearms. He raised his head and blinked, and his eyes watered at the bright sunlight streaming through the kitchen window. When he moved his arm, he sent the empty whiskey bottle crashing to the floor.

"Mr. Decker?"

He turned his head to look at Jenny and sharp pain shot through his head. "Oh, Lord."

"Coffee's almost ready. It'll fix you up real quick, Mr. Decker."

"What time is it, Jenny?"

"It's late morning."

"Where's Eliza?" She always made coffee in the morning. Was she feeling all right? Then he remembered. The pain that gripped him this time cracked his heart. Eliza was gone. "Never mind, Jenny. I remember."

The child set a cup in front of him and he watched the steam rising. "Be careful. It's real strong and real hot. I always made it that way for Pa."

Cobwebs still clung to Matt's brain, but he knew he didn't like the comparison between himself and her father. Eliza had been gone only a day. It hadn't taken him long to sink so low.

"Thanks."

The child sat down in the chair beside him and regarded him with big, solemn blue eyes. She didn't say a word but he could feel her accusation. He just wasn't sure if it was because of his drinking or because Eliza was gone.

"Whatever's on your mind, you might as well spit it out," he said, then blew on his coffee.

"Do all men like whiskey, Mr. Decker?"

He flinched. "I don't suppose all men do."

"I didn't think so when Pa left me with you. But now I'm not so sure."

"Jenny—" What could he say to her?

"It's all right. You don't have to explain. I won't be here long anyway."

"Why's that?"

"Eliza said when she got settled I could live with her."

"Is that what you want?"

"Not exactly," she said, looking at the shattered bottle still on the floor. "Pa said you weren't a drinkin' man." She blinked and sat up straighter. "It's because Eliza left, isn't it?"

"It has nothing—"

"Pa wasn't a drinkin' man neither till after Ma died. He told me that once."

Matt gritted his teeth and a muscle in his cheek contracted. He shifted in his chair. "A man just likes a drink every now and then."

She shook her head. "I'm not a baby, Mr. Decker. She said you don't want her here. If that was true, you wouldn't have that awful look in your eyes and you wouldn't be needin' whiskey."

Jenny was wise beyond her years. She'd seen through the lies and found the truth.

He loved Eliza.

"Since you're not talkin', that must mean I'm right and you do want her here."

"It's not that simple, Jenny. There are things you don't understand."

"I know what's important. You love her and she loves you."

"Did she tell you that?"

"No, sir. But, all the same, I know she does. People who love each other should be together."

"They should. But sometimes that's not possible."

"Only if you're dead." She rested her forearms on the table and laced her fingers. The wisest eyes he'd ever seen in one so young stared at him. "You gotta grab everything you can while ya got it."

"Who told you that?"

"Pa. I wasn't sure I wanted to stay here. The last thing he said before he left was you shouldn't turn down a chance to have a dream."

"What if your dream can't last?"

She thought for a minute, then met his gaze. "I don't suppose it matters how long you have the dream, just that you find it and enjoy it while you got it."

He took a sip of his coffee. "What's your dream, Jenny?"

Without hesitation she answered, "A ma *and* a pa. I had it for a little while, too."

He flinched for the third time since she'd sat down. She carried a powerful punch for such a little thing. Just like another small woman he knew.

"Was it worth having, even just for a short time?"

"Yes, sir," she said without the slightest hesitation.

"So you think I should go after Eliza and bring her back?"

Her gaze quickly lifted from her fingers to his face. There was a hopeful expression in her blue eyes that cut clear through him. "I didn't say that."

"You didn't have to. Wiley beat you to it."

"I think that's a fine idea of Mr. Powell's."

Matt was beginning to agree with her. Eliza belonged with him. The cost in misery later would be worth whatever time he could have her in his arms. He damn well intended to make every minute she spent on this earth happy. And he couldn't do that if she was in Silver Springs cozying up to Ed Whitaker.

He went to the cupboard and pulled out his shaving basin, straight edge, and mirror.

"What are you doing?" Jenny asked.

"Did you know I'm a knothead?" he asked, as he lathered up the soap and spread it across his cheeks.

"Yes, sir." She giggled. "But I think you're doin' all right now."

His hand stopped in midstroke just above his jaw. "Do you know how to iron?"

"Yes, sir. Why?"

He grinned. "You'll see."

*   *   *

"Word sure got around fast." Mrs. Buchanan brushed the black hair that had come loose from the knot at her nape off her face.

"What do you mean?" Eliza wrapped a cloth around the coffeepot to refill cups in the dining room.

"Never seen so many folks here in the boardinghouse for supper. And most of 'em men."

"Word of your good cooking has spread."

The woman laughed heartily. "I've been cookin' in these parts for a lot of years and I ain't never had me a dinner crowd like this. Word spread, all right: that you're here."

Eliza's gaze shot to the other woman. "Me? Why would people come here for supper because of me?"

"'Cause most of them people's men."

"But I'm a married woman." *And I'm carrying Matt's child.* If Mrs. Buchanan was right about the men being interested, that would scare them off fast enough. It sure had scared Matt.

"Doesn't seem to bother Ed Whitaker and Brad Slicker none. 'Sides, I don't see no sign of your husband."

"And you won't either. In any case, it doesn't matter. Mr. Whitaker and Mr. Slicker are just being friendly."

"Somethin' tells me they'll hang around as long as you keep refillin' their cups." Ethel Buchanan's big bosom jiggled when she laughed again. "Them two have had so much coffee as it is, they ain't gonna get a wink of sleep tonight."

"They both seem very nice."

"Just make sure you got a free hand when you're pourin' from that pot."

"They do seem to like their coffee, just like . . ." Eliza sighed.

"Like who?"

"No one." She wouldn't let herself miss Wiley, Jenny, the ranch, and most especially not Matt.

"I'll go fill cups again," Eliza said, going to the door

that led to the dining room. The murmur of voices carried to her from the other side. "Then I'll start clearing the plates."

Mrs. Buchanan nodded. "Eliza?"

She stopped and looked up. "Yes?"

"I don't know what's wrong 'tween you and Matt that made you hightail it into town. But his loss is my gain."

Eliza smiled at her. "Thank you."

She went into the next room, where a long table covered with an oilcloth seated twelve and every place had been filled. Most of the evening's diners had finally left and Eliza was relieved. For several hours, she had done nothing but run back and forth to the kitchen. The only people left now were men: Mr. Whitaker, Mr. Slicker, and two she'd never seen before.

She refilled the strangers' cups first, since they were closest. Then she moved to Ed Whitaker sitting at the end farthest from the kitchen. On her way there, she felt his eyes on her, making her nervous after what Mrs. Buchanan had said. When she stopped beside him, he smiled up at her, showing white teeth below his mustache. She remembered Matt telling her to stay away from him, but she couldn't very well do that when it was part of her job to serve Mrs. Buchanan's customers.

Besides, Matt Decker had given up any say in her life.

She started pouring the coffee and felt Whitaker's arm come around her waist. With her right hand carrying the coffeepot, she tried to remove his grip with her left. He refused to budge and the harder she tried, the tighter his grip became and the angrier she got. The audacity of the man. And her a married woman!

"Will you kindly remove your hand, Mr. Whitaker?" It took every ounce of her self-control to keep her voice steady.

"Feels real good there, ma'am," he said, and squeezed her waist.

The other men in the room just watched. Brad Slicker

had a gleam in his eye that told her he wanted to see what she would do.

"I don't like it," she said.

She stopped pouring and half turned toward him. Then she tipped the pot, letting a stream of hot coffee go into his lap. He let out a yelp and stood up.

"Jesus H. Christ!"

"Don't you dare take the Lord's name in vain, sir." She set the pot on the table. "And don't you ever lay a hand on me again."

She curled her fingers into a fist. It had worked once on Matt, maybe it would show this man a thing or two. She pulled her arm back and jammed him in the stomach as hard as she could. He let out a whoosh of air and doubled over as he grabbed his midsection. It was soft as bread dough, not nearly as firm and hard as Matt's had been. Along with the memory came a rush of regret and longing so powerful, she herself almost doubled over from the force of it.

"Mr. Whitaker, I think it's time you said good evening."

"Yes, ma'am," he gasped. Still half-bent, he grabbed his hat and coat from the tree in the corner of the room and hobbled out the door.

She picked up the pot and rounded the table to Brad Slicker, then poured coffee in his cup. Before she could move away, he took the pot from her and set it on the table.

"I'm not finished with that," she said, reaching for it. Instantly, his arm snaked around her waist and he pulled her onto his lap, with her back toward the table. Her hands were jammed up against his chest as he held her in an iron grip.

"Let me go, Mr. Slicker." She tried very hard to keep the alarm from her voice. But it wasn't easy since he'd effectively eliminated all her weapons. The pot was out of reach even if she could get her arms free. And her secret punch was out of the question for the same reason.

"You're such a bossy little thing," he said.

The one time she'd met him she'd been so desperate for work, she hadn't noticed how small and beady his eyes were. His brown hair barely skimmed his white linen collar and now she knew the ever-present gleam in his eyes had something to do with her.

Matt had warned her about this man too. Horsefeathers. She hated that he was right about the two of them. Now she had to figure out how to get this brute to let her go.

"Mrs. Buchanan has a shotgun in the kitchen, so I strongly suggest you unhand me."

"Everyone knows Ethel wouldn't use that thing." He sniffed her neck. "You smell real nice." His gaze rested on her face. "Pretty as a picture, too."

She cringed away from him as far as his too-tight grip would allow. "What does that have to do with anything?"

"Last time I saw you, Matt Decker was carring you out of the Silver Slipper ass over teakettle." He shook his head, regret in his expression. "Too bad. Coulda had us a pile of fun if you'da come to work for me."

If Matt hadn't done what he had, she would have had to work for this man. Eliza shuddered.

She looked at the two strangers who watched with grins on their faces, as if they approved of this man's ill-mannered behavior. "Would one of you please help me?" she asked politely.

The young blond shook his head. "Never piss off the saloon owner in a one-saloon town." He tipped his head in a courtly gesture. "Sorry, ma'am."

She looked at the other man, who nodded vigorously in agreement.

"Then I shall be forced to call Mrs. Buchanan and we'll find out once and for all if she's willing to use that thing."

Eliza felt a flutter of air cool the back of her neck and

ruffle the wisps of hair that had shaken loose during the supper rush. Her struggle to get away from the man holding her far too tightly threatened to make the rest of her hair fall. Then she heard the dead silence in the room. The other two men looked at the doorway and went still. The steely arms keeping her prisoner tensed for several moments, then released her.

"A wise decision, sir." Quickly, she jumped off Brad Slicker's lap and backed away. She smoothed her apron over her skirt. "I didn't think you'd truly want to test Mrs. Buchanan's skill with her shotgun."

Brad Slicker slowly stood. With narrowed eyes, he still stared at the doorway behind her. The others did as well.

Eliza turned. "What is so interesting—" Her breath caught in her throat when she saw Matt standing there. His black hat rested low on his forehead, just above his brows. She'd never seen him look so angry, and Lord knows better than anyone that she'd given him plenty to be angry about.

"'Evening, Decker." Mr. Slicker's voice was pleasant but there was a tinge of wariness around the edges.

Matt nodded. "Slicker."

If not for the murderous look in his blue eyes, Eliza would almost have thought he was greeting a friend.

"I think we need to get something straight," Matt said.

"What's that?"

"You ever lay a finger on my wife again, you'll wish you hadn't. That clear?"

Mr. Slicker shifted his feet, but never took his eyes from Matt. "Yeah."

"Good."

The barkeep nodded to Eliza. "'Evenin', ma'am. It's been a pleasure, but I gotta be gettin' back to the Silver Slipper."

He held out his hand to her, then looked at Matt, who took a slight step forward. Instantly, Mr. Slicker pulled his hand back and left the room in a hurry. The other two men followed close on his heels. The only sound came from dishes rattling and pots banging in the kitchen. Mrs. Buchanan was busy cleaning up. Eliza knew she should go help, but for the moment she was alone with Matt. Only the long trestle table separated them. She wanted to savor the feeling, just a little, before she got mad and sent him packing.

"Matt, there was no call for you to threaten Mr. Slicker like that. I made him see reason and he let me go."

"You really think threatening him with Ethel's shotgun made him cut you loose?" Amusement danced in his eyes for an instant.

"Why else would he?"

"Because he saw me standing here and knew I'd tear him apart if he didn't."

Eliza knew he was telling her the truth. That man had been no more intimidated by the threat of Ethel's shotgun than by a fly. "You had no right to get involved. I would have handled it."

He snorted. "I could see Brad Slicker was shaking in his boots."

"Well, he would've been if you had taught me how to use a gun when I asked you."

"If you hadn't run away, I might have."

His words brought a stab of guilt, then a rush of longing for the ranch and Jenny. She leaned to the side to peek around him.

"What are you looking for?"

"Jenny."

"Why would you think she's here?"

"I figured the reason you're here is because you brought her into town."

"I came alone."

"Is she all right?" she asked.

A small smile lifted one corner of his mouth. "She's really somethin'."

Just then the kitchen door to her right slammed open

and she jumped. Walter Buchanan, the dark-haired, brown-eyed fifteen-year-old, hustled into the room. He stopped when he saw Matt.

"Howdy, Mr. Decker."

"Walter."

The boy looked around. "Jenny come with you?"

"What made you think she'd be with me?"

"Eliza told us her pa left her at the Double C. Is she with you?"

"No. I left her with Wiley."

The young man breathed a sigh of relief. "Good. When she stayed here with her pa, she took t'followin' me all over town."

Matt's gaze flicked to Eliza for a second, then his mouth turned up at the corners. "Did she?"

"She surely did. A real pain in the—" He stopped. "Sorry, ma'am."

"That's all right, Walter. I'm getting used to it."

"Ma needs me to chop kindling. I'll see you later, ma'am. Mr. Decker," he said, moving past Matt and out the door.

When Matt turned back to her, she asked, "If you didn't bring Jenny into town, why are you here?"

Before he could answer, the kitchen door opened again, and Mrs. Buchanan came into the room. Her dark brows lifted in surprise when she saw Matt.

"Look what the cat drug in," she said, and smiled.

"Ethel." He looked at all the plates on the table. "Looks like business is good."

The woman glanced at Eliza. "Never seen it so good."

"Ought to be careful who you let in here."

"Why?"

"When I came in, Brad Slicker was manhandling Eliza."

"I didn't hear nothin'." Mrs. Buchanan looked at her again. "Why didn't you holler?"

Eliza shifted uncomfortably from one foot to the other. "I was taking care of the situation."

Matt snorted.

Eliza started to gather plates from the table. "I'm sorry. I'll get these right in the kitchen."

"They'll keep." Mrs. Buchanan waved her off and glanced at Matt with a big grin. "I think you've got more important things to do."

"No. Wait—" Before Eliza could stop her she was back in the kitchen. They were alone again—him on one side of the table, her on the other.

"Let's go somewhere we can talk." Matt lifted his hat and set it on the back of his head.

"Right here is fine."

"Too public. Everyone and everything's come through here except the stage from Cheyenne." He grinned suddenly. "I saw Ed Whitaker leaving. You have any idea why he was walkin' funny and holding his stomach?"

She tried not to smile back but couldn't help it. "No idea at all." Then she remembered Matt telling her he didn't want her or her child. Her amusement died. "I don't want to talk to you anymore. You said everything already."

"I never said good-bye."

"Good-bye." She started to walk toward the kitchen.

"Not so fast." On the other side of the table, he moved to head her off.

"Don't you touch me."

"Then stay and hear me out."

"When hell freezes over."

He smiled. "Really, Eliza. Such language. You've only been here two days and already your manners could use some polishing."

She turned and ran for the kitchen door. He got there ahead of her and stopped her from opening it.

"I'm not giving you a choice." He took her hand off the knob and bent at the waist to put her over his shoulder.

"Don't you dare!" she cried.

He looked at her abdomen and hesitated. The baby.

She tried to back away but he still held her hand.

"There's more than one way to skin a cat." He pulled her against him, put his arm behind her knees, and lifted her into his arms. "Doesn't matter if the whole damn town comes traipsing through here." His nose was inches from hers and a steely glint of determination shone in his eyes. "One way or the other, we're gonna talk."

20

Eliza pushed against his chest and kicked her legs, trying to break his hold. "Maybe someone in this town will traipse through here and help me."

She smelled of fresh bread, fried chicken, and flowers, and Matt was so relieved to have her in his arms again, he almost didn't care that she was fighting like hell to get away. Fact was, if it hadn't been for the baby, he *would* have put her over his shoulder. She was slippery as a trout fresh out of the stream.

When her struggles slowed as she tired from the exertion, he looked around the dining room. There must be someplace in the whole damn boardinghouse where he could be alone with her and make her listen without interruption.

He shouldered his way through the kitchen door. Odors of supper hung in the air and he felt his stomach rumble. He hadn't eaten since early morning. But he couldn't think about that now. There would be enough time later to take care of that.

"Matt Decker, you put me down this minute!" Eliza cried out.

Standing in front of the window with her back to them Ethel Buchanan vigorously scrubbed a plate. She turned at the sound and stared at him with the wiggling woman in his arms.

"Mrs. Buchanan, is your shotgun handy?" Eliza asked.

"Trouble, Matt?" the other woman asked.

"Nothing I can't handle," he said. Eliza tried to lift her legs free. He swung her up and tightened his grip. "Stop that before you hurt yourself or the baby."

Eliza crossed her arms over her breasts, making herself deadweight in his arms. "Mrs. Buchanan, if your shotgun *is* handy, will you please shoot this man and make him leave me be?"

The older woman lifted her soapy arms from the bucket and rested her elbows on the rim. "Baby?" A gleam stole into her black eyes. "You didn't waste any time, Decker."

"Yeah, well—"

He wished he could be proud about it and act like any other expectant father. Fact was, if he had it to do over he'd make sure to keep Eliza safe to grow old with her. He also knew, after the rage that had eaten him alive when he'd seen Brad Slicker holding her, there was no way in hell he could have annulled their marriage. The thought of her in the arms of another man tore him apart inside.

He'd found his dream in Eliza. Whatever time the good Lord gave her on this earth, he wanted to spend it making her happy.

"Mrs. Buchanan, I'd appreciate your assistance. This man is holding me against my will."

The widow ignored Eliza and looked at Matt. "Decker, 'pears to me that you've got your arms full of trouble. Anything I can do to help?"

He nodded. "Is there somewhere I can take this little pain in the"—he grinned at Eliza—"I mean this trouble-maker so we can talk without the whole town listening?"

"I put her in the same room you took your weddin' vows in. You can go there."

He nodded in thanks since his arms were indeed chock-full of trouble. "I owe you one, Ethel."

"Name that baby after me."

"I'll consider it." He prayed he'd have both the child *and* his wife to raise it.

"Really, Mrs. Buchanan, I don't want to go anywhere with him. Could you please—"

He left the room and the closing door cut off her words. He turned down the dim hallway to his right. It took him only moments to find the room. Standing in the shadowy corridor, he recalled the night he'd waited with Reverend Wilson for Eliza to come and marry him. If he'd known it was her, he would have hightailed it out of there, but he was certain that no other woman could have made him feel again. He didn't know if that was good or bad. It all depended on how good a talker he was, and whether or not he could convince her that he'd had good reason for everything he'd done to her.

He opened the door, carried her inside, then kicked it shut. The room was dark except for moonlight filtering through the crisscrossed muslin curtains.

"I demand that you—"

Matt removed one arm from her legs and let them slide down. He backed up against the door so she couldn't get past him and out into the hall. With his other arm still clamped around her waist, he held her to him while her feet dangled several inches above the floor. Where his sheepskin jacket gaped open, her soft breasts rubbed against his chest. He pulled the feeling inside him and inhaled her sweet female scent.

He wanted so bad to kiss her, he hurt inside. And the only time he seemed able to get her to do what he wanted was when he planted his lips on hers. Matt decided to do it; he figured he didn't have much to lose.

When she took a breath, then started to speak again, he

stopped her with his mouth. She tensed and squirmed against him, but he spread gentle kisses over her lips. When he touched the tip of his tongue to her top lip, urging her to open to him, she sighed, then obeyed as she rested her arms around his neck.

He stroked the inside of her mouth and tasted her sweetness. Heat swept over him and built inside him until he couldn't contain the feeling.

He lifted his head and watched her eyelids flutter open. When he told her what was in his heart, he prayed that she would believe him. "I love you, Eliza."

The smoky expression vanished from her eyes, replaced by wariness. She shook her head slightly. "You're lying again."

"No, I—"

"That's quite a bad habit you've developed, Matt." When she pushed against his chest, he set her on the floor.

"I wish I didn't, but I do," he said. "That's the truth."

"The truth is you've never forgiven me for telling my father about you and Emily O'Leary. Because of that, you don't want me or my child."

"I'll admit I've been less than honest with you and with myself, but you have to believe this—I got over that a long time ago. Coming to Wyoming was the best thing that ever happened to me, until the night I married you, right here in this room."

"Then I don't understand why you won't let me be your wife. You wanted one. I wouldn't be here at all if you hadn't asked your mother to help you find a wife."

He took his hat off and tossed it on the chair beside the door. "We're going to be here awhile. If I light the lamp, do you promise to stay and listen?"

She backed up to the foot of the bed and nodded. When he passed her to get to the night table, her feminine fragrance stirred in the room. He turned to look at her. Standing there in the moonlight, she was just about the prettiest thing he'd ever seen. If he couldn't make her understand, he'd—Hell, he had to, that's all there was to it.

Eliza watched him watch her. The light was behind him and she couldn't see his expression. A voice inside her told her to run, cautioned her not to listen to him. Another, stronger, one said to make him kiss her again. She listened to the second one. The least she could do was stay and hear him out. She had nothing to lose. Her heart was already broken.

The lantern chimney clinked loudly as he lifted it. Then a match scratched, flared to life, and brightened the room when he touched it to the wick.

"You did want a wife, didn't you, Matt?"

He nodded. "But I wanted a stranger, someone I wouldn't care about."

"That's what you got. You don't care about me."

"You're wrong. As soon as you took off that hat and I recognized you, I knew I was in trouble. Especially with you in that skimpy little nightgown, standing in front of the light looking practically naked—"

"Matt!" In spite of her protest, a small, pleasurable shiver slipped down her spine.

"You wouldn't want me to lie." One corner of his mouth lifted in a smile. "Anyway, after that bobcat attacked Wiley and I saw blood all over you, I was so scared. I realized I did care about you. I wouldn't have felt that way about a stranger. You're something special, Eliza. You always have been. You're like a ray of sunshine from the past."

"But you don't care about me. You said so—"

He shook his head. "Wrong again. I knew I loved you the second I laid eyes on your freckles and the prettiest pair of green eyes I've ever seen."

"You loved me so much you moved out of the house? Doesn't sound to me like a man who cares. Unless—"

"What?"

"Unless I'm not the problem. It's the baby." Eliza

watched his expression carefully. If Wiley hadn't told her, she never would have recognized the shadow that crossed his face for what it was. Fear.

"But you wanted a wife *and* children, Matt."

"With a stranger. Look, you might as well know the whole story." He raked his fingers through his hair. "Before Carrie's time was due I had to get the herd to market. I had to go. Had a big bank payment due on the ranch. I wanted her to stay in town here at the boarding-house." He stopped for a second and a muscle in his cheek contracted.

Eliza's heart went out to him. She wanted to tell him to stop, not to put himself through this. But he was feeling again, and she knew he had to let all of it go.

"She wouldn't stay here?" she prompted him.

He nodded grimly. "Said havin' a baby was the most natural thing in the world."

"What happened?"

"I left her. When Wiley and I got back . . ." He stopped and took in a big breath of air, then let it out in a rush. She was dead. She'd bled to death and the baby died with her."

"Oh, Matt." She did go to him then and put her arms around him. He was rigid, wouldn't let himself be comforted. She pressed her cheek to his chest and held him. "Wiley said she was tall, but her hips were narrow, not built to have babies. I don't think a doctor would have made any difference."

"I should have been with her. I wish it had been me."

The muscles in his back flexed, and Eliza felt as if she was holding his pain in her hands. "But it wasn't. You went on. And you wanted to try again."

"Only because of the land. I didn't want to die and have no one to leave it to."

She took one step away from him and reached for his hand. Then she placed it on her belly. "Now you have someone."

He pulled away as if she'd burned him. "Don't you see? It's starting all over again—just like with Carrie. It's all my fault, because I couldn't stay away from you. Because I love you. I think"—his voice choked—"I think even more than I ever loved her."

She stood on tiptoe and took his face in both her hands. Moisture collected on his cheeks and she brushed it away with her thumbs. She searched the depths of his blue eyes and saw that he was telling her the truth. He thought he was responsible for Carrie's death. That was why he had pushed her away and said he didn't want her or the child.

It was *because* he loved her, and the baby.

"Look at me, Matt, and listen carefully. I'm not Carrie. I'm built for having babies. If it will make you feel better, I'll see the doctor here in town and he'll tell you the same thing. Nothing is going to happen to me or our baby. I swear to you."

"How can you be so sure?"

"I just am." She smiled and pushed the hair off his forehead. "Besides, you're a good man. God would never be that cruel."

He didn't look completely convinced by her argument. "So you believe me? You believe that I love you?"

She nodded. "Why did you come after me?"

"Jenny. She said no one should turn their back on a dream. You're my dream, Eliza."

"I just wish it hadn't taken you so damn long to say it."

His brows lifted in surprise as a lopsided grin turned up his mouth. "Eliza, Your language!" he said, pretending to be affronted. "I must be a bad influence on you."

She nodded ruefully. "I guess so. The worst part is that by the time we've been married for fifty years, we'll be too feeble to fight it when our grandchildren take the soap to our mouths."

He chuckled then, the first true merriment she'd seen

out of him since he'd rescued her from Brad Slicker. Then he started to laugh, until every corner of the room echoed with the deep, hearty sound.

"You're so good for me, Eliza."

"That's why your mother sent me here."

"You think so?"

"I'm sure of it. She knew I was right for you. And you're the only man I could ever love. It's not going to happen, but if I died tomorrow, I want you to know I've been happier in your arms than any woman has a right to be." When he pulled her to him, she snuggled against his strength. "As wonderful as this feels, I think Mrs. Buchanan is expecting me to help her in the kitchen."

He backed her toward the bed and lowered her to the mattress. "She better get used to doing dishes by herself. You're gonna have your hands full at the Double C."

She laughed. "Oh, I hope so."

"Believe it. I love you, Eliza."

"And I love you."

When they left the doctor's office, Matt grabbed Eliza around the waist and swung her around on the board-walk. She laughed at the grin of pure pleasure on his face. Dr. Raskin had assured him that Eliza was healthy and as far as he could tell would have no trouble delivering a fine, healthy baby with no risk to herself.

"I told you so," she said.

"That you did." He looked down at her. "Would you mind if we made one stop before we go back to the ranch?"

She shook her head. "Where?"

"You'll see."

They walked hand in hand to the telegraph office and stepped inside out of the cold wind. The man behind the counter looked up. "Howdy, Matt, Mrs. Decker."

"Horace." Matt nodded to the other man.

"Hear tell you and your bride got some news to celebrate."

Matt sighed and shook his head. "Wonder if this town will ever get so big that it'll take more than a half hour for news to get from one end to the other."

"Can't rightly say, Matt. Congratulations on the young 'un."

"Thanks, Horace. In fact, that's why I'm here. I'd like to send the good news back home."

The man nodded as he pulled out a pencil and a pad of paper. "You think it's gonna be a cold winter this year, Matt?"

He looked down at Eliza. "No. Not now."

"So who's the wire goin' to?"

"Send it to Mrs. Laura Decker, Boston, Massachusetts."

Horace nodded. "What's the message?"

"Just say 'Thanks.' Sign it 'Love, Matt.'"

The man shot him a puzzled look. "That's it?"

"Yup. She'll know what it means. Right, Eliza?"

"Right." She smiled her wide-open smile, the one that was as big and bright as the Wyoming sky and made his heart beat until he thought the whole town could hear it.

"Thanks" would have to do. He didn't have any other words to say how grateful he was for his winter bride.

Epilogue

Silver Springs, Wyoming Territory—October 1, 1878

After a stop at the telegraph office, Matt halted the wagon in front of the Silver Springs Mercantile. He glanced into the wagon bed behind him and smiled at his sleeping almost three-year-old son, Luke. Jenny pulled a blanket up around the boy's neck.

Little Laura, just a year old, was swaddled in a quilt in Eliza's lap.

His wife smiled at him. "When your son wakes up, he's going to be a handful."

"Just like his mother."

After three years of having Eliza beside him, Matt sometimes forgot how lonely his life had been before. He reminded himself of the months of worry he'd known when she carried Luke and how he'd tried to hide it from her. But Eliza knew and kept reassuring him. She'd been right. Their firstborn had made his entrance into the world without a hitch. Baby Laura, named after Matt's mother, came soon after, as easy as you please, Eliza had said. There was a part of him that would always worry about her, but he tried to live his dream from day to day without asking questions.

He jumped down from the wagon seat and took the sleeping baby from Eliza. After handing the bundle to Jenny, he lifted his wife down, letting her slide intimately against him.

"You're such a scoundrel, Matt," she said with a grin.

"Can't help it. With you rubbing against me all the way from the ranch, why—"

She looked at Jenny beside her and shook her head slightly in warning. But her wink told him she didn't mind in the least and that she'd show him a thing or two later.

Just then Luke sat up and rubbed his eyes. "Papa," he said, reaching his arms out.

Matt lifted him out of the wagon, then smiled as his son rested his cheek on his shoulder and promptly went back to sleep. The brisk wind sent them all trooping into the store. Ethel Buchanan stood at the counter paying for her goods. She looked up as the door closed behind them. "Howdy."

"Hello, Ethel," Eliza said. "How are you?"

Before she could answer, Jenny eagerly stepped forward. "Mrs. Buchanan, where's Walter?"

The other woman frowned thoughtfully. "I reckon he's over at the livery."

"Thanks, ma'am," Jenny said. She moved over to Eliza. "Ma, can I go say hello?"

"That would be the neighborly thing to do."

"Thanks," she said, handing the still-sleeping baby to Eliza. Then she raced from the store.

Matt looked down at Eliza. "Aren't you going to stop her? The way she follows after that boy worries me."

"It wouldn't do any good." She smiled. "Quit acting like an overprotective father."

Matt knew from the twinkle in his wife's eye that she

was remembering the way she had followed after him when she was about Jenny's age. Still, he wasn't so sure about this. He loved that girl as if she was his own flesh and blood. If anyone hurt her, he'd make it his business to see that they had cause to regret it.

Ethel picked up her packages from the counter. "Does Jenny ever talk about her pa?"

"Not since after that first winter, when we had to tell her he'd died. She seemed to know already," Eliza said. "She said he was happier now with her mother."

The older woman gazed at the door the young girl had gone through. "She's a fine young woman. In spite of how that no-account father of hers raised her."

"He did right by her," Matt said. "When he left her with Eliza, he knew just what he was doing."

"Reckon so." Ethel grinned at Matt. "Now, don't you worry none about my Walter and that little girl."

"I'm not," Matt said quickly.

"In a pig's eye." Ethel Buchanan laughed. "Walter is workin' hard and savin' every penny. He's plannin' to buy that parcel of land you offered him, Matt, and start ranchin'."

"Me and my big mouth," he said, rubbing the back of his neck.

"Now you stop that, Matt Decker," Eliza gave him *that* look. "Walter is a very nice young man. He'd never do anything to hurt Jenny. Why do you think she has to follow *him*? He's waiting for her to grow up."

"Are you always right?" He brushed a hand over his son's downy hair, which was exactly the color as his mother's.

"Always. Just like your mother." She smiled and shifted the baby in her arms.

"Is she getting too heavy? In your condition, maybe you shouldn't—"

"Condition?" Ethel Buchanan's black eyes lit up like coal in a potbelly stove.

A soft glow came over Eliza's face. "I'm going to have another baby."

"Hot diggity. Maybe you'll name this one after me." The other woman put her packages down and hugged Eliza as best she could with the sleeping child between them. Then she pulled back and looked at Eliza. "You're gonna have your hands full."

Eliza looked down at the precious bundle in her arms. "Don't I know it."

"If anyone can handle it, Eliza can," Matt said. "She's taken to life on the Double C the way a duck takes to water. Besides that, she's awful bossy."

"Someone has to keep you in line. And I don't do it alone. Jenny is a big help. I don't know what I'd do without her." She grinned up at her husband. "If only this one wouldn't worry so much."

"Can't change a man's nature," Mrs. Buchanan said. "Nice chattin' with you folks. But I gotta get ready for the supper crowd."

They said their good-byes and watched her walk out the door.

Eliza looked up and studied the man she loved so much as he tenderly cradled their small son in his strong arms. She counted her lucky stars once again. Matt had told her of the conversation with Jenny that had sent him to town after her. She didn't want to think about where the two of them would be without that generous, sweet-natured child. They'd given her a home; she'd given them each other.

Just then, the door opened and Ed Whitaker walked in. He had married the schoolteacher a year and a half before, but still looked a little sheepish every time Eliza ran into him. He tipped his hat. "Matt, Eliza. Hear tell congrats are in order on the news."

"How'd you know?" Matt asked.

"Heard from someone down at the telegraph office."

Matt pulled his watch from his vest pocket, studied it, then shook his head. "Sure can tell this town's grown. Took almost an hour for that news to spread."

"Thank you, Ed. We're very excited about it," Eliza said.

The other man reached into his coat and pulled out a piece of paper. "Almost forgot. This is for you," he said handing it to Matt.

As Matt read the wire, a wide grin split his face. "Mother's coming. Says she missed the wedding and the first two births. She's damn—" He stopped and looked down at Eliza. "Sorry, Eliza, but that's a quote, damn well not going to miss seeing her third grandchild come into the world."

"That's wonderful!" Eliza cried. "We owe her so much, Matt. She's a very wise woman."

He stared down at her, the intensity of love shining in his eyes. "Just like you."

"I love you," she said.

"Thanks to my mother and that hat, I'm lucky enough to have you to love." He smiled and shifted Luke so he had a free hand. With a tenderness she always found amazing in a man so strong, he touched her cheek. "Winter isn't lonely and cold for me any longer. Not since you became my bride. I love you, too, Eliza Jones Decker."

Alone in a Crowd by Georgia Bockoven

After a terrible accident, country music sensation Cole Webster must undergo reconstructive surgery which gives him temporary anonymity. Before he can reveal his true identity, Cole loses his heart to Holly, a beautiful woman who values her privacy above all else. Cole must come to terms with who he is and what he's looking for in life before he can find love and true happiness.

Destiny Awaits by Suzanne Elizabeth

When wealthy and spoiled Tess Harper was transported back in time to Kansas, 1885, it didn't take her long to find trouble. Captivating farmer Joseph Maguire agreed to bail her out on one condition—that she live with him and care for his two orphaned nieces. Despite the hardships of prairie life, Tess soon realized that this love of a lifetime was to be her destiny.

Broken Vows by Donna Grove

To Rachel Girard, nothing was more important than her family's cattle ranch, which would one day be hers. But when her father declared she must take a husband or lose her birthright, Rachel offered footloose bounty hunter Caleb Delaney a fortune if he'd marry her–then leave her! Cal knew he'd be a fool to refuse, but he would soon wonder if a life without Rachel was worth anything at all.

Lady in Blue by Lynn Kerstan

A delightful, sexy romance set in the Regency period. Wealthy and powerful Brynmore Talgarth never wanted a wife, despite pressure to restore the family's reputation by marrying well. But once he met young, destitute, and beautiful Clare Easton, an indecent proposal led the way to a love neither knew could exist.

The Long Road Home by Mary Alice Monroe

Bankrupt and alone after her financier husband dies, Nora MacKenzie's life is shattered. After fleeing to a sheep farm in Vermont, she meets up with the mysterious C. W. Friendship soon blossoms into love, but C. W. is keeping some dangerous secrets that could destroy them both.

Winter Bride by Teresa Southwick

Wyoming rancher Matt Decker needed a wife. His mother sent him Eliza Jones, the young woman who had adored Matt when they were children. Eliza was anxious to start a new life out west, but the last thing Matt wanted was to marry someone to whom he might become emotionally attached.

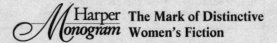